TURNBULL HOUSE

What Reviewers Say About Jess Faraday's Work

The Affair of the Porcelain Dog

"*The Affair of the Porcelain Dog* is an excellent mystery. The characters are complex and in general not what they seem on first sight. Many unexpected twists and turns keep the novel intriguing right up to the end. The historical setting of late Victorian London is portrayed accurately. It is recommended for mystery collections at public libraries, especially those in gay- and lesbian-friendly areas, and college and university collections."—*Gay, Lesbian, Bisexual, and Transgender Round Table of the American Library Association*

"*The Affair of the Porcelain Dog* is so much less than a happily ever after and so much more than just a simple ending. In fact, if I find out there's no intention to write a sequel to this book, I think I just might cry."—*The Novel Approach*

"Jess Faraday takes you into a very bleak, dangerous, and inhuman realm. A world without mercy. But despite all this, she's able to deliver a beautiful and romantic story. ...This clever multi-layered mystery skillfully combined with some very strong characters will definitely keep you in suspense until the very end."—*Booked Up Reviews*

"It is a book that keeps you riveted to the page."—*Reviews by Amos Lassen*

"The author builds a credible plot through the actions of diverse, fully-nuanced characters, which keeps the reader interested. ...Excellent first novel by a promising new author, which I give five stars out of five."—Bob Lind, *Echo Magazine*

"Sherlock Holmes Meets Oscar Wilde. Faraday has written a brilliant Victorian mystery. ...The careful plot is arranged like set of nesting boxes. With Faraday's smashing writing and research, Victorian London comes alive through the eyes of a 19th century outlier."—*The Bright List*

Visit us at www.boldstrokesbooks.com

By the Author

The Affair of the Porcelain Dog

The Left Hand of Justice

Turnbull House

TURNBULL HOUSE

by
Jess Faraday

2014

CREDITS
EDITOR: SHELLEY THRASHER
PRODUCTION DESIGN: SUSAN RAMUNDO
COVER DESIGN BY SHERI (GRAPHICARTIST2020@HOTMAIL.COM)

Acknowledgments

Many thanks to the kind readers who have taken Ira and his friends into their hearts. You make it all worthwhile.

Thanks also to my two writing groups for their invaluable insights and unflinching critique. Couldn't do any of it without you.

And many thanks as well to Jean Utley and Book 'Em Mystery Bookstore for your unflagging support of authors big and small.

Dedication

For Roy. Always.

PROLOGUE

November of 1891 was the autumn of my discontent. Melodramatic, yes. But if one is to understand the chain of foolish and self-destructive actions that I undertook over the course of that month, one must first understand the depths of that discontent, as well as its roots.

The past five years had taken me from furtive back-alley gropes in the shadows of Whitechapel to a life of luxurious indolence amid the lace curtains and aspidistras of York Street, then much of the way back down again. I'd spent a pleasant two years being spoilt by Cain Goddard, London's best-educated and possibly best-dressed crime lord. But ultimately, even a gilded cage begins to press in on a person—especially when one's nascent conscience decides, in spite of one's fondest wishes, to expand. How fortunate I was that, in his generosity—and in an effort to add realism to his claim that I was his live-in confidential secretary—Goddard had also taught me a trade.

And that was where I found myself that November: in a flat on Aldersgate Street, which, though squalid, was mine—paid for by the sweat of my brow or, more precisely, by the ink on my fingers—with no obligation to any man. The single room was drafty in winter, sweltering in the summer, and the landlord thought indoor plumbing was an idea best left to the fevered imagination of that Gallic popinjay, Verne. Still, it was preferable to sleeping on my feet, leaning against a rope with twenty other men in some Dorset

Street doss house. And I had no interest in living off the generosity of some rich man until he grew bored with me. Until my situation changed, my present lodgings were the only palatable option. And until Wilde paid me the outrageous sum he owed, my situation would not be changing any time soon.

That was another element of my discontent. I'd spent the summer revising and typewriting that masterpiece of fluff and fatuousness, *The Picture of Dorian Gray*, only to have Wilde flounce off to Paris with his entourage the week before he'd promised payment. The betrayal had surprised me. Up to that point, he'd been a singularly congenial employer, even after I'd turned down his advances. I had my theories regarding his sudden change in character, but theories don't keep the tobacco tin filled, don't subsidize evenings out, and don't pay the rent.

If it wasn't enough, my carnal needs had gone neglected for a very, very long time.

So when you ask me why in the name of Guy Fawkes and the Queen I would open the door to a newly unshackled felon, invite him inside, and plow him like a fertile field against the wall, you will understand not only how I would endanger myself and my meager possessions in such a careless manner, but also how I could fail to foresee how this one lapse in judgment would set in motion a cascade of events that would shake the very foundation of what I'd thought was my world.

You might also understand how even if I had foreseen it, I probably wouldn't have given a fuck.

CHAPTER ONE

MONDAY

His name was Marcus. He was beautiful. He was also a thief, which I could have guessed, and should have. But when he showed up at my door in that Aldersgate Street hellhole, I was too chuffed at my luck to give it much thought.

It was my third week of unemployment since Wilde had left London. My work at Turnbull House didn't count. That's not to say I didn't love helping our urchins learn their numbers and letters, nor that I wasn't bursting with pride that the youth shelter Tim Lazarus and I had started was still, after two years, a beacon of hope for the entire East End. But it didn't pay, and it certainly wasn't putting me in the path of any well-dressed confirmed bachelors with fat wallets and similar tastes in amusement. There had been no evenings at the Criterion for quite a while, and until Wilde answered my demands for payment, it was doubtful there would be. I was distraught.

I was mapping cracks in the ceiling when the knock came. It was an anemic-sounding rap, with the timidity of one who expected rejection. Rightly so, I thought, when I took in my visitor's ill-fitting clothes and fresh-from-chokey coiffure.

"Evenin', Mr. Adler," he said, twisting his frayed cloth cap in his hands. Outside it was pissing down rain, and he was wringing water onto the floorboards before my front door. "You prolly don't remember me, but..."

Oh, but I did remember.

Marcus had been a slip of a lad the last time I'd seen him, all of twenty, eyes red-rimmed from cocaine, arms bruised and scabbed from the needle. I'd broken into his brothel in search of a missing friend. He'd been attempting to chuck me out. Then the police came. Sitting there in the dark, side by side on the wooden bench of the Black Maria bound for the cells under Bow Street, I'd been moved by bleak visions of his imminent imprisonment and withdrawal. I'd told him to look me up when they let him out.

And now he had.

Someone else's trousers puddled at his ankles. Someone else's coat-sleeves covered his fingers to the second knuckle. Rain had plastered his fair hair to his head. Far from being unattractive, however, his countenance, translucent from two years without sunlight, now had an alabaster sheen that glowed angelically in the light of the lamp in my hand. He was still thin, but labor had put meat on his bones and had given the chest beneath the work-worn shirt an attractive new breadth.

You can understand how a man might be moved to charity.

"Harrington, isn't it?" I asked.

"Yes, sir. Marcus Harrington."

"Just out of Pentonville?"

"Not two hours ago, sir."

"And I suppose you have nowhere to spend the night."

"That's right, sir."

I cleared my throat, wondering what I was to do with him. There were any number of men who would have had a ready answer to that question, but I'd extended my offer in good faith and without agenda. I'm no saint, but I am a man of my word. And quite frankly, I was happy for the distraction. "Well, come in, then."

He extended a nervous hand, fingertips callused and split from picking oakum. I gave it a quick shake, noting the delicate bones, and murmured something about not calling me "sir."

He seemed genuinely touched when I removed his coat and hung it on the rack next to my own. Just inside the door, he slid off his waterlogged boots, self-consciously stuffing his socks inside. It wasn't much, my humble little slice of Central London. But despite the traffic holes in the carpet, the soot-blackened window, and the tattered screen hiding the cracked commode in the corner, it was better than Marcus had seen in the past two years, or maybe even in his short, desperate life.

"Well," I said again.

He was looking around my nasty little room as if it were a palace. I must admit I rather liked the feeling. It distracted me from the fact that, having invited him in very late on a dark and stormy night, I was now, seemingly, responsible for him. It was one thing to extend a helping hand to the Turnbull House gang before releasing myself on my own recognizance at the end of the day. Plucking someone from the streets and taking them into one's home was quite another.

Fleetingly, I wondered if Goddard had felt the same hesitation before whisking me from our corner on Commercial Road and installing me in his Regent's Park home all those years ago. But that had been a different arrangement altogether. There had been privileges and expectations. I had no expectations of my guest, and the only privilege I was offering was a night's hospitality. But what did that entail? My cupboard was empty, I'd whisky only enough for one, and my sway-backed bed was barely big enough for me.

"If you don't mind, sir." He interrupted my musings.

I turned. "You mustn't call me sir," I said once more.

"Would it be too much trouble if I had a quick scrub?" He nodded toward the basin and pitcher on their stand next to the commode-screen.

"Of course not," I said, relieved that he'd found his own momentary entertainment. "If you'd like, I'll boil some water, and you can have a proper tub-wash."

He seemed delighted by the prospect, and as he gave his face and hands a preliminary rinse, I set out a copper tub in front of the fireplace and hung a bucket of water above the coal-fire to boil. When the water began to bubble, I poured it into the tub, added an equal part of cold from the jug beside the fireplace, and arranged the commode-screen to provide him a modicum of privacy—an act that moved the poor man almost to tears.

"Thank...thank you...sir...I mean...Mr. Adler."

He had completely disrobed by that point, his oversized trousers and shirt in a pool on the floor. Although he'd thought nothing of standing naked before who knew how many other men, he was peeking out at me from behind the age-yellowed screen like a virgin. It was charming.

"All things considered, I think it's best if you call me Ira."

A shy smile broke over his face at that, and I found myself mirroring it. I do enjoy standing on ceremony, as anyone who has scrabbled his way up from the gutter inevitably does. But with Marcus, it didn't seem quite fair. Perhaps because he was in the same gutter I'd occupied at his age—in my early twenties. No, I'd never been one for the needle, but I had peddled my arse all over the East End, and it was only luck and the patronage of a certain Cain Goddard that had kept that arse out of Pentonville.

"All right, then, Mr...Ira."

I swear I heard a tinkle of bells when he smiled that time. He ducked back behind the screen, and, shaking my head, I set about gathering a towel, an extra blanket, and a pillow, so my guest could make a bed before the fire. The great clock struck one thirty, and soon my lonely flat was alive with happy splashing sounds. I set the bedding on the floor and hung his clothes over one side of the screen to dry.

Only when I crossed to my chest of drawers to find him a spare set of nightclothes did I notice the shapely silhouette the fire was casting against the fabric of the screen. A better man would have averted his eyes. He certainly wouldn't have let his gaze linger on the shadow of young Marcus's supple limbs, or imagined his own hand guiding the cloth over his smooth skin.

"I can't tell you how grateful I am, Mr. Ira."

My pulse raced guiltily. Grateful. He was grateful, and I was raking my eyes over the delicious curve of his silhouetted arse. I turned my back to the screen.

"I'm sure we can find some way for me to repay you," he continued.

"That's not necessary," I stammered. When I say it had been a long time, I'm not speaking in terms of days. A better man would have immediately dismissed the images parading past my mind's eye. A better man would have manufactured some crisis to excuse himself from the flat until young Marcus was safely clothed and asleep, alone and unmolested beside the fire. I've said before that I'm no saint, but I like to think I'm no cad, either. The irony of my current predicament—seeing as Turnbull House was in the business of helping people out of the flesh trade rather than into it—was certainly not lost on me.

"Come now," Marcus said. The splashing had stopped and—God help me, he was toweling himself off—he had traded his supplicating tones for a knowing purr. "There must be somefin' I can do to show me gratitude."

A better man would have run, then.

A better man would have at least kept his hand out of his trousers.

My heart leaped to my throat when I heard him emerge from behind the screen. It stopped dead when I felt his warmth at my back, his chin resting on my shoulder, saw his eyes sparkle with delight as they found the clear and turgid evidence peeking out of my waistband that I am not a better man.

"I...ah...er..."

"I can help you with that," he breathed into my ear. My heart pounded. The tables had turned, and now I felt like the callow virgin. "It's no bother."

He dropped to his knees and took me in his mouth. For the first time, I was able to fully appreciate the gentle ripple of muscles beneath his skin—skin, which, over the past two years, had lost the ravages of the needle and become smooth and soft once more. A fine coat of light, curly hair covered his forearms and legs, with just a tuft on his sternum, glistening in the lamplight. And...oh, God. I really would have to look away from *there* if I wanted to enjoy his attentions for longer than an instant. After several toe-curling moments, I set a hand on his head.

"Too much?" he asked.

Oh, God, no. But yes. There's something to be said for a man who sucks cock for a living. I should know. Goddard was a skilled and ardent lover, but he didn't have the almost supernatural mind-reading skills of a professional.

"You want I should—"

I nodded. "Over there, by the wall." I gestured with my head and laughed weakly. "And don't talk with your mouth full."

CHAPTER TWO

TUESDAY

I woke to the smell of sausages—hot sausages, fat, juicy, and straight from the brazier. Thinking it was a dream or, at best, a sausage-man pushing his spring barrow along the sidewalk beneath my window, I turned over and buried my face in my pillow. But the smell persisted, and it was close. There was another smell as well—musky and clean, and related, without a doubt, to the light hairs on the mattress. Someone else's hairs, no doubt, as my own were dark and tightly curled. I smiled. That part of the evening, at least, had not been a dream. Rolling over, I stretched lazily.

It had been so long since I'd experienced that specific, all-encompassing bodily satisfaction—that delightful, leaden fatigue—that it took me a moment to recognize it for what it was. Yawning languorously, I glanced at the pocket watch that had spilled out of my waistcoat onto the floor sometime the evening before. Midmorning, already, and I was still wrapped in a cocoon of postcoital sloth. It was going to be a good day.

A sharp rap on the front door shattered my all-too-brief bliss. Who on earth could it be? I had precious few visitors. I liked it that way. Tension crept into my neck and shoulders as I considered the possibilities. The police, for instance. Though Marcus had arrived after my neighbors—working people, all—would have retired for the night, it was always possible our festivities had awakened someone. The flat to the left housed a baker's assistant—an exceptionally early riser, who would not have been at all amused, had he put his ear to the wall and listened carefully.

The knock sounded again. My trousers were on the floor near the bed. The bedsprings creaked as I put out a toe to attempt retrieval. Then came a sudden, angry volley of pounding, which stopped abruptly as someone opened the door.

I sat up quickly. Not out of fear this time, but out of curiosity. To be honest, I was surprised that Marcus hadn't moved on to his next destination. But perhaps it was still raining. Or perhaps, I realized with growing apprehension, he didn't have a destination in mind.

"Who the devil are you?" demanded my friend and business partner, Tim Lazarus, from the very spot in the hallway where young Marcus had wrung out his hat the night before.

"I might ask you the same question."

"I'm looking for Mr. Adler. This is his flat."

"And who, might I ask, is callin'?"

Despite my trepidation, the image that came to mind made me chuckle. Lazarus was tightly wound at the best of times. Though he knew—intimately—my taste in bed partners, he'd never met one that hadn't set that vein on his forehead throbbing. If I didn't know better, I might think he was jealous.

"Who am I?" Lazarus demanded. "Who am *I?* I'm about to summon a constable, that's—"

"It's all right, Tim," I called over a barely suppressed laugh. I shimmied into my trousers and padded to the door. Marcus was bare to the waist, and he smelled like his sweat and my soap. He was wearing my other pair of trousers. As I came up beside him, he relaxed his guard-dog stance and crossed his arms over his thin, though nicely defined chest.

As Lazarus took in the tableau, his expression went from outrage to realization. Watching the color rise along his neck toward his recently trimmed salt-and-pepper hair, I felt equal parts pity and glee. Lazarus might look like any other starched-shirt East End do-good, but our past together was not so far behind us that he could pretend he didn't know, from personal experience, what Marcus was doing here.

"Of course," he said, taking a sudden interest in his boots. "Forgive me, Adler."

"Come in, Tim," I said charitably. "How's the wife?"

The word "wife" worked a miraculous transformation on young Marcus, and he suddenly smiled and ushered my friend inside like a genial host.

"Yes, do come in, er, Mr..."

"Lazarus," I supplied.

"*Dr.* Lazarus," said Tim.

"Do come in, Dr. Lazarus. I just been 'round to the shops an' picked up some comestibles. Nuffin' fancy, but what's ours is yours, like."

Ours?

Lazarus and I exchanged a look. I was as curious about this unforeseen presumption as Lazarus was—even more so about the fact that Marcus had been "'round to the shops." With what money, was my question. One didn't receive a stipend upon leaving chokey, after all. But before I could open my mouth, Lazarus had subtly backed my guest up against the fabric screen—the screen that still concealed the vat of now-cold bathwater—and had initiated an interrogation of his own.

"And you are—"

"Harrington, sir. Marcus Harrington."

"Mr. Harrington." Lazarus stroked his neat moustache thoughtfully. He was about the same height as Marcus, but with a strong, compact musculature. He practiced some sort of fighting art and was looking at Marcus as if he were sizing up a partner for the ring. Fortunately, Lazarus was a man of intellect first; any blows he threw would be verbal. "The state of your hands suggests a recent stint picking oakum. You don't look well-enough fed to have come from a workhouse, which tells me you're recently from prison."

Marcus blinked dumbly. I couldn't blame him. Lazarus's observations have affected me the same way at times.

"Pentonville," I said, suddenly feeling protective. "Marcus was a guest of Henri Labouchere."

"Oh." Lazarus relaxed. Two years ago, Lazarus and I had both been living under the Damoclean specter of Labouchere's law—a law that punished both actual and attempted indecency between men on the word of one lousy witness. A single, decade-old photo had almost cost four of us our freedom. The press didn't call the law a blackmailer's charter for nothing.

"You might remember that business at Fitzroy Street," I added.

"Oh!" Lazarus said again. Lazarus had been indirectly involved in the raid on the brothel where young Marcus had been apprehended on the job. I'd have gone down as well, if not for some quick thinking on the part of Lazarus's employer at the time, a self-styled "consulting detective" named Andrew St. Andrews. Was it evil of me to enjoy seeing the faint flush of guilt in the man's cheeks as he realized the consequences of his actions? "So you're staying here for the time being, then. What are your plans after that?"

"Tim, the man hasn't been out twenty-four hours. Let him be." Actually, the longer the morning wore on, the more I wanted to know the answer myself. But I wanted to be the one to ask the question. Tim shot me a look that said he'd guessed as much.

"Forgive me, Mr. Harrington," he said, not sounding at all sorry. "I didn't mean to pry. In my line of work—"

"Dr. Lazarus and I run a home for young people trying to make their way out of the flesh trade," I explained. "Turnbull House. You may have heard of it."

"We provide a bed, meals, education, some vocational training. You yourself might be—"

Marcus laughed. His voice sounded rusty, as if he hadn't had a laugh that good in years, which, considering where he'd spent those years, might well have been true. "Sounds good for them wot needs it. But I ain't lookin' for a way out. More like a way back in, if you know what I mean. Fitzroy Street's all boarded up, an' I ain't going back to selling me arse on the corner if I can help it." He graced us again with that twinkling, angelic grin. "But I'm sure it's a jolly nice place."

Lazarus blinked. In the almost two years since we'd established Turnbull House, I'm quite sure no one had ever turned down his offer for that particular reason. As I watched him attempt to comprehend that Marcus was actually quite happy with his vocation, laughter welled up inside my chest, and it was all I could do not to let it loose in his face.

I really did need to see to my carnal needs more often.

"Indeed." Lazarus turned to me with a look that said he and I would revisit this discussion later and said, "Which brings me to the reason I stopped by. There's an emergency meeting of the board of directors today, Adler. As a member of the board, you should be there."

"What time?"

"As soon as we arrive. Put your coat on."

Tim and I had founded Turnbull House, along with Tim's wife, Bess, and Pearl Brandt, the nurse who ran Tim's Bethnal Green clinic like a pirate captain. Over time, Tim had taken on the administration of the place, along with any medical care our charges needed. Bess, who had trained as a teacher in America, taught reading, writing, arithmetic, and basic life skills. Pearl had gone back to more or less single-handedly overseeing the Bethnal Green clinic. As for me, well, my skills had been more necessary in the beginning. Having come out of the trade myself, I had firsthand knowledge of the kind of support our charges would need. But as the different components of the project began to come together, my specific knowledge wasn't as necessary anymore. Now, more often than not, I provided a friendly ear or an extra pair of hands.

I certainly saw no reason to waste what was left of the morning in a meeting.

"Tim—"

"No," he said before I could protest further. "This concerns you, too, Adler. I knew you'd try to argue your way out of it, so I came to take you personally."

Marcus protested. "But I just brung sausages." Lazarus glared. "And fresh rolls, too."

"Fresh rolls, Tim," I said.

"You're telling me your stomach is more important than the future of twelve disadvantaged young people?"

Oh, for God's sake. Who could have argued with that?

"Fine," I said. Stalking across the room, I snatched my shirt and waistcoat off the floor and shoved my feet into a pair of socks. "But I'm not leaving without a sausage."

Smiling triumphantly, Marcus tore apart a roll and smashed a thick brown link between the halves. Ignoring the symbolism, I grabbed it out of his hand and took a petulant bite. Still warm. He grinned. "I'll show meself out, then?"

Lazarus, already at the door, turned, eyebrow cocked and loaded. Without waiting for my answer, he said, "We'll follow you."

CHAPTER THREE

W hat are you grinning about?" Lazarus demanded as we trudged up Raven Row, shoulder to shoulder, umbrellas angled into the downpour. It wasn't the narrowest street in Whitechapel, nor was it the darkest or most dangerous, though in retrospect, we might have chosen somewhere more convenient to my room on Aldersgate Street. On the other hand, the previous night's pleasures had left me positively giddy, and a brisk walk through the rain was just what I needed to clear my head to confront whatever looming disaster Lazarus had dragged me there to address. "Well?" he asked.

"Wouldn't you like to know?"

"Pretty sure I know already. I was just hoping you could suggest a more attractive image to replace the one that's lodged itself in my mind."

"How about Bess's face when she sees the mud you're about to track inside?"

I stopped at the doorway of Turnbull House and waited for him to rattle the lock open. In the distance, the Great Clock struck half-eleven. Just beneath the rain, I could hear the students reciting the Bible verse Bess had chosen to end the morning lessons. I closed my umbrella while Lazarus stepped through the door, then followed, wiping my feet on a mat some of our residents had made by knotting together worn-out sheets, and rested my umbrella against the wall.

Turnbull House was a narrow brown brick building, distinguished from the surrounding narrow brick buildings only by the plaque near the front door, bearing our organization's name. Lazarus and I had named the place after my oldest friend, Nate Turnbull, who had died trying to rescue the trafficked children who had been the shelter's first residents. The ground floor housed the classroom, a meeting room, and a small nook that Lazarus claimed for his office. The dormitories were on the second floor, and a small, ill-equipped kitchen and bathing area were in the basement. The only source of heat was the hearth in the classroom, and Bess kept the door shut. I hung my sopping coat and hat on the hook next to Lazarus's but kept my gloves on.

"I'm back," Lazarus called, knocking on the classroom door. "And I've brought Adler with me."

The door opened. While Lazarus went inside to make conversation with his wife, I adjusted the loose pane of glass in the front window. The paint Lazarus and I had carefully applied around the frame was already starting to chip, and the wood was warped where ice had invaded last winter. By springtime it would sport a handsome new crack. At least the glass was still intact, which was more than could be said for any number of windows in the neighboring buildings. It would have been insensitive to call the place a shithole—as I sometimes referred to my own flat. For one thing, I'd help build it myself, so if it wasn't very nice, it was my own fault. For another thing, at least one keen, youthful pair of ears was always listening at the keyhole. And no matter how true it might have been, no child likes to hear that they are living in a, well, you know.

It was a far cry from the brilliant start we'd made two years ago, though. Lazarus and I had been heroes for a spell after we uncovered the child-slavery ring that had provided Turnbull House with its first residents. We'd ridden high on a flood of donations for an entire year, thanks to the bouts of ecstatic generosity that followed each newspaper article as the story unfolded. But eventually the case settled and Turnbull House became old news. The charitable classes are fickle, forgetful, and easily bored. They have no concept of the fact that two guineas will not end child slavery forever, and yet they become annoyed if reminded of that fact often enough to actually make a dent in the problem. It doesn't help that every month seems to bring a new, more exciting, more fashionable cause that desperately needs their patronage. We nearly lost September's rent, for example, when one of our lady-angels decided, on a whim, that her money would do more good supporting an old-age home for retired pit ponies.

We managed to squeak through that crisis, thanks to Lazarus's careful husbanding of our resources and Bess's extraordinary persuasive powers. But September was just the first crack in the ice. I'd no doubt that whatever problem Lazarus had called this meeting to discuss, money would be at the root of it.

"Good morning, Mr. Adler," Bess called, waving to me from the front of the classroom. She was standing in front of a blackboard crammed with notes—an extravagant gift from Lady Pit Ponies—while her charges, a dozen young people aged twelve to seventeen, cleaned their slates and placed them neatly on the benches.

Bess was in her early thirties, solidly built—even more solidly than usual, being six months pregnant—and had bright brown eyes that sparkled with intelligence and wit. Her mouth was a bit too wide, her features too pronounced for her to be described as pretty. Nonetheless, her warmth, earnestness, and unshakable self-confidence made her irresistible to students and potential donors alike.

"Morning, Bess."

"The meeting is ready to begin at your convenience, dear," Lazarus said.

"Very well. Students, I trust you can find your way downstairs for luncheon. One roll to a customer, and no pushing."

The midday meal was nothing to be excited about, but many of the students were happy to be assured of any kind of food on a regular basis. Mumbling *Yes, Missus* and *Good morning, Mr. Adler*, they filed past me through the door and made their way down the hall.

Mrs. Lazarus wove through the rows of benches with a floaty sort of agility one wouldn't expect from a woman in her condition. Tim had been opposed to her continuing to teach after her condition began to show. But she had argued—as persuasively as she argued everything—that her pupils had seen infinitely more shocking things in their lives. In fact, she went on, because she never did anything halfway, given their backgrounds, it would do them good to observe the happy result of healthy, loving, marital congress. And if the women who lived in the neighboring tenements didn't have the luxury of hiding themselves away for a few months when nature took its inevitable course, how could they take her seriously if she claimed the privilege?

Most importantly—though by this point in the argument Lazarus had already waved the white flag—she provided her services for free. If Turnbull House wanted to continue its school, there simply wasn't a budget for an outside teacher.

No Englishwoman of means would have argued so passionately against the confinement that many women regarded as right and fitting. But Bess was not a lady of means, nor was she English. And if we were to benefit from her American forwardness in soliciting donations, we would also have to put up with the more outrageous results of that forwardness as well.

"How are the lessons coming along?" I inquired as she propped the door open to let in a bit of fresh air.

"As well as can be expected. The younger ones are soaking it all up like sponges. The older ones are having a bit more difficulty reading and writing, but are doing well with the vocational component."

Mrs. Lazarus had worked some sort of arrangement for the residents to attend a local industrial school in the afternoons. I'm not sure how it worked. We didn't have the money to pay the students' fees, and the school received no assistance from the government on our behalf. But when Mrs. Lazarus set her mind to something, she not only accomplished it but made everyone involved feel like they'd come out the better for it. If she weren't such a stalwart in her church, I'd call it witchcraft. But as it is, I'll just say it's a gift we're all grateful for.

We followed her back inside. Like the rest of the building, the classroom walls had been painted a year ago and washed regularly since. There was a bank of east-facing windows from which I had personally scrubbed at least a decade of soot. Though the windows looked out onto a wall of the inevitable brown brick, they let in enough light to keep the lamps off during the day.

While I rearranged the student benches to better suit a meeting of four directors, Pearl walked in. She looked like she'd come straight from a night shift at the clinic—dark circles around her deep-set eyes, the wrinkles on her face more pronounced, steely hair sticking out at all angles from under her cap. She still wore her apron, clean though stained, and her forearm cuffs had taken a beating. Laying her dripping coat over one of the benches near the fire, she greeted me with an exhausted smile.

"Thank you all for coming," Lazarus began, once we had all taken our seats. He fiddled with his cuffs, a sure sign something was bothering him. "It's no secret that Turnbull House is struggling. Donations have dropped off—"

"Lady Pit Ponies," I muttered. A general grumbling rose around the room as the others named donors whose support had been flagging recently. Lazarus held up a quelling hand.

"And Lady Sporting Hall, and Lord Fallen-Women. It's not our place to judge the worth of other charities or the people who choose to give to them. But it does force us to face reality. We've done the best we could. Not one of us takes a salary, and we all give generously of our time and resources. But even so, Turnbull House is in danger of becoming insolvent."

"How soon?" Pearl asked.

"By the New Year. And that's optimistic."

Silence fell over the room. We all glanced at each other: Pearl, who had no doubt faced this issue at the clinic as well; Bess, who appeared offended that all of her hard work and careful planning had led to this place anyway; and Lazarus, who just looked tired.

"What about the residents?" I asked. It was all too easy to imagine where they would end up and how they would support themselves.

"Bess and I can only take four or five," Lazarus said. Bess's eyes widened. Her expression made it clear what she thought of *that* idea. "And perhaps one or two could stay at the clinic on a temporary basis. But that leaves half." He turned to me. "I wouldn't presume to ask you to take in any, Adler, given your new living situation."

All heads swung toward me.

"Charity takes all forms," I said, straightening on my bench. The particular charity of Adler's Flat wouldn't last more than another night, if I had anything to say about it. But even if it did, it certainly wasn't any of these people's business. "And speaking of charity, what about your friend St. Andrews? Isn't he always good for a few quid?"

Andrew St. Andrews, Lazarus's one-time employer, was the third son of an earl. Surely he could cough up a nice lump of cash for us.

"St. Andrews always gives generously to the Christmas fund," Lazarus said. "This is considerably more serious than that."

"Couldn't we ask Mr. Porter for an extension, then?" Our landlord had always seemed a sensible sort to me. And he had really taken to Bess's idea that he'd be helping needy children by renting to us at a discount.

Lazarus looked distressed. "And that, as they say, is the rub. Mr. Porter informed me yesterday evening that he's had an offer on the leasehold."

"An offer?" I cried. "Who would want this shithole?"

Lazarus glared. "Apparently some factory owner wants use it to house workers. Mr. Porter is sympathetic to our cause, but he said the man made him an offer he couldn't refuse. Mr. Porter likes us," he said, trying to speak over the rising chorus of protests from our little group. "But he has his own expenses to think of. He did say that if we could match the offer, he'd sell to us instead."

"With what money?"

Lazarus shook his head. "That's why I've called you all here. I'm asking you to go home this afternoon and think. Try to come up with a solution, no matter how improbable or unorthodox. Think. Twelve lives are depending on it."

At that point by a loud clout on the front door interrupted the meeting. Everyone looked at me.

"Why is this always my job?" I asked. No one said anything. "Fine." I pushed myself up from my bench.

When I opened the door, the rain had stopped, though it had puddled on the doorstep. In the puddle stood a constable with a bushy ginger moustache, his fist clenching the collar of possibly the most objectionable-looking urchin I'd seen in a long time. And I'd grown up on these streets.

"This Turnbull House?" the constable asked. A drip of water fell from the roof and splattered on the top of his tall hat.

"It's what the sign says."

"Right." He pushed the child forward. "Found this one nicking oranges in Spitalfields Market." The lad looked twelve, which meant closer to fourteen or fifteen. Standard grimy face, greasy brown hair, and clothes likely taken from someone's line. He fixed me with a piercing blue eye, as if daring me to say something about it. His sharp chin was shiny with orange juice and a stray bit of pulp. He looked positively feral. "I don't like to take 'em to prison so young," the constable explained, with a rueful glance at the young man. "I got four of me own, you see. Way I see it, sending 'em to school keeps 'em out of trouble. Gives 'em a chance when they gets older. You got a school here, and beds. They say your Mrs. Lazarus works miracles with the hard cases. Now, you going to take him or what?"

Still glaring at me with that unnerving gaze, the boy spit a pip at my boot.

"Don't they have residential schools for that, Constable...?"

"Mathers, sir," the constable said as I stepped out of the path of a second expectorated pip.

"Your philosophy is a popular one these days, Constable Mathers," I said. "But there have to be any number of residential schools in London, where a boy like this could have a bed in cold weather and learn a trade, and not be a burden on our already strained resources."

"I been to three this morning. Ain't no places at none of 'em, and even if there was, ain't nobody to pay the fees. And it's *Sergeant* Mathers, if you please, sir."

"What about a reformatory? You said you caught him committing a crime."

Mathers fixed me with a glare of righteous indignation worthy of Bess herself. "There are some what'd say stealing food when you're starved ain't no crime. Help a boy like this now, and you could be the saving of him. Start treating him like a criminal, and that's what he'll grow up to be."

I had seen for myself how true this was. And normally, I wasn't so uncharitable. I had played Father Christmas for the residents last year, after all. I think some of the little beggars might have even taken a shine to me. But we weren't in a position to take on more students. And Turnbull House had been set up for a very specific kind of person—not for just any little orange thief.

The boy looked like he couldn't care less what we decided. He looked like he would be out the back window the minute we turned our heads anyway. Lazarus and the others had begun speaking again. I glanced over my shoulder, then looked back at *Sergeant* Mathers.

"We really do have a very specific mandate set forth in our charter. Young people who want out of the flesh trade—not just any urchin off the street. And besides, we don't have any open beds."

Mathers looked at me for a long moment. I talk tough, but it's no secret that when all is said and done, it's pretty easy to get around me. Besides, we were there to help, not to judge. Who knew—perhaps if this little monster couldn't support himself stealing produce, he'd resort to something worse. The sergeant's mouth quirked, as if he were reading my thoughts.

"Oh, hell," I said.

Lazarus would grouse, but perhaps next time he'd make the effort to answer the door himself.

"Just leave him with you, then, shall I? Right, lad. Be good, now." The sergeant gave the young man a push toward me, then turned. We watched him disappear into the early afternoon crowd, whistling a little tune. Lovely.

"Well, why don't you come in for a moment, anyway?" I said. "I'm sure we can at least find you a bite to eat. I'm Mr. Adler. What's your name?"

The boy sneered. "None of your business, you nosy bugger." But he turned on his shabby little heel and pushed past me through the door anyway. As he shuffled down the hall, I heard him mutter, "What a shithole."

❖

Having only added to our worries by taking in a mouth we couldn't afford to feed, I thought to make myself useful by paying a call to our landlord. Mr. Arthur Porter worked out of a small, tumbledown storefront office on Cheshire Street. He was a kind-hearted man, at least until he'd taken to chucking children onto the street. And though I was no Bess Lazarus, perhaps, I thought, I'd be able to reason with him.

"Mr. Adler!" he cried, hefting his heavyset frame out of his chair as I walked in. His joviality was habitual—I usually brought the rent. He seemed to have forgotten that he'd just stabbed me in the back. When he saw my expression, his thick, gray moustache drooped and the twinkle left his eyes. "I see you heard the news."

"How could you, Mr. Porter?" I asked, hoping that I sounded hurt and disappointed rather than ready to rip off his mutton-chop sideburns. "I thought you believed in what we were doing."

"Oh, but I do. I surely do, Mr. Adler." He sighed, pulling a red handkerchief from the pocket of his waistcoat and mopping his forehead with it. The fire in the grate was hot and bright. Our landlord had money to burn, it would seem. He self-consciously pulled his waistcoat tighter across his large belly and held up his hands in a helpless gesture. "But the plain fact of it is, I need the money. I was happy to help the shelter, still am. But the missus and I are trying to put something away, and every bit helps. When this gentleman came along wanting to buy the leasehold, his offer was too good to pass up. Perhaps I could give to your Christmas fund instead."

"Who wants the building?" I demanded, not deigning to dignify the Christmas-fund remark. If Porter couldn't see reason, perhaps I could deal with the buyer directly.

Mr. Porter sighed again. "I'm afraid I can't tell you that. It was part of the deal. He wanted to remain anon-anin-an—"

"Anonymous."

"Precisely. He was very insistent about that."

I frowned. Apparently the buyer had anticipated that someone from Turnbull House might want to contact him. Which suggested that he knew throwing us out was a shitty thing to do, but he didn't want to be talked out of it. Very interesting.

"What sort of factory does he run?" I asked.

"He didn't say."

"And you didn't ask?"

"He seemed a very private man." Mr. Porter was beginning to sweat again, though whether it was from the fire or from my interrogation, I couldn't tell. A drop of perspiration slid down my own neck. I took off my hat and fanned myself with it. I glanced out toward the street, but the windows had fogged over.

"But he says he just wants to house workers." I turned back to him. "You really won't give me his name? For the children?"

Yes, it was a stretch to call our residents "children," but from his expression, the word evoked the intended emotion.

"I'm sorry, Mr. Adler," he said guiltily.

"I suppose he paid you well for your silence," I said. He replied with a helpless shrug. "But why? Why does he have to have our building? There must be plenty of suitable places in the area."

"He said it was close to his factory, and right where he needed it to be."

I caught his eye and held it. "You realize you're tossing children out onto the street. Children, Mr. Porter."

He bit his lip and looked away. "I'm not happy about it, Mr. Adler."

"Then—"

"The missus and I need to put something away. We're thinking to buy a little place by the seaside, let rooms in the summer…"

"But—"

"I don't like doing this," he said. "You're good tenants, and I don't want to do nuffin' to hurt the children. But expenses are expenses. Listen," he said, sighing again. "He's coming in again to sign the papers a week Friday. If you can find the money by then, you can buy the leasehold yourself."

I stopped pacing. "How much?"

"Four hundred pounds. Four hundred eleven, to be precise."

"For that shithole?" It was Tuesday. That left a week and a half. If I were to pull a clerkship out of my arse, I might come up with ninety quid. Per annum.

He shrugged again. "It's what the gentleman offered. And the missus and I…"

I closed my eyes and counted to five.

"Mr. Adler?"

"There's no way you can give me his name? Let me reason with him myself? This mysterious factory owner?"

"Not a chance, Mr. Adler. I'm sorry."

Now it was my turn to sigh. "Then I'll just have to go tell the children to pack their bags and start looking for a doorway."

I swept through the door, cheeks burning, his sincere apology ringing in my ears.

CHAPTER FOUR

It wasn't my first instinct to go running to Cain Goddard, I assure you.

Even as I found my feet following the once-familiar path back to his home near Regent's Park, I knew it was a bad idea. I'd left Goddard more than two years earlier, following a sudden moral epiphany. To wit, the child-slavery ring Lazarus and I had uncovered—the event that had led to the establishment of Turnbull House—had belonged to one of Goddard's associates. Goddard himself didn't traffic in children, but he had no objection to others doing so. I couldn't reconcile the fact that, to him, it was no worse than trafficking in turnips, so I left. There had been no shouting, no recriminations, but I'd departed in a very final way and not returned. I was quite sure the Duke of Dorset Street was unaccustomed to being dismissed so summarily.

Never mind that I was returning hat in hand.

Goddard had a long memory and a short temper. But he also had a lot of money. Four hundred eleven quid was a drop in his bucket. And he had loved me once. I had loved him. If he'd given the reasons for my departure any thought at all, he might appreciate the chance to help these children, having failed to help the ones who came before them. He might jump at the chance for a bit of moral redemption.

Or so I kept telling myself as I stood at the bottom of his scrubbed front stairs, trying to convince myself I wasn't making the worst mistake of my new life.

The front door opened, and Goddard's former girl-of-all-work stepped out onto the landing. After the butler's untimely death, Goddard had promoted Eileen Murphy to housekeeper, and she now wore a uniform of starched black bombazine. Her lowly mobcap was gone, and her hair was swept up in a tight, chestnut-colored bun at the back of her head. She looked left then right, then cast an imperious eye down the stairs to where I stood. Recognizing me, she cracked a crooked smile that betrayed her age. She was only eighteen, though between the dress and her new mantle of authority, she appeared quite imposing.

"Mr. Ira? Wot you doin' down there?"

I crept up the stairs like a dog expecting a kick, but relaxed when I caught a glimpse of the familiar vestibule, with its recent paint job and black-and-white tile. The Duke of Dorset Street was ruthless in his business dealings, it was true. But Cain Goddard, my former lover, was intelligent, witty, and generous. It was he who had scraped me off the mean Whitechapel streets. It was he who had taught me to speak and dress like a member of the educated middle class. He had turned an illiterate street rat into a decent confidential secretary—skills with which I support myself to this day. And when it was all over, it was Goddard who had gifted me with the astonishingly expensive Remington keyboard typewriter with which I currently ply my trade.

Surely he'd put aside enough of his anger by now that he'd admit to similar memories. Surely he'd be, if not happy to see me, at least willing to receive me on an urgent matter of business.

"Hello, Eileen," I said, leaning against the doorjamb. She stepped back with a smirk but knew not to take my flirtation to heart.

"Good day to you, Mr. Adler," she said coolly. "An' it's Mrs. Murphy, now, thanks all the same."

"Mrs. Murphy." I bowed my head in acknowledgement of her new title. Cooks and housekeepers customarily styled themselves "Mrs." even if, like our Eileen, they had never so much as shared a cab with a man. "I always knew you'd get on. I trust Dr. Goddard hasn't been abusing your dedication too much."

"Oh no, sir. 'E do work us 'ard, always did. But last summer," she leaned in conspiratorially, "'e got me a cook an' a girl."

"Really?"

When I lived at York Street there had been but two employees—Eileen and my arch nemesis, Collins the butler. To retain a staff of three when only Goddard was living there was a sign that Eileen had distinguished herself indeed.

Or it was a sign he was no longer living alone.

"I can't imagine," I said, "that Dr. Goddard would maintain such a large staff when it's only him."

"That's wot 'e said, until I tol' 'im wot 'e could 'ave a 'ot dinner every night or a clean 'ouse in the mornin', but not both unless I get some 'elp."

"You didn't!" I laughed out loud.

"I 'ad to. It were gettin' ridiculous! You ain't got no idea wot it takes to run a 'ouse, does you, Mr. Adler? None of you men does." She sniffed. "After Mr. Collins...well....after 'e *departed*, like, it were just too much work, no matter 'ow much the master were payin' me. An' I tol' 'im so."

"And he listened."

"Too right, 'e listened," she said. "'E agreed on a cook an' a girl for cleanin', but in exchange, I was to spend me afternoons off learnin' to read an' write, so's I could keep the tradesman's books like a 'ousekeeper should. An' 'e wants me to do somfin' about me haitches."

I laughed again. Only Goddard would feel that *he'd* gained something by offering his employee an education.

"So it's just him living here," I said.

She cocked an eyebrow. She may have been devout, but she wasn't stupid. "Just 'im," she said a little wistfully. "Ever since you...well, ain't been no one 'ere but 'im."

It seems silly that the thought should relieve me—after all, I was the one who had left—but relieve me it did nonetheless.

"Is he at home now?" I asked.

"'e hain't. But if you want to leave a message, I'll make sure 'e gets it."

"Just give him this," I said.

Straightening, I took a card case from the pocket of my waistcoat and opened it toward her. I'd had the cards made up at Wilde's insistence, though when it came to the design, I'd put my foot down. Instead of the florid typeface and obnoxious colors he'd suggested, I kept it simple: my name and address in neat black script on cream-colored stock.

"Oh, wot's this, now? Very fancy, Mr. Adler! Gone into business for yourself, 'as you?"

"I have."

She narrowed her eyes, lips twitching mischievously. "Is that what you come for, then? To offer your services?" She emphasized the last word with a hint of cheekiness that made me choke back a laugh. Coming out of her shell, our Eileen, no doubt about it.

"Just tell him I stopped by, if you please."

❖

Marcus wasn't waiting by the door when I returned to my flat. I was relieved. Two years ago, when I'd pledged him my assistance in the cramped, dark confines of that police wagon, I hadn't intended to solicit a roommate. The way he'd prattled on to Lazarus about "us" and "ours" after a single evening made me nervous. I hadn't the resources to take in another hungry mouth, no matter how talented that mouth was. More importantly, I had come to cherish my freedom and my privacy. I'd be damned if I let some handsome little baggage beguile me out of them.

Glancing up and down the hallway, I let myself into the flat and locked the door behind me. I hung up my coat, hat, and umbrella, wondering if they would ever be completely dry again. While I was wiping my boots on my knotted-rag doormat—last year's birthday present from the Turnbull House gang—I saw two envelopes that had been slid under the door in the evening post.

I sighed with relief at the sight of a French postmark accompanied by Wilde's sloppy, widely spaced scribble across the face of the first envelope. Relief turned to disappointment when, upon tearing the missive open, I found he hadn't sent a measly centime. Rather, the envelope contained a photo, which was not only quite obscene, but was creased over the interesting bits and frayed at the corners. The back was decorated with little splotches of wine, and Wilde's handwriting careened across the empty space, the drunken letters spelling out a single word: BRAM.

I crushed the photo in my fist. Clearly he meant for me to collect my remaining pay from his friend Stoker. I'd met Stoker once or twice. He was a reliable individual—a family man with a steady and lucrative job managing Henry Irving's theatre. No doubt he was good for any debts he himself might have incurred. But as much as all of Wilde's friends loved him, did any of them love him enough to shell out that kind of money on the word of an acquaintance who had been peripheral—at best—to their chummy little circle? Somehow I doubted even Stoker's good nature would stretch that far. I supposed I should have been grateful that Wilde hadn't directed me to Bosie. Now that young man was trouble. I'd tried to tell Wilde as much, but he seemed determined to learn the lesson on his own.

The second envelope—addressed in Goddard's tidy hand— was a pleasant surprise. Goddard hadn't, it seemed, wasted any time responding to the calling card I'd left with Eileen. I took this as a positive sign. Granted, I'd taken the long route home, by foot, and even stopped by the library in St. James's Square along the way. The price of subscription was exorbitant, but fortunately Wilde considered it a necessary business expense. At any rate, I'd stayed long enough for the letter to arrive. I slipped my finger beneath the flap of the envelope and lifted the seal.

Come to dinner at the usual time.—C

Dinner at Goddard's was at eight o'clock sharp. Early to bed, early to rise, as the Americans say. I lifted my watch from my waistcoat pocket and glanced at it. I'd quite lost track of time while perusing the library's offerings. After breathing its rarefied air, I always found it difficult to force myself back out onto the sooty, traffic-clogged streets. Could I make it back across town in forty minutes' time? It was doubtful. And yet, as I'd been the one to initiate contact with the man, I knew better than to not even try. Shrugging my wet coat back on, I grabbed my umbrella, locked the door behind me, and ran for the bus.

❖

I arrived back at York Street just as the Great Clock was striking eight. It wasn't a long dash from the omnibus to Goddard's front steps. Nonetheless, I took a moment at the foot of the stairs to catch my breath, straighten my cravat, and smooth down my hair. I was nervous. Not only because I was coming to ask Goddard for money, but because his response to my card had been to summon me to dinner. My chest fluttered with what might have been anticipation. I'd missed him. It might also have been fear. If Goddard wanted revenge, I'd assumed he'd have already taken it. At the same time, a good dressing-down wasn't completely out of the realm of possibility. Especially since, in his mind, I probably deserved it.

But I'd started this. Now it was time to take what came.

I gave the brass knocker a few taps.

"Good evening, Mrs. Murphy," I said, when she answered the door. "You're looking authoritative tonight." She preened, patting her still-tight brown bun. Even at day's end, her black housekeeper's uniform was impeccable. "Good Lord, if I hadn't known you when you were the mousy little under-house girl, I'd be shaking in my boots."

She grinned, breaking character. "Thanks. I been workin'... rather, I should say, I *have* been working diligently to better myself, sir."

"Well, it's paying off." I held up the invitation. "I do hope I'm not too late."

She gave me a don't-be-ridiculous frown, then winked. "Aw, I don't s'pose 'e'll mind." Her words, and her slip back into informality, made me smile. "Would you care to wait in the vestibule while I announce you, sir?"

"Yes, please. I should like that very much."

The entryway of Goddard's house was little changed from when I'd left my keys and farewell letter on the little silver mail tray and walked away. The coatrack, where Eileen hung my things, still stood beside the door. Next to it was a bench made from cherrywood and padded with a velvet cushion held down with brass tacks. Black-and-white checkerboard floor tiles. A round table of polished, quartersawn oak stood opposite the door. The silver goblet of flowers that I remembered was gone; in its place at the center of the table stood a globe with colorful fish. A nice touch. Stairs to my right led up. To the left, a corridor led to Goddard's sanctum sanctorum. It was a strange sensation, returning as a visitor to a place where I'd once lived.

Eileen returned shortly. "Right this way, sir." She winked again. "'Ope you brung your appetite."

"Thank you, Mrs. Murphy."

Goddard stood when I entered, surreptitiously closing his *Literary Quarterly* on the table. His features looked softer than I remembered, the lines at the edges of his eyes more relaxed. The dignified gray that had dusted his temples the last time I saw him now peppered his moustache and precisely cut dark hair. He was dressed for dinner, which I hadn't expected. But then again, I was a guest now. And he always looked dashing in black. His expression was curious but open, as if he wasn't sure why I might have turned back up after so long but was willing to entertain an explanation.

"Thank you for asking me to dinner," I said once Eileen had seated me at my usual place at the foot of the table, left, and closed the doors behind her.

"I figured it might have been a while since you'd enjoyed a proper meal."

"Two years, to be exact." Wilde had, of course, included me in his restaurant parties from time to time, but it wasn't the same as an intimate meal at someone's table.

A moment later the double doors opened again, and Eileen entered with a girl I didn't recognize. The girl was carrying a small tureen, and Eileen instructed her to set it on the table. My stomach growled as succulent smells filled the air. The food would be plain but well prepared and tasty. Goddard might have had the money to eat like Prince Eddy, but he always upheld strict standards of healthfulness and frugality. As the girl ladled out a hearty vegetable soup under Eileen's watchful eye, Goddard said, "The beard suits you."

My hand went unbidden to my chin. I'd been barefaced when Goddard had met me, and so I'd remained at his request. But as soon as I'd left his house, I'd embarked upon a spree of eccentric facial-hair stylings. The one I currently sported—a close-cropped "box beard" with thin lines of hair running up each side of my jaw to the ear—was admittedly rashly conceived. It also needed a trim.

"It's kind of you to say so."

"Although I prefer you clean-shaven." He lifted a spoonful of soup to his lips and blew. "Keeping busy?"

"You could say that."

We circled each other with the delicacy of diplomats until the end of the second course, carefully avoiding each other's eyes or topics that might lead to conflict. Eventually, however, we reached a state of mutual comfort, and conversation ensued. My stories of Wilde's hijinks amused him, and he was appropriately impressed by my more serious undertakings at Turnbull House. He told me all about his latest passion—a special greenhouse he'd designed, which now took up much of the back garden. He'd cultivated roses for years, but since I'd left he had expanded his interests to include flowers and plants in general. The greenhouse allowed him to experiment with creating new varieties, he explained, and even to grow out of season. He didn't mention teaching. Apparently he'd finally given up the last vestiges of the academic career that had been ruined by scandal so long ago. If so, he was well shot of it. If the intellectual world didn't appreciate his accomplishments by this point, it was their loss.

Before I knew it, my belly was fuller than it had been in two years, and my head was full of exceptional wine. I leaned back in my chair, nearly sleepy with satisfaction.

"And now," said Goddard as the girl cleared away the dessert bowls, "the time has come for gentlemen to adjourn to the parlor."

So the morning room was a parlor now.

It wasn't important, I suppose, what the room was called. When I'd lived at York Street, he'd given it over to me. I'd been too intimidated to alter the decor, but over time, Goddard's preference for clean-lined, masculine furnishings had become my own. As I followed him inside, I noted the two boxy Morris chairs he'd commissioned during my tenure. The design had come from America, and in its straight slats of wood and crisp corners, I sensed echoes of the bold forthrightness of Bess Lazarus's countrymen. Off to the side stood the olive-colored velvet divan, always a favorite of mine. The double desk remained before the window that faced out onto a small patch of dormant roses and a rather impressive-looking greenhouse. Only one side of the desk was in use. A cheerful wood fire burned in the fireplace.

"The usual?" Goddard asked as I took a seat on the divan. I nodded.

Many men would have taken cigars at that point, as well, but for health reasons, Goddard abstained from all but the occasional Egyptian cigarette. His one indulgence was fine whiskey, which he served in the cut-crystal glasses I remembered well. He walked over to hand me the fuller of the two glasses and then, to my surprise, sat down rather close beside me.

"So," he said, taking a long sip from his glass. "You never told me why you decided to contact me after all this time."

"Well…" As I searched for the right words, he quietly set his drink on the polished wood floor. "It's funny you should—"

The kiss came as such a surprise that I scrambled backward across the divan and almost tumbled over its rounded arm. Whiskey sloshed over the rim of my glass, splashing silently onto the Chinese rug. What remained I belted back in one go before setting the glass on the floor and wiping my shaking fingers on my trousers.

It wasn't that I was averse to the idea of kissing him, but I really hadn't expected it. In fact, if I'd seen him start toward me in the first place—he was remarkably quick for a man in his mid-forties—I'd have assumed he was going for my throat.

Goddard chuckled under his breath. "Sorry. Did I startle you?"

"You might say that."

I was also taken aback by the presumption. I had always liked it when he took control, and the hard, whiskey-flavored slickness of his mouth had left me aroused. All the same, I was no longer his plaything. Part of me felt as if he should have at least asked permission.

I forgot my objections when he leaned in a second time, slowly, and cupped my face in his smooth, muscular hands. Now that I was expecting it, the kiss felt like coming home after a long, unpleasant journey. For just a moment, all of my troubles dissolved, and nothing existed except his fingers in my hair, the traces of his jasmine and bergamot cologne, and the smooth, familiar contours of his mouth.

And then as suddenly as he had moved in, Goddard pulled back, leaving me confused, disappointed, and blinking in the gaslight and shadow.

"Why did you come, Ira?"

"To ask you for money," I said.

I know. *I know.* But every drop of blood in my head had surged to my cock, and I found myself incapable of the higher functioning required for either diplomacy or deceit.

Perhaps that had been the idea.

Goddard raised his eyebrows and reached for his drink. From his expression I imagined he must have been asking himself if he really hadn't taught me any better than that. He swirled the last swallow of whiskey around the bottom of his glass, regarding it with seeming disappointment.

"It's not for me. It's for Turnbull House. Our landlord wants to sell the leasehold. If we can't raise the money to buy it, we're out."

"I see."

"Then you'll help?"

"No."

Really, should I have expected a different answer? And yet clearly I had, or I wouldn't have come in the first place. Sighing, I stood.

"Then I'm sorry I wasted your time. Thank you for dinner."

"I've no doubt it's a good cause," he said, laying a hand on my forearm with a firmness that told me the conversation wasn't over. Warily, I sat back down. "Dr. Lazarus wouldn't involve himself if it weren't. But tell me, Ira, how are you living right now?"

"Not like this." I gestured around the elegant room where I had frittered away many a day.

"But no more Whitechapel doorways."

"No, but—"

"You did it all on your own."

"I couldn't have done it without your help," I said pointedly.

"But there's help and then there's help," he said. He leaned back against the arm of the divan, crossed his arms over his chest, and regarded me with a gleam in his eye.

"I don't follow."

He shrugged. "Give a man a fish. I gave you tools. I gave you the education necessary to become a secretary, and then I gave you a first-rate typewriting machine. You did the rest."

"But—"

"Despite the way you left, there were times I was tempted to funnel some money your way. Not a lot, perhaps no more than a secretary's salary. But if I'd done that, how would you be living right now?"

"I'd certainly have better quarters," I said petulantly. "And nicer clothes. And meat more than once a week, and—"

"Wrong," he said triumphantly. "You wouldn't have worked as hard as you have, and you know it. You'd be living exactly the same way you are now, only you wouldn't have two years of work experience behind you. You'd have no references. You'd be, for all intents and purposes, a kept man. Only I wouldn't be reaping the benefits of that kind of arrangement."

"I suppose." No supposition about it, I realized with chagrin. He was right.

"So it is with all charitable causes. If I were to buy your friends the leasehold, there would be great celebration. Things would be fine for a while, but then the building would need repairs. Or Mrs. Lazarus would go off to have her baby, and you'd need money to actually hire a teacher. Or something else would come up. What your shelter needs is a path to self-sufficiency."

I opened my mouth, but no sound came out. Twelve youths, a pregnant woman, and a doctor who was running two charities without pay. If any of them were remotely self-sufficient, they wouldn't be there. I'd always known Goddard was pragmatic. I'd never thought him cruel as well.

And I wasn't even going to ask how he knew about Bess's baby.

"You need a product your residents can produce and sell," he said. "A service they can perform. You could teach them to shine shoes."

"Shine—that's fine to say, Cain, but we need the money now. The landlord is about to chuck us into the street. If we don't have a building, how are we going to set up a workshop?"

A slow smile spread across his lips, and I could tell he'd been leading me to this point all along. "You could buy the leasehold, Ira."

"If I could buy the leasehold, why the devil would I have come to you?"

His dark eyes grew black, and I knew I'd gone too far. I'd not used that tone with him before. Probably few people ever had. I was suddenly, painfully aware that I was in the presence of the Duke of Dorset Street, and I'd do well to harness my tongue.

"I'm sorry," I said, reflexively bowing my head. "I've spoken out of turn."

He let a long, heavy pause settle between us, then said, "More whiskey?"

"Please."

He reached behind him to the trolley and found the decanter. After he'd poured us each a strong belt, he said, "I wasn't being facetious, Ira. Have you forgotten my offer?"

"That letter you left on my desk more than two years ago?" I hadn't forgotten. I hadn't read it, either. But neither had I thrown it away.

"If I know you, the envelope is still on your desk, probably still unopened." He tutted. "You really should try to see to your correspondence in a timely manner."

When I'd left, I'd made it ever so clear that I'd no intention of participating any longer in his criminal activities. My feelings hadn't changed. But for some reason I'd held onto the letter. I'd thought about tossing it—almost every day. Yet somehow it had always ended up tucked safely beneath one stack of papers or another.

Smirking, he clinked his glass against mine and took a sip.

"This is how it will work. I'll give you the money to buy the leasehold, and you'll pay me back in installments. With a few specific conditions. How much did you say your landlord wants for it?"

"Four hundred eleven quid," I said cautiously.

"Right. If you can scrounge up fifty-two pounds per quarter, the leasehold will be yours in two years."

The Duke of Dorset Street was offering an interest-free loan? I narrowed my eyes. It was too easy, and yet the hope it represented was tantalizing. The very small part of my brain that represented good judgment told me it was time to leave. And yet, like a fish, I followed the bait.

"Of course if you wanted to make it go faster, you could run a few errands for me from time to time. Nothing illegal. Probably not even anything that would offend your delicate sensibilities. Deliveries, perhaps. Imagine showing up at Turnbull House tomorrow afternoon with the papers in your hand."

Oh, yes, I could see it—the tears of relief in Bess's eyes as the threat of moving Turnbull House to her own house faded away. Lazarus's disbelief and, ultimately, his admiration as I handed him the documents. I could imagine it all too well. I could also imagine what would happen if we didn't come up with the money. And I could also imagine the trouble that could come from allowing the Duke of Dorset Street back into my life to that degree. If I returned to work for him, even in this small way, what other compromises would he ultimately require?

Briefly I thought of poor old Dorian Gray from that story of Wilde's. A deal with the devil. I remembered the first deal I'd made with this particular devil, on this very couch, when I'd become his creature. It had changed my life in so many ways, good and bad. But there was no need for melodrama. It was just a loan, and possibly a bit of recreational sodomy. If I kept my head, we could leave it at that.

"What's the catch?" I asked.

He patted my thigh delightedly. My heart leaped to my throat. It was terrifying the flood of images, sensations, and memories that his mere touch raised in me.

"I'm glad you asked that. Should you accept this loan, I would expect Turnbull House to come up with a plan, within the next week or so, for a business it could use to support itself. Numerous charities right here in London have done so successfully. I could give you a list if you'd like. It wouldn't be difficult."

"A list." I mused. Well, why couldn't Turnbull House come up with something, then? Especially if we were no longer laboring under the threat of eviction. But fifty-two quid a quarter was still a lot of money. "And you said something about running errands to offset the principal?"

He seemed pleasantly surprised at my use of appropriate financial terminology and patted my knee again. Then he gave my thigh a squeeze, letting his hand remain. "You can start by making a delivery for me tomorrow. I'll send someone to Turnbull House with instructions. I'll pay you some now and the rest upon completion."

"A delivery."

He took two half-shilling coins from his pocket and laid them side by side on my thigh. The symbolism wasn't lost on me. Two half-shillings was what he used to slip into my trousers back in Whitechapel before disappearing into the night.

"Nothing illegal, I promise. I'll write you out a cheque before you leave. You can have the leasehold in your hand by the end of tomorrow."

It sounded easy, but the devil always made it sound easy. No one sold his soul for the opportunity to work hard.

"And what if we're unable to repay the loan?" I asked.

"Then you would come to work for me until such time as the debt was paid."

"Work...for you? Doing what?"

He chuckled. "Oh, I'm sure we'd find something. But let's not give up before we've begun, hmm?"

He moved his hand to the crease of my thigh, causing an instant, if involuntary response. I swallowed hard, still not completely sure his offer was the best idea, but absolutely certain I didn't want him to remove his hand. He leaned toward me, slowly again, and nuzzled my neck. His jasmine and bergamot cologne made my head swim, and the smoothness of his freshly shaved chin raised goose bumps all along my flank.

"Most importantly," he murmured into my ear, "once you've accepted my terms, you'll be able to accompany me upstairs without feeling you've whored yourself."

I swallowed, my face turning to meet his. "Only deliveries," I whispered against his mouth. He nodded. "Nothing illegal." He shook his head, lips smiling against mine. "I suppose there's no harm in that, then."

CHAPTER FIVE

WEDNESDAY

The following afternoon was the finest I'd ever seen in November. The air was clear and crisp, the sky a dazzling pale gray. The stink of the Thames was muted that day, and a breeze stirred the soot in the cracks and corners of the buildings. As I approached Turnbull House, my boots rapping sharply on the cobblestones, I felt like a returning hero. Not only was my stomach full and my libido fully sated, but the inside pocket of my coat—which Mrs. Murphy had miraculously found a way to dry the night before—was bulging with the documents transferring ownership of the Turnbull House leasehold to me. Sighing satisfaction, I flung the door wide, looking for someone to impress.

What quashed the urge wasn't my own sense of decorum—you know me better than that—but the argument that exploded in the corridor the moment I stepped inside.

"No, Bess!" Lazarus shouted in that harried tone that said he'd shouted it four or five times already. "Absolutely not!" He was in that broom closet he used as an office, and his voice barreled through the open door, down the hall toward me like a freight train. He had been such a quiet man when I'd first known him. But his wife's outspokenness seemed to be rubbing off on him lately. Or perhaps the stress was finally causing him to crack.

"I don't see what you have to say about it!" Bess returned.

"I'm your husband!"

"It's *my* hair. And at least a month's rent!"

"It's out of the question!"

"It's none of your business!"

Lazarus slammed the door.

I could imagine him sputtering away in that back room, his face turning as red as a strawberry, that vein throbbing away on his forehead. He liked to think he was in charge, but he knew better. We all did. And that bothered him, too. I wondered what they were arguing about this time, but when she burst out of the classroom, eyes blazing, I knew better than to ask.

"Hullo, Bess," I said.

Her face was flushed, and the tightly curled dark hair in question was falling out of its bun in unruly ringlets. She looked me up and down, her expression fierce. "Hmm. Finally roll out of bed, did you?"

Just how late was it? I glanced at my pocket watch. Oh, dear. "You look lovely this morn—er, afternoon." She must have sensed the amusement in my voice, or perhaps it was the spring in my step that annoyed her. "All right, then?"

"You try talking some sense into him. I have lessons to organize."

She bustled back into the classroom and slammed the door. I looked down the hall again. Whatever was bothering Lazarus, he'd need a moment to let his temper die down. I hung my coat and hat, gingerly removing the building documents from the coat's inner pocket. A sudden movement toward the end of the hall caught my attention. The boy Sergeant Mathers had brought by the day before emerged at the head of the basement stairs, an apple in his thieving little hand.

"Wot? The missus said I could have it." Looking me straight in the eye, he took a generous bite.

I didn't feel like arguing, so instead I asked, "Where are the rest of you?"

"Afternoon trainin'. Ain't found me a place yet, have they?"

"So you're staying behind, making yourself useful here?"

"That's right."

He stuffed the apple into his waistcoat pocket and leaned against the wall. From another pocket he brought out a piece of string and began to weave a scratch cradle.

"Still wearing yesterday's clothes, I see," I said.

"What's it to you?"

"Nothing. But everyone gets at least one extra set of clothes. Bess likes everyone to be well turned out."

He shrugged, looking down at the elaborate pattern of loops he was weaving around his surprisingly delicate fingers. "Nuffin' wrong wiv' the ones I got," he mumbled.

"Suit yourself. But if you start to stink, Bess'll have you in the bath so fast it'll make your head spin."

He sucked in a quick breath, fear flashing across his face. Yes, it was definitely fear. But why? Before I could ponder it further, he forced his features back into an insouciant smirk. "Doubt anyone could smell me in this shithole anyway."

His words stung, but his reaction to the idea of a bath brought me up short. Plenty of boys—and grown men, for that matter—saw soap and water as an unnecessary bother. But I'd never met anyone who lived in terror of it.

"This is my shithole," I said evenly. "Bought and paid for. So if you're eating my apples and sleeping under my roof, I'll thank you to show a little consideration, if not for yourself, then at least for the rest of us. By the way, I never got your name."

He regarded me for a moment. When it was clear I wasn't going away, he slowly unwound the string from his fingers, stuffed it into his trouser pocket, and held out his hand. "Jack." The bones of his hand were fine, though the muscles felt strong. His nails were bitten to the quick. "Jack Flip."

I frowned. "What kind of name is that?"

"It's my name, innit? And you are?"

"Ira Adler."

"You a Jew, then?"

He didn't approach the subject with the disdainful tone I'd heard from one or two of our donors. Rather, it was the tone in which one might ask, *you're joking, right?* Polish and Russian Jews were plentiful in this part of town, but having brought their skills with them, and being generally hardworking and ambitious, they usually didn't stay in East London long. If I—unemployed and inclined toward indolence—were a Jew, then I was a poor example.

"Sounds like a Jewish name, anyway," he said.

I shrugged. "My mother might know, but she left me in a workhouse when I was three. Then she died."

My throat tightened unexpectedly around the last few words. It was something I hadn't thought about for quite a while, and I was surprised that it still had an effect on me. It seemed to have an effect on Jack Flip, as well. His eyes widened for a split second, and his jaw lost a hair of its hardness. He cocked his head and looked at me a bit differently—as if perhaps I might be more than just another slumming do-good.

"Me mum's dead, too," he said.

"Sorry to hear it. Your dad?" A dark look crossed his face, and I knew I was better off leaving it be. "Sorry. It's none of my business."

Shrugging, he said, "Way of the world, innit?"

"That it is." The last traces of our argument drained away, leaving me feeling a bit drained as well. I clutched the documents tighter in my hand. Hopefully once I presented them to Lazarus, it would set things right on a number of levels. As we approached the door to Lazarus's office, I heard him stirring behind it. I turned to Jack, dropping my voice. "So before I go face the lion, what're they arguing about this time?"

Jack leaned in conspiratorially. "Money problems. She wants to sell her hair. He's dead against it."

I snorted. Our money troubles weren't funny, but arguments between Tim and his wife could be downright entertaining. I was this close to admitting that, when I was bored, I sometimes stirred the pot a little to get them going. But imminent eviction held no humor. And at that moment, I was the only one who knew that it was no longer a threat.

"I shouldn't worry about it," I told him, holding up the papers. "How are you settling in, anyway?"

He propped a shoulder against the wall, took out his apple, and rubbed it against his waistcoat. Examining the shine, he said, "'S'all right, I guess. Don't much like sittin' with the little ones to learn me letters."

"You don't read, then?" Bess grouped the students by ability, rather than age. Jack shook his head. "You'll catch on quick enough. How old are you?"

"Sixteen," he said, sticking out his chin.

"More like fourteen, I should think. I was almost ten years older than you before I could write my name."

He looked up from his apple.

"Really?"

"Absolutely. There was a teacher came 'round the workhouse, but I didn't pay much attention. And then when I was your age I ran away."

"But they said you're a secretary. How'd you—"

"I had a friend," I said, smiling as I pictured Goddard the way I'd left him that morning, propped languidly in the parlor doorway, smirking like that cat who'd drunk the cream. "A very, very patient friend, who taught me everything I know. If it wasn't for him, I don't know where I'd be."

He looked me up and down appraisingly. "Aw, I reckon you could get at least sixpence if you dressed up nice, took yourself off to Piccadilly, an'—"

"*Sixpence?*" I cried, rather too loudly. The sound of Tim's paper-shuffling stopped for a moment. I coughed and straightened my collar.

Jack Flip cracked a crafty smile. "I knew it. But don't worry, Mr. Adler, your secret's safe with me."

I exhaled heavily and shook my head. "It's no secret, Jack. But that part of my life is over. And I wouldn't wish it on anyone. That's why Dr. Lazarus and I started this place."

He seemed to think that over for a moment. "He the 'friend' you told me about?"

"No."

He opened his mouth, no doubt to ask another grossly impertinent question, when I heard Lazarus sigh and flop down into his chair.

"Look, we can continue playing getting-to-know-you later, but right now, I need to talk to the doctor." I couldn't resist patting the deed again and adding smugly, "In all likelihood, Mrs. Lazarus will just have to keep her hair on."

He grinned as I put my hand on the doorknob and let myself in. Inside, Tim Lazarus was sitting in a chair behind a desk that nearly touched the walls on either side. His arms hung limply, the lapels of his jacket flapped untidily, and he was staring at the ceiling. "And what good news do *you* have for me this afternoon?" he asked without looking at me. I was bouncing up and down on my toes as I thought about how to word my story for the greatest effect. "I suppose you're thinking to head down to Commercial Road to make a quick sixpence?"

"Why does everyone assume that's the only way I can make money?" I demanded. If not for the papers in my hand, I'd have been mortally offended. "Worse, why does everyone think my favors come so cheap? You look awful, Tim."

He turned to face me and pushed his hair back over his forehead. He'd rolled up his sleeves and had clearly been looking over the mess of papers on his desk until he couldn't think straight. "I'm sorry, Adler. I didn't sleep a wink. Please tell me we don't have rats or a fire or some other damn thing that needs money and attention."

"No." It went without saying that he worked too hard. But I'd never seen him looking this grim. I forgot all about my self-aggrandizing story. "Were you here all night? You should go home. And stop by the clinic on your way. Really, Bess and I can handle things for a day."

He shook his head and attempted a weak smile. "It's fine, Adler. What did you need?"

"Here." I pushed the deed across the battered table at him. "Perhaps this will make your day a little brighter."

He leaned across the desk, squinting at the paper in the dim light from his lamp. Then he snatched it away and read it for himself. Twice.

"I...I don't understand." He looked at me, clearly afraid to believe his eyes.

I grinned. "We own the leasehold, now. Or rather I do. So tell everyone to stop packing. Turnbull House is here to stay."

He blinked his red-rimmed eyes. Clearly he was thinking of the exact words he would use to tell me how brilliant I was and how I had been the saving of Turnbull House, himself and Bess, and perhaps all of Western civilization. At long last he opened his mouth and said, "Get out."

"What?"

He stood. Lazarus isn't tall, but he is quite fit, and when he gets his dander up, he can be intimidating. "Get out."

"Tim—"

He backed me up against the door, then reached around me to open it. "Don't you understand what we're trying to do here, Ira?"

"Tim?" Bess was at the door, now, too, looking alarmed. Perhaps she was wondering whether the lack of shouting was due to Lazarus's long-overdue collapse. I didn't see Jack Flip, but he was probably skulking about somewhere. "Ira? What's going on?"

"I purchased the leasehold." I turned. "Really, I'd thought people would be happy about this."

"Happy?" Lazarus demanded. "Happy? We're running a youth shelter here, Adler. We are trying to show these young people a way to earn a living with their hands and their minds. We're trying to show them that they don't have to *debase* themselves to get on in the world. *You* were our great success. You were our example. 'Look at Mr. Adler,' we'd say. 'He used to be in the same position you were in, and just look at him now.' But now you've gone and—"

"Gone and what, Tim?" I didn't raise my voice often—at least not as often as Tim had been doing recently. I shuddered to think what he'd be like after the baby came. I snatched the deed back and shook it in his face. "How do you think I got this, anyway?"

"Well, let's see." He crossed his arms across his chest, arranging his features in that patronizing expression that always made me want to strike him. "You leave yesterday evening, come back this morning in the same clothes—more disheveled, of course—and smelling of another man's cologne. You're wearing that same stupid grin you always wear when you've had a particularly good—"

"Tim, please," Bess said quietly.

"When you've *had it* particularly well. And now you come skipping in, waving the deed to the building. What else am I to think, Adler?" He stopped for a moment and scratched his stubbly chin—the presence of stubble only showing just how deranged this entire situation had made him. "Of course I'd never have thought it of Mr. Porter."

The image of our bewhiskered landlord standing with his trousers at his ankles flashed through my mind. It was terrifying.

"Mr. Porter sold me the deed for four hundred eleven quid, nothing more or less," I said primly.

"Aha! And just where did you get that kind of money? I suppose Wilde returned from France and decided to pay you for ten years of work in advance? Aha! Aha, I say!"

I opened my mouth to speak, but no words presented themselves. "I...ah..."

"I thought so! Get out! Get gone and never come back!"

He pushed me back through the door and slammed it in my face. I heard the lock engage. Bess was to my right. Jack was suddenly at my left elbow. They were both looking at me expectantly. I pounded on the door with my fist.

"You're being childish, Tim!"

"You have no respect! You have no respect for me, for Turnbull House, or even for yourself!"

"You're making a mistake!"

"Who did you...who did you...*for four hundred quid?*"

"Four hundred eleven! But I didn't—Tim, even I'm not that good!"

Jack Flip looked up at me, cracking a grin.

"Where *did* you get the money, Ira?" Bess asked, quite reasonably.

"From Goddard."

"*Goddard?*" Tim shouted. His tone made me suddenly glad there was a door between us.

Bess's eyes widened and she gave the door a few dainty, open-handed smacks. "Tim, calm down. Remember your heart." She turned to me. "He gets such palpitations."

"He...he...Goddard! *For four hundred quid!*"

"Four hundred eleven!" I shouted, giving the door a kick. "And it wasn't like you make it sound. I did...well, we did...but...it was two different transactions, Tim!"

There was silence after that. Bess and I looked at each other, both waiting for the crash as Tim keeled over dead. But the crash never came. After a few more moments of silence he said in that exhausted voice of his, "Ira, I don't know what to say."

"How about thank you?"

"What?" He opened the door.

"You could say, 'Thank you, Ira, for saving Turnbull House and for keeping me, my pregnant wife, and twelve young people off the streets.' That'd be a good start."

He looked from me to Bess. Bess nodded encouragingly, though I had a feeling that once she got me alone, she'd subject me to her own interrogation.

"You didn't do anything illegal to get that money," he said warily.

"I promise."

After a long pause, he sighed.

"Then that's all right, I guess."

"But I did sign a contract," I said.

"You *what?*"

"Tim, your heart..."

"You didn't think that Goddard would just give me the money, did you?"

"Oh, God." He moaned, leaning his forehead against the doorjamb.

Mrs. Lazarus hung her head.

There's a long, sordid history involving me, Goddard, and Tim Lazarus. Even if you didn't know the full story, it would be easy to tell what our roles had been, from Tim's reaction to the idea of Goddard getting into my trousers. A history he must surely have shared with the missus, judging from her knowing look.

"I signed a contract," I repeated. "For a loan. We're supposed to come up with a plan to make Turnbull House self-supporting."

"Self-supporting?"

"It seemed more reasonable when he explained it," I mumbled.

"Ira, if we were self-supporting, we wouldn't be in this mess!" Did he think I didn't know that? Was it my fault I couldn't argue the point as convincingly as Goddard had? Perhaps I should put my hand on his knee and show him! Once again I was reminded of Dorian Gray's bargain—a deal with the devil that had ultimately ended in destruction. I'd made such a deal with Goddard once: my autonomy in exchange for being spoilt absolutely rotten. It might have ended in destruction, had I not left. Had I done it again? No. The first deal hadn't cost me my soul, and this one wouldn't either.

"That's the condition of the loan," I said, straightening. "We come up with a business plan by the end of next week, and I submit it to him. Then we have two years to pay him back, in quarterly installments."

"That's fifty quid every three months."

"Fifty-two. He's not running a charity, Tim."

"No," Lazarus said. "We are."

"But if we manage, the building is ours, free and clear."

"And if we don't?" he asked.

I swallowed. I didn't particularly want to think about that. "If we don't, then I go to work for him. For Goddard."

"In what capacity?"

I sighed.

"Well, I, for one, think it's a great idea," Bess said, stepping between us. This wasn't the first time her American outspokenness came as a pleasant surprise. "No, seriously, Tim. Pennies from heaven might have saved the building, but what about next time?"

"That's exactly what Goddard said!" I said.

Lazarus shot me a black look.

"You did a good thing, Ira," Bess said.

"I wouldn't go that far." Lazarus grouched. She returned his black look tenfold. "Well," he said, "it does, at least, give us something to work with." He looked at Bess. "And you can keep your hair where it is."

"It's settled then." Bess clapped her hands together. "I'll call a meeting of the board for tomorrow. And in the meantime, I suggest you three get this place clean."

❖

The rest of the day passed without incident. Jack and I helped Bess tidy up, while Lazarus beavered away in his broom closet, trying to reconcile our reality with the new state of financial affairs. The few times he and I crossed paths in the hallway, he at least attempted to be civil, but his mind was clearly somewhere else. Eventually the sun set, the streets grew dark, and the daytime sounds of lorries and hawkers' cries gave way to the jangling, out-of-tune piano in the pub around the corner, voices rising with gin and temper, and the whispers of back-alley dealings. Pearl had arrived for the night watch, Bess was upstairs doing one final bed check, and it was time for me to go home.

But not until I'd cleared the air with Lazarus.

"Do you need something, Adler?" Lazarus asked from behind the closed door, as I raised my hand to knock. Figuring it was as close to an invitation as I was likely to get, I opened the door myself.

"Is everything all right now?" I asked. I hated when we argued—really argued—not least of all because it was usually my fault. Tim was one of my only true friends. We might have spent a lot of time sniping at each other, but it was more like the banter of an old married couple than actual conflict. And we almost never came to raised voices and slamming doors.

He sighed and gestured me inside. I waited while he turned up the flame of his desk lamp, and then for another moment while he shuffled the papers on his desk into a neat stack. "I apologize for my earlier outburst," he said, not looking up from his papers. I opened my mouth to respond, but he cut me off. "If you wish to enter into an ill-advised, legally binding agreement with a known criminal, that's your business."

"I did it for Turnbull House," I said.

He closed his eyes. "I know." He turned back to his desk, separated the stack of papers, then restacked them in a different order. In the dim paraffin glow, I caught snatches of ledgers, correspondence, and tradesmen's forms all mixed together.

"This place is a mess," I said.

"Thank you."

"Perhaps if you kept your papers better organized—"

"You're the secretary. Isn't that your job?"

"Actually, I'm the owner of the leasehold, now," I said, hoping to tease him back into his usual good-natured irascibility. Instead, he looked down, pinching the bridge of his nose. That vein began to pulse on his forehead again. "Well, Goddard is, I suppose, until we repay him."

"That's really not helpful."

"Let me try again. You're tense, Tim. No, more than tense. You look like you're ready to rip the ears off the next person who speaks to you."

"Then why are you still here?"

"Better me than someone who doesn't deserve it."

That earned a weak smile. Still looking down, he propped his elbows on his desk, his shoulders slumped. He had unbuttoned his jacket, despite the fact that his office was cold enough for me to see my breath in the air. He had loosened his tie as well, and his cuffs were grimy with perspiration.

"That time of month?" I asked.

I wasn't being crude. For many years, Tim Lazarus had taken a monthly injection of poison just in case an old enemy came for him. The injections made him cranky as a bear for a few days afterward, but his enemy—a superior officer from his Afghanistan days, whose corruption Tim had uncovered—did end up trying to settle the score a few years ago. And the injections had saved Tim's life.

Of course the officer was long gone, now. The poison was just a joke—a joke that I thought increased in hilarity every time I told it.

Except that day. That day, Tim was really distressed.

"Don't think I'm not grateful for what you did," he said. "Even though I suspect it's going to end up causing us more trouble than it's worth. But sometimes…" He sighed, staring over my shoulder into the darkness beyond the doorway. "Sometimes I really resent how easily everything seems to come to you."

"Excuse me?"

"You know what I mean."

"No, I'm not sure I do. What, exactly, about my life has been easy, Tim? Growing up sleeping in doorways? Selling my arse for a shilling on a good night?"

"Being swept into the lap of luxury by a disgustingly wealthy crime lord?"

"Then giving it up because you'd infected me with a terrible case of *scruples*?" I shuddered. Nothing was more counterproductive to lasting material happiness than scruples. Except, perhaps, the clap.

Lazarus stood, stretching out his kinks and cramps, and squeezed through the meager space between the edge of his desk and the wall. He leaned against his desk, facing me. I could feel the heat radiating from his body, despite the November chill seeping through the outside wall. I could see the shadow his stubble cast against his chin. And I was suddenly very, very aware of just how unnecessarily close he was standing.

"You've always known who you are," he said, his voice gravelly soft.

I swallowed. "Doesn't everyone? I mean, it's no great mystery—"

"Stop." He took a deep breath and laid a heavy hand on my shoulder. "Ira Adler, you have all the perceptiveness and all the emotional complexity of a peppered moth."

I frowned. I didn't have a poet's tortured soul, it's true. Emotional depth brought nothing but misery. Just look at Tim. He was grayer than Goddard, now, despite being a decade younger. It suited him, somehow. It suited him well.

"Are you insulting me after I just bought you a building?" I tried for flippant, but the words were heavy on my lips. As he dragged his hand along my shoulder to my neck, cupping my cheek with one hand, I froze. Taking my face in both hands, he kissed me, suddenly, in a way that was simultaneously violent and tender.

A surprise, to say the least, though not an unpleasant one. I'd missed his peppery kisses and the astonishing way, for such an otherwise unassuming man, that he liked to take command. But that part of our association was long in the past. What was he thinking? And could he have picked a worse time, or place, to indulge in this particular bit of nostalgia?

He broke the kiss and stumbled back, leaving me slack-jawed with shock and more than a little aroused.

"There," he said softly. "See? You know exactly who you are."

"What on earth are you talking about?" If anything I was less sure now than I'd ever been in my life.

"Nothing. Forget it."

Forget it? I might have been a shallow-hearted insect, but this wasn't something I'd be likely to forget. We hadn't been on intimate terms for many years, and he hadn't given any indication since then that he desired to revisit that part of our past. Not that I'd have objected under different circumstances, but both of our lives had moved in very different directions since then. In particular, one of us was about to become a father.

On the other hand, perhaps this had nothing to do with me. Perhaps any man might have done so at that moment—any man in a smoky back room. Or on a Whitechapel street corner. My arousal drained away, and cold anger replaced it.

"Shall I disrobe now?" I asked.

"No."

"Is that a sixpence in your pocket? Will you leave it on the desk when you're finished?"

He looked away. So did I.

This was a stupid argument. Lazarus hadn't meant to insult me. He hadn't been himself lately, and my acting like a child wouldn't solve whatever was bothering him. Perhaps it was time for me to play the adult for a bit.

"Shall I pour us a whiskey?" I asked, gently this time.

For a split second, he looked as if there were nothing he wanted more in the world. Then, pulling himself together with great effort, he said, "No, thank you, Adler. As you can see, I've quite a bit of work to do. Wouldn't want the new landlord to think we're a bunch of deadbeats." He laughed weakly. "Anything we have to say to each other can wait until tomorrow. Now get out. I'm sure at least one of your men is wondering where you've gone."

❖

What the devil was happening?

As I shut the door to Turnbull House behind me and locked it, a cold drizzle began to fall. Fitting for my mood, I supposed. November was turning out to be unaccountably wet and stormy. Resisting the temptation to force myself to walk home through it purely out of spite, I trudged to the corner and found a stop for an omnibus that would take me to within a block of my building on Aldersgate Street. The bus came quickly. I hopped on in the back, paid my fare, then sat, carefully and apologetically, in the only remaining seat, next to a young woman who appeared to have had as trying a day as I had, though probably not for the same reasons.

I'd spent so much time in a celibate desert that I'd almost grown used to it. Wilde's raucous suppers had been an easy substitute for a social life. Fending off his advances had become a game that simultaneously fed my ego and made me feel as if there were a warm set of arms for me to tumble into any time I should choose to abandon my silly principles regarding business and pleasure. I felt the occasional wistful pang when I caught Lazarus gazing besottedly at his loudmouthed wife or noticed her sneak an extra spoonful of costly sugar into his tea. But for the most part, I'd been able to convince myself that this ersatz life, this ambient intimacy, was, in fact, everything I wanted.

And then suddenly I was no longer wandering in a celibate desert but drowning in a sea of men. Normally, I'd have congratulated myself on my good fortune. But each of these men came with his own set of complications. And complication was the last thing I wanted at this point in my life.

Marcus's arrival had been a gift—as had been his departure. I'd been closer to despair the night he'd turned up than I had been in quite a while. I'd been broke, unemployed, and lonely. With Wilde in Paris, the circle of acquaintances that had seemed so cozy had disintegrated, and my evenings had become quite dull. A handsome young blond had been the perfect pick-me-up. That said, it was good he'd taken his leave when he had. The way he'd blathered on to

Lazarus about "us" and "ours" after a single night's pleasure had set me on edge.

Goddard had been a pleasant surprise. Knowing he disciplined his emotions as strictly as he did his employees, I wouldn't have thought he'd allow himself so much as a flicker of interest after all this time. The sex had been outstanding, as always. And he hadn't sent me back out into the cold, wet night the moment it was over. No, he'd seemed as content to lie next to me until mid-morning as he had been to weave a net of financial obligation that would tie us together for the next two years. That gave me pause. With Goddard, pleasure and obligation had always been intertwined. I'd do well to remember that—and to avoid falling into old habits.

But it was Lazarus who was making my stomach churn as I stepped off the bus and made my way up Aldersgate Street that evening. What on earth had possessed him to accost me like that? Years ago, even before Goddard, Lazarus had been my client. He hadn't been a virgin, but neither was he widely experienced—not with men or women, and certainly not with paid companionship. What I offered was easy and safe. He could satisfy his urges whenever he could afford it, and I would never make any inconvenient demands. As a bonus, we enjoyed each other's company. It really came as no surprise that he, in his inexperience, would fall in love with me eventually. Nor that I, knowing that this illusionary sentiment never ends well, would leave him when something better—in this case, Goddard—came along.

He'd harbored such a grudge for so long after that, that I'd avoided that section of town altogether. It sounds ludicrous, but until events brought us together again almost three years ago, I could literally feel his hatred ringing through the streets of Bethnal Green. Circumstances had forced us to put aside our animosity and work together, though. And now, as friends and business partners, we got on quite well.

But I never expected sex to enter the equation again. And especially not under these circumstances.

And then there was his wife.

Ordinarily, the fact of his marriage wouldn't have bothered me. Many of my past clients had been married—a fact they would reveal in choked, guilty whispers while pounding my arse from behind. I hadn't minded as long as they'd paid. It was different with Lazarus, though. Not only had I come to care about him personally, but I considered Bess my friend as well. And though I might have had the emotional depth of a butterfly and the moral sense of a rock, even I recognized that crossing that line would cost me the two true friends I had in the world.

Lazarus wasn't stupid, and he wasn't the type to let his emotions get the better of him. Usually. Surely he realized that his game was toying with the destruction of three lives—four, if you counted the baby. He wasn't normally reckless or uncaring. So what was he playing at? He was under extraordinary pressure, that much was clear. The shelter's imminent dissolution had been hanging over his head like a Damoclean sword. And his wife's growing circumference, on display for all the world to see, must have been a constant reminder of what was at stake for him personally, should he have failed.

Perhaps he was feeling nostalgic for the carefree days when he had only himself and his backstreet practice to support. No fraught network of intertwined responsibilities, all depending on him. I'd been part of those happier times—an uncomplicated bit of fluff to warm the cold nights. I could sympathize, truly I could. At the same time, the thought made me burn with indignation. If Lazarus had wanted me back—me, specifically—I might have entertained the thought—at least until the next time I heard Bess's dulcet tones ringing through the rafters. But this had nothing to do with me. My instinct had been right. I might have been anyone. Or no one at all. A fantasy. Or Lazarus's right hand.

If he expected me to take on this level of aggravation, he might at least offer to pay me for it.

By the time I reached my building's front door at Aldersgate Street, I was in a right state. I'd long since forgotten the cold, the rain, and the filth. I squelched up the stairs, heedless of the wet trail I was leaving behind. So absorbed in my thoughts was I that I barely registered the man crouched on the floor of the corridor next to my door.

"Just where the devil have you been?" Marcus demanded, struggling to his feet. He'd apparently been in that same position for some time, and it appeared that his legs had cramped.

My stomach sank, and my ire rose. "I beg your pardon?"

"Waited for you all night, didn't I? And most of the day, too…" As I drew closer, slowly, his angry expression drained away, and his blue eyes widened with what could only be described as concern. "Blimey, Mr. Ira, you look like you've lost your best friend. Come inside. I'll fix you a drink, an' you can tell me all about it."

The logical part of my brain said that this was the very last thing I should do. Marcus wasn't my friend. He wasn't my lover or confidant. More likely than not, he was after nothing more than another night's lodging and a chance to argue himself into a more permanent situation. At the same time, the stresses of the day—the unaccustomed conflict and profundity of emotion—overcame me in a heavy, fast-moving wave.

"Come on, then," I said, now thoroughly exhausted. I fumbled the lock open, and he held the door for me, taking my coat, hat, and boots once inside, as if I were a small child.

"You go sit down. I'll take care of you." I trudged across the room and lowered myself onto the bed like a load of very painful bricks, while he poured me a careful drop of whiskey from my meager supply. Kneeling beside the bed, he pressed the glass into my hand. "Don't worry, Mr. Ira," he said softly, brushing a bit of hair from my forehead. "Everything will work out. You'll see."

The glass was cool, and the whiskey was hot. I handed the empty glass back, lay down, and closed my eyes. My muscles, now warm and tingly, melted into the lumpy mattress.

"That's right," Marcus said, as sweet unconsciousness overtook me, "you let it all go." I felt him reach across me to take the extra pillow. "I'll be right here on the floor next to you, if you need me."

CHAPTER SIX

THURSDAY

The meeting was set for the usual time—eleven o'clock— and this time no one needed to drag me there. Though I still cringed inside when I thought about my exchange with Lazarus, the novelty of being the hero, at least for an hour or so, was enough to inspire me to wake up early. I was out of bed by eight. By nine, I'd had a quick wash in the basin, trimmed my whiskers, dabbed on a bit of cologne, put on my cleanest clothes, and bolted down a bit of the bread and tea Marcus had waiting. By ten o'clock, I was ready to go.

"S'pose I'll be on my way, then," Marcus said, as he handed me my coat. He'd already laced up his hand-me-down boots and draped his ratty coat over his arm. He was trying to put on a brave face, but I could tell he was dreading my turning him out again. We'd carefully avoided any discussion of his standing while performing our ablutions, but of course, one can't put these things off forever. He looked so forlorn, there by the door, holding out my umbrella like a faithful butler. The memory of his kindness last night hardened into guilt over what had to be done this morning. "Thank you so much for your hospitality, Mr. Ira."

"So you have somewhere to go?" I asked.

His mouth tightened, and he seemed to struggle between truthfulness and pride. "Not as such," he said, straightening. "But don't you worry 'bout me. You've done your bit, you have. Ain't fair to ask more 'n that."

"I suppose not. Well—"

"It's just the thought of going back to Commercial Road," he said, his voice cracking over the last two words. "You been there, Mr. Ira. You know what it's like. And with the Fitzroy Street brothel closed, and all me contacts scattered to the wind, and the rain…" He turned away, seeming to make a Herculean effort to gather his wits.

The thought of spending the night, perhaps many nights, on the mean East End streets made me break out in a cold sweat. My own time on that wicked quarter mile wasn't so far in the past that I couldn't close my eyes and hear the rats scrabbling behind me in the alleyways, or smell the refuse that ran through the gutters on rainy days. Aldersgate Street might not be a palace, but it was a damn sight better than that.

Marcus swallowed hard, let out a short breath, then turned to face me. "I'll be fine, Mr. Ira. No need to worry."

I stole a glance at my pocket watch. Forty-five minutes to get myself to Whitechapel. Why did hell always break loose when I was trying my damndest to do the right thing? I wasn't looking for a lodger—especially one who wouldn't help with the rent. At the same time, who was to say that, with training, the man might not be capable of contributing to expenses? Pennies, at first, of course. But if he learned to read and write, perhaps discovered some hidden talent—some talent that did not involve the removing of clothes— who could say how far young Marcus might go? Hadn't Goddard shown me the same kindness once?

"There's always a place for you at Turnbull House," I said. Though in truth, I didn't know where. We'd put two of the youngest ones head to toe in the same bed to accommodate Jack. And Marcus was quite a bit older than our oldest student. "You could learn to read and write. You could have a bed, and meals—"

"Thanks all the same," he whispered, staring out into the darkness of the hallway. Of course he knew, as I did, that it wouldn't be a good fit. In addition to the fact of his age, bumping into him on a daily basis would be very, very awkward.

There had to be some other option. I glanced again at my watch, knowing I had no time to give it adequate consideration. I had to get to the meeting, and even I wasn't stupid enough to leave him in my flat unattended, with a fifty-quid typewriter and all my spare clothes. And yet how could I just turn him out, when I might be able to help him in the same way Goddard had helped me?

"You really don't have anywhere else to go?" I asked.

He looked at me with sorrowful eyes. And then an idea struck me.

I shook my head. I was an idiot. But at least I wasn't heartless as well. "Right. Here's what you'll do. Spend the day looking for work. Honest work. I won't have you bringing back a pox, and I can't very well fetch you from jail. Go down to the docks. They're always looking for people to help with loading and unloading." I cast an evaluative glance at his torso. He was skinny, but probably good for a short spell of heavy lifting. "If that doesn't work, go down to Spitalfields Market and see if you can help out there. I should be back in the evening, seven, eight o'clock. Come by. We'll talk. And here." I handed him the heel of the loaf we'd shared earlier. "You'll need to keep your strength up."

Relief lit his face. His smile was radiant. My chest swelled with accomplishment. Not only had I returned kindness for kindness, but I'd reached between two untenable options and pulled out a completely different and wholly workable solution.

"Thank you, Mr. Adler. Thank you!"

"Call me Ira," I said, as he strode down the hall, no longer holding himself like a condemned man.

❖

By the time I arrived at Turnbull House, Pearl, Bess, and Lazarus had already cleaned the blackboard and straightened the rows of benches. Normally, at this time of morning, our charges would have been scratching out arithmetic problems on their slates, biting their tongues in concentration, their fingers covered in chalk dust. Today, however, they all sat ramrod-straight at the rear of the room. They all had scrubbed their faces and hands. The young men had slicked their hair down with water, and the young ladies were combed and plaited to Sunday standards. As I walked in, thirteen hopeful faces swiveled toward me—well, twelve hopeful ones and Jack, who wore his usual cocky smirk. And I felt just a touch of the staggering expectation under which Lazarus must have labored, day after day.

Pearl Brandt, Lazarus's nurse, and co-founder of Turnbull House, regarded me with a wary optimism. She sat patiently, rough hands clasped in her ample lap atop her freshly ironed apron. She'd given herself a good spruce-up when she'd done the residents—fresh cuffs and cap, steely hair combed into a neat bun beneath it. But she was still yawning from the night watch and wouldn't suffer idiocy in silence. Bess flitted about the room—as much as a six-months-pregnant woman can be said to flit—already having absorbed the news and ready to move on to the day's next task. She tossed me a quick smile between straightening the drapes and poking the coals in the fireplace.

Lazarus was the only one who didn't look over when I came in. Instead, he busied himself rearranging the desk at the front of the room. Eventually he cleared his throat and officially asked for silence. I took my place near the blackboard to address the room.

"Hello, everyone," I said. "Yes…well…erm…" I fiddled with my cuffs and considered taking off my jacket. It really was quite warm in there. "Some of you might have heard that Turnbull House is undergoing financial difficulties. It's understandable you would be concerned. However, I'm pleased to say you can now lay those concerns to rest."

Everyone seemed surprised when I announced that I had purchased the building's leasehold. I'd never put on airs, never pretended to have much more than the residents themselves had. No one would have trusted me if I'd done that—that much I remembered from my own rough-and-tumble childhood. But they did trust me, which was why their expressions when I told them their home was safe will stay with me for the rest of my days.

"The papers are in Dr. Lazarus's office, under lock and key. The building is safe, and so are all of us. But the fact remains that the money was a loan. We have a repayment schedule of fifty-two pounds per quarter—that's a little more than seventeen a month. We have to find a way to make that money and keep it coming in for a minimum of two years. Ultimately, though," I glanced at Lazarus, who was pointedly looking away, "it would be to our benefit to continue to support ourselves even after the loan is paid." Twelve pairs of wide eyes blinked at me. Jack didn't say a word, but his raised eyebrow said that that would be a pretty trick indeed. "So, over the next few days, I'd like you to think about ways we could earn money, honest money, and keep it flowing in. No idea is too ridiculous. Ah…that's all, I suppose."

"Thank you, Mr. Adler," Bess said, rescuing me. She turned to her charges. "Please give Mr. Adler's request some thought, while you enjoy your luncheon downstairs. You are excused."

The residents filed out, uncharacteristically subdued. One or two of them stopped to exchange a few words with me on their way. Jack Flip, I noticed, had traded his place on the bench for a back corner, where he stood, watching with an air of detached amusement.

"I still can't get that boy to take a bath," Bess said to Lazarus, *sotto voce.*

"I shouldn't worry about it," Lazarus replied. "He'll change his mind when the others start to complain. They won't be as gentle about it as you are."

"I think the more pressing problem," said Pearl, who stretched as she heaved her buxom form from her bench, "is how we're going to manage seventeen quid a month."

"Perhaps something the older residents have been learning in their vocational programs," I suggested.

"Shoemaking? Tailoring?" Pearl rubbed her square jaw. "Can't see how that could bring in much, especially since they're only learners themselves."

"The girls are learning needlework," I offered.

Pearl shook her head. "We might get a few commissions, a few more if they're good, but…"

"What about service?" Bess asked. "The girls can sew and mend, and all of the residents are accustomed to keeping the premises tidy."

Pearl shook her head. "Maybe in America, but here, the only people what would have our charges in their homes are the ones who'd put them right back to work doing what they was doing on the streets."

"We could try to find apprenticeships for the boys," Lazarus suggested.

"That would be good for the boys, but it wouldn't do much good for our quarterly obligation," replied Bess.

Just then, someone knocked at the front door. All heads swung in my direction.

"Is that my job now?" I asked. But before I could protest further, Jack was out of the classroom door and down the hall.

"Was he there this entire time?" Pearl asked as the front door rattled open. After an exchange of voices, two sets of footsteps walked back to the classroom. A moment later, Jack appeared with a muscular, ginger-haired man in an olive suit and matching bowler.

"He says he has a delivery for Mr. Adler," Jack said.

Well, well, well, Mr. Watkins.

The last time I'd seen Henry Watkins, one of Goddard's employees, he'd been throwing me to the ground as a building exploded in front of us. The bomb had been meant for Goddard, who had walked away with minor injuries. My new hat, which had been trampled in the subsequent mêlée, had not been so fortunate. I'd later told Goddard how Watkins had saved my neck. As I've said, Goddard rewards loyal employees handsomely, and though Watkins still walked with the swagger of an East End tough, his well-made shoes and neatly trimmed beard spoke of a man with a bit of cash to spread about. I couldn't reward him in the same way, of course. But I could at least refrain from betraying his identity and our prior acquaintance.

"I'm Mr. Adler," I said.

"Delivery for you, sir."

With a flourish, he produced a bouquet of flowers from behind his back. It was a strange grouping: pink rhododendrons, a few pink and white Christmas roses, and one very large purple thistle, all lying on a bed of straw. The straw looked as if it had been stepped on, though the rest of the flowers were pristine. Rather an unpleasant combination, especially considering it had come from Goddard, who had very distinctive and—up until this point—very good taste. But my confusion quickly gave way to embarrassment. Sending flowers, as one might to one's ladylove, was a bold gesture. We'd spent but a single night together after two years of separation. And I'd made very clear that I hadn't come for reconciliation, but for a loan. Moreover, considering the fact that we could both could get two years at hard labor on mere accusation of indecency, the gesture was as dangerous as it was mortifying. My face and neck went suddenly hot, and I began to stammer.

"Per your contract, you are instructed to deliver these to the address on the attached card." It sounded as if Watkins had rehearsed the words, to give them a dignity worthy of his new suit.

I blinked as he handed me a card with an address written in Goddard's tidy hand. Then, finally understanding, I slumped against the doorframe, relieved. "Oh, thank God. That is, yes. Yes, of course. Thank you. I shall deliver it immediately."

Thank God, thank God, *thank God*. Goddard hadn't sent *me* the flowers. He'd never be that indiscreet. Perish the thought! Delivering the flowers—to someone else—was my first task, my first step toward repaying the loan. I turned to the assembled group, whose expressions ranged from wry amusement to I-told-you-so.

"I did mention I'd be doing a little work on the side to speed things up a bit," I said.

"You mentioned it," said Lazarus.

"Will that be all?" I asked Watkins.

Leaning in conspiratorially, Watkins said, "Except he wanted me to give you this as well." He surreptitiously slipped a small, rectangular bundle into the pocket of my jacket.

"Thanks." Then a thought occurred to me. I took a scrap of paper from my pocket and motioned for something to write with.

Watkins pulled a pencil from behind his ear. I scribbled out a quick note, then carefully unfolded the crumpled photo across the back of which Wilde had scrawled his friend's name. Handing them both to Watkins, I said, "If you would please take this to Mr. Stoker at the Lyceum Theatre on Wellington Street." I flipped him a thruppence. Watkins tucked the note into his own pocket and nodded. "Yes, sir. Good day, sir." He tipped his hat and left.

As the front door shut behind him, I could feel the eyes of Lazarus, Bess, Pearl, and Jack on my back. I fingered the parcel through my pocket.

"Wot's that book, then?" asked Jack.

"Book?"

"In your pocket. It is a book he gave you."

"Oh...yes..." The heat crawled back up my neck. This was surely a gift, though a much more innocent-looking one. Nonetheless—

"I think that's private, Mr. Flip," Lazarus said. His tone was that of a schoolmaster issuing a correction. But when I glanced at him, his dark eyes bored into mine. "You don't have to tell us if you don't want to, Adler."

Well, really, who wouldn't rise to that?

I wrenched the little volume free of its paper and twine and held it up. "Poetry," I said, relieved at how safe and stuffy it sounded. Poetry from a former literature scholar. It wasn't Goddard's fault he'd been expelled from the ivory tower all those years ago. Well, perhaps it was a bit. Still, no one would have batted an eye at his transgression, had it involved some girl from the village instead of the third son of an earl. I wondered if the university fathers knew that in banishing Goddard from Cambridge, they would be unleashing upon all of Britain one of the most ruthless, efficient, and fearsome criminals the world had ever known.

"Coleridge or Catullus?" Lazarus asked under his breath.

Could have been either. Goddard had included an introduction to the better poets when he'd educated me. I flipped to the front of the book—a handwritten book, rather than a published one. Handwritten by Goddard. There it was—the table of contents. If I remembered correctly, Goddard had indeed harbored a fondness for Catullus. Ah, yes.

"What of it?" I asked. Lazarus smirked. I flipped back to the front, where there was an inscription. "What's 'XV'?"

"The Roman numeral fifteen," Bess said.

"Please say you're joking," muttered Lazarus.

"What?" I asked again. "What's wrong with that?"

"The fifteenth poem." He shook his head. "Just...read it. Later." "I intend to."

"This gives me an idea," Jack Flip suddenly said, relieving us of this awkward conversation. Four heads swiveled toward him. "Runners."

"Excuse me?" Lazarus said.

"Mr. Adler said wot Turnbull House needs to come up with some sort of a business, right? How about a messenger service? Everyone here grew up on the streets. Who knows London better? Who knows how to get somewhere fast? And who hasn't taken a penny to deliver a message now and then? We could start a messenger service to get the money."

"A penny here and there isn't going to get us very far, Jack," I said.

"Naw, we'd charge more'n that. 'Cause it wouldn't be just any little beggar, give him a penny an' never see him again. We'd be answerable to you." He turned to Lazarus. "People trust you, sir. You're a doctor. An' missus, you're a teacher. A nurse," he nodded at Pearl. "An' you," he turned to me. I gave him a cautioning look. "Well, now you're all respectable, like. Folks know if they pay you to deliver a message, it'd jolly well get there."

For the first time that day, Lazarus looked as if he wasn't, in fact, contemplating throwing himself off the roof. "That just might work, Mr. Flip. How much do you think we could charge?"

"I'd pay sixpence if it'd guarantee the message would get there safe and quick," Pearl said.

"And we could charge more for important messages, or messages that needed to get there within the hour," said Bess.

"If we had regular customers, we could charge them a single rate for a week or a month," I suggested.

Ideas began to fly hard and fast. Pretty soon, seventeen quid a month didn't seem like much at all. Jack Flip leaned back against the wall, crossed his arms over his chest, and grinned. When he caught me looking at him, his grin widened. I ducked my head in acknowledgement and in relief that, quite possibly, my deal with Goddard would not turn out to be the stupidest thing I'd ever done in my life. In the midst of discussion, Lazarus looked up at me.

"Adler, don't you think you should deliver those flowers before they wilt?

❖

I stepped out the door of Turnbull House into a bath of that strange illumination that comes between storms, as if the sun, discovering some untapped well of fortitude, were attempting one final push through the clouds. It didn't succeed, of course. The streets were still gray, though a lighter shade of it, and the air still smelt of blood and metal. The card Goddard had sent with the flowers directed me to an address so close that I was surprised Goddard hadn't simply instructed Watkins to make the delivery himself. The strange bouquet of straw and thistle was meant for Rudolf Lothar, who worked at the sugarhouse on Flower and Dean Street.

Now this was curious, I thought, as I tramped westward through the mud and grit, elbowing my way through a spontaneous odds-and-ends market that had sprung up in an alley. What on earth business did Goddard have with a sugarhouse? The Germans had London's sugar production locked up tight. Though there were as many sugarhouses on the East End as there were able-bodied beggars, Englishmen employed by them were few and far between. The owners preferred to hire their own tight-lipped, stoic countrymen for the backbreaking work. As for the business aspect of it, they preferred to keep that in the family as well.

The sugarhouse on Flower and Dean Street comprised six forbidding stories of brick and wood, with slits for windows and great smokestacks that pumped hot, sweet-smelling vapors into the air. The main structure and its associated outbuildings stretched across an entire side of the street from one intersection to another. The clanking of machinery was loud enough outside the facility—inside, it must have been deafening. A whistle sounded as I approached. The main doors opened, and stout-bellied men in shirtsleeves—and some in no shirts at all—spilled out into the midday cold.

Despite the toothsome results of these men's labor, sugar refineries were hot, unpleasant, dangerous places to work, and given to gruesome accidents. Just the other day, *The Times* reported an incident in which a sugar baker fell into in a vat of boiling cane juice. By the time they fished him out he was as red as a lobster and thoroughly poached. I shuddered. One might think that a place like that, where hundreds of people worked unconscionably long hours for less than a docker's tanner, would be fertile grounds for the nascent labor movement that had been sweeping the city. But if a movement was afoot to organize sugar bakers, I hadn't heard about it.

Goddard hadn't included a description of the man expecting my flowers, so I paced slowly back and forth in front of the factory until I'd caught the attention of a ruddy-faced, bushy-bearded man in a leather apron. He strode toward me, neither welcoming nor unfriendly—like a resident dog, prepared to bark or wag, depending on what I did next.

"I have a delivery for Mr. Rudolf Lothar," I said.

"Herr Lothar?" He brushed at a grimy streak on one of his meaty forearms.

I produced the bouquet, which, by this time, was beginning to droop a bit. He frowned at it, then, after a moment, turned and whistled to one of his compatriots. After a short conversation, the other man darted back into the building and returned with a slighter man in his forties, who wore a clean suit and expensive shoes. His thinning light-brown hair was pomaded and neatly arranged, and his sideburns had been recently trimmed. If not for his air of authority, I'd have guessed him a clerk. But Herr Lothar was clearly a manager of some sort. He pushed his spectacles up on his nose—his hands were smooth, I noticed, the fingernails clean—and regarded me officiously.

"I am Rudolf Lothar," he said.

"A delivery from Mr. Mephistopheles." I handed him the flowers.

Goddard used a number of false names in his criminal dealings, many drawn from literature. This one seemed a bit dramatic, especially in light of my recent work on *Dorian Gray*. But then again, how many sweaty Hanoverians had read *Dorian Gray?* Or the story by Goethe it was based on, for that matter?

Herr Lothar had, apparently, for his pale face went even paler as he perused the card and examined the arrangement of flowers. He licked his lips nervously and glanced about, as if Goddard might suddenly hiss up from the cobblestones in a cloud of sulfur-smelling smoke.

"Is there a return message?" I asked. His reaction concerned me. The bouquet was obviously not a lover's token.

"No message."

I watched with increasing trepidation as Herr Lothar turned and stumbled back toward the factory, obviously shaken to the core. Clearly he knew who he was dealing with. And clearly he knew that whatever he had done—or failed to do—Mr. Mephistopheles was not best pleased.

The thought of Goddard's displeasure would shake me to the core as well.

"Do you require anything else?" the bearded man asked, cracking his thick knuckles.

"No," I said. "My business here is finished."

❖

Late that afternoon I sent word to Goddard that I'd made the delivery. Good manners might have recommended I give Jack a chance to try out his messenger-service idea, but the Turnbull House gang was my responsibility. It felt wrong, somehow, to send someone who was trying to reform his life into the Aladdin's cave of ill-gotten treasure that Goddard's home would represent. A vague disquietude had settled over me in the wake of my interaction with Herr Lothar. Goddard had kept me out of his criminal dealings when I'd lived at York Street. I hadn't thought about it one way or another at the time, but now I was grateful. His were not, by and large, victimless crimes. Looking a person in the face who was quite possibly a future victim had left me unsettled, to say the least. I was also hungry.

I'd already spent a few pennies of Goddard's two half-shillings. But what remained bought a few hours' relaxation in a smoke-filled cider house, along with ale and a slightly overcooked chop. While I enjoyed my food and the as-of-late-unaccustomed solitude, an out-of-tune chanteuse belting out popular songs at an equally out-of-tune piano across the room, I rolled myself a cigarette and took out Goddard's book of poems.

The tome was actually much more than an ordinary book. Goddard had long railed against prevailing sensibilities, which allowed only the most flaccid translations of anything even remotely interesting. A publisher would probably find himself and his entire staff behind bars, should he attempt to put out any translation at all of what Goddard had considered Catullus's best work. What Mr. Watkins had passed me was, in fact, a bound book of empty pages, into which Goddard had hand-written the most ribald of the poems—in Latin and his own unblinking English translation—along with copious historical, cultural, and linguistic notes. He must have known I'd skim the notes. Still, I appreciated the effort. I flipped through the pages until I came to the fifteenth.

And then I choked on my ale.

"All right, love?" a waitress asked, noticing my distress.

I gave her a sheepish smile and stuffed the book back into my jacket pocket.

The fifteenth poem was a missive from Catullus to a friend, regarding the poet's young lover. Basically, it said, *Watch over him, treat him well, but keep your cock in your toga or I'll stick a radish up your—*

Was Goddard trying to be funny? He knew smutty verse always gave me a laugh. Even more so when it was accompanied by earnest and thorough academic research. I doubted he'd compiled the little volume for my benefit alone. More likely it was notes for a monograph that would never see the light of day.

Or was it a warning? The poem itself was certainly a warning. In our past, Goddard would have been in the poet's role, and I would have been the young man under his protection. Was he trying to tell me that I was under his protection once more? Or that I could be? Or was he warning me off someone else? I thought fleetingly of Marcus. He was just Goddard's type: hapless, malleable, and sexually adept. But Marcus had come to me straight from prison. Even if he hadn't, Eileen—Mrs. Murphy—had said that Goddard had been living alone since I left.

And Goddard himself had made no such mention.

No, I thought, checking my pocket watch—eight thirty—Marcus had come to me because I'd invited him. To think any different was paranoia. Although if Goddard really did want me back…No. It was useless to speculate. I stood, made eye contact with the waitress, and laid a few coins on the table. I'd told Marcus to come back to my flat about eight, and he was no doubt already there, working himself into a lather that I hadn't yet arrived home. Though I still thought I'd done the right thing by sending him out to look for work, I'd no idea what to do if he'd not found it. Perhaps, I decided, that would depend on how hard he'd tried.

❖

It was close to nine by the time I stepped off the omnibus. Every other streetlamp seemed to be on the blink, and no matter how deeply I cringed into the upturned collar of my coat, the rain still managed to drizzle down the back of my neck. As I hurried up Aldersgate Street and back up the stairs of my building, my boots plunged into every black puddle, tripped over each upturned cobblestone, and snagged on every loose board. Yet I pushed on, hoping that if Marcus was there, the sandwich and bottle of beer I'd brought back from the cider house would serve as an adequate apology for keeping him waiting.

My tardiness turned out to be the least of his worries.

The corridor of my building was about as well maintained as the dodgy end of Aldersgate Street. That is to say that in a hallway serving eight flats, only a single lamp worked, and it was at the far end. Marcus sat huddled beside my front door, as he had the night before. But this time, when he lifted his head to regard me with those how-could-you eyes, the dim, flickering light accentuated the bruises that marred his beautiful face and the lumpy mess that was his right cheek. He rose gingerly along the wall, sucking on a scuffed knuckle, and greeted me with a sickly smile.

"Went down to the docks today, like you said, Mr. Ira." He winced around a split lip. "They ain't much for casual work."

My God, how could I have been so stupid?

The dockworkers' strike had only been a year and a half before. Marcus wouldn't have heard about it in prison. As for me, though I sympathized with their cause, the strike hadn't made as much of an impression as it might have, had I not deliberately arranged my life to avoid physical labor. Before the strike, the Port of London would have been a fantastic place to pick up casual work. But now, especially with the labor movement picking up steam all over the city, I'm surprised they hadn't killed poor Marcus just for asking. And I'd sent him there.

"Oh, God. I'm so sorry." I reached for my key. "Really. Come in, let's get you cleaned off. Here," I said, handing him the sandwich and beer.

Hands shaking, I unlocked the door and quickly crossed the room to turn on the lamp and build a hasty fire. He slumped in my chair, and I poured water into the basin and set out a clean cloth for him while he attacked the sandwich. Understandable, I guess. The last thing he'd eaten had been the heel of bread I'd given him before sending him out. What had I been thinking?

"Thank you, Mr. Ira." He gasped between long pulls of beer. "I ain't et all day."

"I'm so sorry about sending you to the docks. I should never— I'd quite forgotten—is anything broken? Do you need a doctor? I'll send for Lazarus straight away—"

He smiled crookedly. He was missing a tooth. "It looks worse than it were. Leastways it can't be too bad. Walked back, didn't I?"

"You walked—" My mind reeled. Of course he had walked. I hadn't given him bus fare, had I? What if the dockworkers had beaten him so badly he'd not been able to walk? I had a brief, horrible image of him staggering, lost and disoriented, through the dark, twisty passages of the dockyards, weaving his way past opium dens and roving groups of rough-handed sailors. "I'm so sorry, Marcus. I should have—" What? What should I have done? Once again, in trying to help, I'd only made everything worse.

"Tried Spitalfields Market after that," he said. "But weren't nuffin' for someone who looked like he's been in a fight. Thought about tryin' Piccadilly later—" I inhaled sharply. Somehow the attentions of green-carnation-wearing toffs struck me as worse than being left to the tender mercies of sweaty sailors. "But I figured you wouldn't like that."

I didn't like it. Not one bit. But no longer because of how it would reflect on me or on Turnbull House. I felt responsible for Marcus now, and for my mistake. And the thought of him attempting to ply his trade after having been beaten to within an inch of his life...

But if Marcus stood on a street corner to earn his daily bread, it really was none of my business. I had no claim on him and wanted none. Truth be told, if he was as good at his vocation as our encounters suggested, it would be the quickest way for him to line his pockets and be out of my hair. Yet the idea of him offering up his bruised and battered form for some other man's pleasure—I exhaled slowly and forced myself to unclench my fists.

It had been a constable who had beaten me that night, so long ago, when Goddard had made the last-minute decision to take me into his home. Only one officer had assaulted me, but I'd looked much the same as Marcus did now. I wasn't in love with Marcus, as I'd later learn that Goddard had been with me. Yet somehow, against my will and better judgment, I found myself warming to him. Like a younger brother, perhaps.

"Sorry," he said. He looked like he meant it.

"Nothing to be sorry for," I replied shakily. "It's a quick way to make a few coins, but that's behind you now. Isn't it?"

He ventured a split-lip, cracked-toothed smile. "It is if you say it is, Mr. Ira."

But what other skills did the man have? He didn't read or write, and didn't, as far as I knew, have contacts in any of the trades unions. It was too late in the year for hops-picking. A shame, for not only could he have earned money, but he'd have had to ship off to Kent for at least a month. I almost suggested mudlarking, but the banks of the Thames—a rich source of scavenged treasure—were fiercely guarded by people who would be less kindly disposed toward an interloper than even this morning's dockworkers. "What else can you do?" I asked.

He looked at me coyly from beneath his long, light eyelashes.

"No," I said firmly.

Shrugging, he folded the paper from the sandwich, rolled it up, and tucked the roll into the neck of the empty beer bottle. He set the bottle on the floor next to the chair and began to unlace his boots. If only I were employed in some regular industry—a factory, refinery, or shop. But I moved in different circles, and my own employment was irregular at best. I wondered how long it would take me to train Marcus to be a useful assistant—provided he was interested in learning. And provided I had the patience, or even the ability, to teach him.

My pathetic little coal fire was glowing in the grate, giving off a slight but persistent warmth. Marcus, now barefoot, stretched his toes toward it and sighed with satisfaction. He glanced up at me, clearly noticing my agitation. "We don't have to fix the problem tonight, Mr. Ira. Why don't you tell me about your day, while I open the wine?"

"Wine?"

Grinning, he produced a bottle from the folds of his oversized coat. Red wine—and a rather nice one at that.

"Where'd you get that?" I asked. He pretended to be too involved with fishing the corkscrew out of the mess of papers on my desk to hear me, but I saw the ghost of a smile on his downturned face. "Did you steal it?"

"It mighta fell off the back of a lorry while they was loadin' it." He found the corkscrew and applied himself to the task with alacrity. "Serve 'em right for jumpin' on me like that, don'cha fink?"

"Marcus!" But I couldn't suppress a grin at his nerve.

"Don't tell me you ain't never stole nuffin', Mr. Ira," he said smugly. "Not where you come from."

I turned. "How do you know where I—"

That really surprised me. My background was no secret to people I knew well, but I'd worked hard to eliminate all traces of the East End from my speech. My clothing was well worn, but it had been quality, once. And I certainly hadn't indulged in any drunken, late-night confessionals with my young protégé.

"It's that picture, there," he said, gesturing with his head toward the framed bit of yellowed newspaper on the imitation mantel. He gave the corkscrew one final twist, then dislodged the cork with a *pop!* He decanted some of the lovely red into my wineglass, handed it to me, and then filled the water glass for himself. "That woman. You knew her."

The clipping was more than a little morbid, if you read the caption. The drawings depicted the victims of the 1870 tainted-opium deaths in Limehouse. One of the victims, whose face I'd boxed in pen, was my mother. I'd last seen her as she left me at the door of the workhouse where I'd spent the next twelve years. Throughout those years and beyond, it had been my only solid connection to her, to who I was, and to my past. I'd carried that little scrap of paper around in my pocket, terrified that I'd forget the woman who had forgotten me. Perhaps that wasn't fair. She hadn't forgotten. She'd deliberately left me in that workhouse to pursue her first love—the lotus. She'd probably meant to come back.

"You knew her. You must've done. Otherwise, why keep the picture? And you wouldn't admit to knowin' her if you hadn't come from them streets. So, who is she, then? Not a lover." He chuckled there. "A relative, then? She must've been special if you kept the picture so long it turned yellow. But you ain't seen her in a while or you'd have a proper picture. 1870. Was it your mum?"

I stared at him, blinking. Who could have predicted that this very pretty, very lost young man—a renter and a one-time cocaine fiend—would harbor such a keen deductive sense? It was odd to keep an old newspaper clipping in a frame, I admit. Of course it would catch a visitor's eye. But how many visitors could pull all that information out of a single object belonging to someone they hardly knew? How many would bother, even if they could?

"Sorry," Marcus said for the second time that evening. "Won't happen again, Mr.—"

"Yes. She was my mother," I said. "She's dead now. That was very impressive, Marcus."

"Wot was?"

"The way you extrapolated my entire history from an old newspaper clipping. Do you always observe your surroundings with such detail?"

He tilted his head. Even with the bruises and scratches, it was charming. "I like to fink about wot I see. Look at people an' try an' guess their stories. It's a laugh sometimes, an' it don't cost nuffin'. 'S prolly rude, though. Ain't it rude?"

"It's brilliant," I said. I stood and began to pace, swirling the fragrant wine around in my glass. With no news from Wilde in weeks, I would soon need to start looking for other clients. I'd thought to somehow share the work with Marcus. But why let his sort of talent sit idle, when he could start making himself useful right then and there? "Could you help me with a problem?"

"Me? Help you?" His face lit up with pleasant surprise, a touch of confusion, and an enthusiasm I hadn't seen before. He drained his glass and set it on the desk. "Be happy to, if you fink you can use me."

For once, no innuendo colored his offer. We were making progress. "Splendid. Now, come here, and let me tell you what I had in mind."

Bringing the lamp with him, he crossed the room, set the lamp on the floor, and sat down on the bed next to me. Then he folded his hands in his lap like an attentive student and gazed at me raptly as I told him about the loan to save Turnbull House and the extra duties

I'd accepted to hasten its repayment. Though it was clear that the loan had come through questionable channels, I omitted all reference to Goddard. Coming out of the milieu he had, Marcus would, of course have heard of the Duke of Dorset Street. I was certain that Goddard would be as hesitant as I was to deliberately shed light on any connection between him, Turnbull House, and myself. Not that Marcus had done anything to make me doubt the sincerity of his desire to help, but I knew—personally—the circumstances he was trying to escape. I had felt that desperation myself. It would take more than a few days of good behavior before I believed he wouldn't cause all sorts of havoc, intentional or otherwise, the minute my back was turned.

I did, however, recognize the gift of his acuity. If anyone could give a new perspective on the bizarre bouquet of flowers I delivered to the sugarhouse that morning, it was Marcus.

"So what do you make of it?" I asked, after I'd finished the tale of Herr Lothar and the Swollen Thistle.

He shrugged. "It were a message."

"Yes, yes, of course," I said impatiently. "A present from Mephistopheles is never just a present, but—"

"Mephi...wot?" Marcus asked.

"Mephistopheles. In *Faust*—Right. There's this story where a man makes a deal with the devil, thinking he can win in the end. It doesn't work, because the devil holds all the cards."

He nodded knowingly. "That's always the way."

For the sake of the deal I'd made with Goddard, I hoped that wasn't true. "In that story, the devil's name is Mephistopheles. It's a lot like a book I recently type-wrote for a client." I mused. "A deal with the devil that involved a painting. Anyway, we know the bouquet was a message, but—"

"No. Them flowers had a meanin', each one. You know, like daisies for friendship an' lilacs for love. Me sister were a bouquet girl in Covent Garden," Marcus said somewhat wistfully. "She used to get to the basket woman first every mornin' when it were still dark, get the prettiest ones an' tie 'em togevver herself. She knew all the flowers an' their meanins."

He clearly missed his sister. Hadn't seen her for some time. I didn't ask what became of her. Hawking bedraggled blooms through the streets for pennies rarely led to long life and financial independence.

"We was livin' in that cellar on Drury Lane. She couldn't teach me nuffin' proper, so she taught me the flowers. I fink I remember some of 'em. There were a book she said—"

"*The Language of Flowers!*" I used to flip through Goddard's copy from time to time, but I could hardly ask him for it now. "If I told you the flowers in the bouquet, do you think you might remember their meanings?"

"Might do."

My pulse began to race. "Christmas rose," I said. We'd start with something easy.

"Calm. Only not just calm. Let me fink." His light, dirt-caked eyebrows furrowed across the bridge of his battered nose. "More like 'I'm worried. Tell me not to worry.' Somefin' like that."

"Interesting." I glanced at the bowl and basin, sorely tempted to offer him a wash. But he seemed to have forgotten his pain in the excitement of the task. "How about rhododendron?"

His frown deepened. He absently scratched at a streak of dried blood on his cheek. Little dark flecks sprinkled down onto my bed sheets. "Wot's it look like?"

"About an inch wide, with five pointed petals—pink petals with dark-pink streaks."

Lost in thought, he bit his lower lip, yelping as it split open again. Bright-red blood surged to the surface and pooled there. I sprang up to fetch the cloth and basin. As he continued to *fink*, I dipped the cloth in the water and dabbed the wound clean. Once it had stopped bleeding, I began to address the other wounds and smudges. Unbidden memories flashed through my mind of that night, so long ago, when Goddard had brought me home, tending to my own injuries in much the same way.

"Danger," Marcus said suddenly. He cracked an uneven grin, then winced. "That one were definitely danger."

"So, *Danger. Tell me not to worry.* But Lothar was the one worrying. He looked like he'd worry himself right into an asylum," I said.

"Sounds like he crossed someone, did that Lothar."

"Yes." Crossing Goddard. I shivered. If that was the case, then Lothar would do best to leave London immediately. Perhaps leave Britain altogether. "The bouquet also had some straw—broken straw. Looked like someone had stepped on it. And a big, fat thistle."

Marcus absently took my glass from my hand and, careful of his lower lip, drained it. He turned to me. "Sorry, Mr. Adler. I really couldn't say. I don't fink me sis ever got that far in our lessons."

"That's all right." I patted him on the knee. "You've already given me more than I expected." In so many ways. I picked up his pillow from the floor and lay it next to my own. Settling myself next to the wall, I gestured for him to join me.

"If you're sure, then, Mr.—"

"No more 'Mr.,' and turn the light off when you come."

CHAPTER SEVEN

FRIDAY

The next day arrived amid unbroken steely skies and a biting cold unmitigated by the unusually heavy rains. Marcus and I dragged out our morning tea as long as possible before wrapping ourselves in every article of clothing I owned and hauling our shivering carcasses across town to Turnbull House. We arrived as luncheon was ending and staff members were filtering into the classroom with a few of the older residents to discuss Jack's plans for a messenger service. From all reports, he had been working on the idea with unprecedented industriousness, and everyone seemed to be taking the young man very seriously indeed. I did hope their trust in him would ultimately prove well placed.

Shutting the front door behind us, Marcus and I peeled off layer after layer of sodden clothing and stamped our boots dry on the mat. I dropped my umbrella in the receptacle near the door. The umbrella was well made, though not much use when the rain came at a person almost horizontally. Now that I was clad in only a shirt, waistcoat, and trousers, the hot air pressed in all around me, saturating everything with the smell of burning coal. Someone had left the classroom door open to better distribute the heat. Marcus and I exchanged a pleased look.

I glanced about, keeping an eye open for Lazarus. Eventually one of us would have to take the initiative to set things right between us. Somehow I doubted that Marcus's presence would make this easier. Even before our paths had become a tangled pile of bed sheets, Marcus had seemed to set Tim's teeth on edge. Briefly, I thought to grab my young friend and dash back out the door. Marcus wouldn't have objected. He'd been uncharacteristically quiet since our arrival, though I doubted he'd remembered much about his first meeting with Lazarus. If my own experiences were anything to go by, I would guess the schoolhouse atmosphere was intimidating him, making him feel keenly his own lack of education and direction.

"Ira, hello!" Bess appeared in the doorway that led down a flight of stairs to where her charges were enjoying their luncheon. She strode toward us, her smile widening as she took in my companion. "And you are?"

"Mrs. Lazarus, may I introduce my friend, Marcus Harrington?"

"Mr. Harrington." She smiled in that forthright way of hers and stuck out her hand. Her cheeks were glowing, no doubt as much from the warmth from the extravagant fire as from her condition. This, I realized, was what people meant when they referred to a pregnant woman as "radiant." Momentarily taken back by her enthusiasm, as well as the wool-clad spectacle she made of herself, Marcus stared, wide-eyed, at the hand for a moment, as if it might bite. Then he raised her fingers uncertainly to his lips.

Naturally, Tim chose that very moment to stick his head out his office door.

"May I help you?" He spat the words out like nails as he stomped down the hallway toward us. Marcus dropped her hand and stepped back. "Oh, it's you." Lazarus glanced from his wife to the hand I was placing protectively on Marcus's shoulder, to Marcus's battered face. "That's quite a goose egg you have," he said, his tone suddenly filled with professional concern.

Whatever personal quibbles he might have had fell away as he moved in to examine Marcus's wounds. Marcus shied away at first, but Lazarus gentled him with an expert touch, examining the bruises and lacerations until he was satisfied.

"Looks painful, but you won't need stitches. You're lucky," he said, stepping back. "What happened?"

"I was lookin' for work down by the docks," Marcus mumbled. Lazarus frowned. "Who told you to do that?" Shaking his head, he turned to me. "I don't suppose he's given another thought to joining our program."

"Marcus is fine where he is," I said.

"Mr. Ira's made me his assistant, like."

"Has he really?" Now it was me that Lazarus regarded with concern.

"We don't have room anyway, Tim," Bess said, firmly taking his arm in her own. She glanced at me and Marcus, her intelligent eyes searching, evaluating. Then she smiled. "And we don't have time to stand about arguing. Jack is waiting inside, and look, he's already gathered the others."

I followed her into the classroom, "making a beeline," as Bess would say, for the fireplace. While I toasted myself before the coal fire, imagining the skin of my back and neck turning a crispy brown, I watched Marcus slowly circle the classroom. It was touching, the way he reverently ran his fingertips over the stack of dilapidated textbooks on Bess's desk while gazing longingly at the morning's arithmetic on the chalkboard. His expression suggested both a deep desire to improve himself and a desperate fear that even if the opportunity arose, he would somehow prove incapable of doing so. I remembered that combination of longing and fear. I remembered how patiently Goddard had labored to help me take those first steps.

"Brought a friend, then, has you?"

I jumped as Jack appeared at my side, seemingly out of nowhere. "Announce yourself, will you? It's bad manners to skulk about like that."

He snorted. "Thought I just did."

He'd washed his face for the occasion, and his hands. Stripped of their protective layer of grime, his features appeared almost pretty—full lips, high cheekbones, and a turned-up nose that was charming in a cheeky-wallet-snatcher sort of way. He had very long eyelashes for a boy. Beneath his cap, his lank brown hair had been combed smooth. But he was still wearing the same clothing he'd arrived in. From the wrinkles and the less-than-fresh aroma radiating from him, I guessed he was sleeping in those clothes as well.

"Hasn't Mrs. Lazarus given you a new set of togs, yet?"

Before Jack could lob one back at me, Lazarus clapped for attention. Everyone took a seat on the benches, while Bess wiped the chalkboard clean. Marcus hurried back to join me near the fire, and Jack strode to the front of the room to take the stage.

"By now you all know wot Mr. Adler saved the building," he said. "Now it's our turn to show him wot his efforts ain't gonna be for nuffin'. We need to bring in money, an' keep it comin' in. How, you might ask? Let me tell you."

Jack was a natural performer, and as he went on to describe his very well-thought-out plan, it became apparent that he was also a natural leader.

"You lot," he said, indicating three young men and three young women sitting on the front bench. "Mrs. Lazarus told me you can write, read a map, an' wot you're smart, fast, and dependable, like. That's why I picked you to be the leaders. If it all works out, you'll each run a pair of messengers in your own section of town. Now, has any of you run messages before?"

"Plenty of times," one of the boys said. Edmund. He was the oldest of the Turnbull House gang—seventeen or so, if I wasn't mistaken—though he'd just arrived in the middle of last year.

"An' did you ever lose one? Or maybe just forget the message and pocket the money?"

Edmund shifted uncomfortably in his seat, a guilty smile twitching at the edge of his lips.

"Let me ask you this, then, Eddie. Would you lose a message if you had to answer to the missus?"

A nervous titter resounded throughout the room. Edmund glanced at Mrs. Lazarus, his eyes going wide at the thought. "No, ma'am!"

"I should think not," Jack said seriously. "But even more important than stayin' on the missus's good side is wot people'll pay more if they know we's reliable. An' if we do good enough, they won't use nobody else. Which is wot we want, 'cause we ain't gonna be makin' seventeen quid a month if they's usin' other people."

"Seventeen!" one of the girls cried. "That's more than I'd make in a year as a scully!" Other voices rose to join her objection.

"It ain't that much," Jack cried over the rising tide of argument. "Nurse Brandt said she'd pay sixpence to send a message if she knew it'd get there."

Lazarus cleared his throat. The room gradually settled down. "Even still, Mr. Flip, assuming we could get sixpence for every message, we would need to run—"

"Six hundred eighty messages a month," Jack said, as if it were nothing. "We got twelve of us—six teams of two. That means…a little less than four messages a day per team, if they's workin' seven days."

"How did you do that?" I asked. I'd still been counting shillings. Jack shrugged. "I like numbers."

Bess admonished him. "We can't work on the Lord's day. Sunday is for church and rest."

"Then let's say five a day. In Central London? Bright an' breezy!"

"It does sound easy, when you put it that way," Bess said.

"And don't forget the side jobs I'm doing for our benefactor, which gives us a little leeway for slow days," I said, though I neglected to mention that I'd taken the first payment in cash. Slowly, people began to nod. Voices rose again, but this time in excitement rather than dismay.

Tim turned to me. "I think it just might work." Astonishment lit his face, and for a few seconds, he looked ten years younger. "Ira, this could really work!"

"So I'm not a complete idiot, then?" I asked.

"Of course not, Ira," Bess said warmly.

At the front of the room, Jack was gathering his lieutenants about him. I caught snatches of conversation involving uniforms and letters of introduction. Then I spied my protégé, off in a corner, self-consciously leafing through one of the worn schoolbooks. He looked lost and bored. As I made my way across the room, Jack turned to Marcus and caught his eye.

"You! Mr. Adler's friend, do you know East London? You want to help us divide up the city?"

Marcus glanced at me uncomfortably, setting the book hastily back on the desk. "Actually, Mr. Ira, I was finkin' I might go look for work again."

"Wiv' your face like that?" asked Jack, ever the soul of sensitivity.

Marcus glanced away, looking for all the world as if he'd like to sink into the floorboards. I felt sorry for him. In addition to embarrassment, he had to be feeling his injuries. And then I'd dragged him here. I gestured for him to walk with me into the hallway. Once outside the classroom, he looked profoundly relieved.

"Actually," he said, sounding much more confident now that we were alone, "I was finkin' about what we was talking about last night. You know, the meanins of the flowers an' all. Maybe I could go find that book you told me about."

"*The Language of Flowers.*" I nodded, digging through my coat pocket for a pencil stub and a scrap of paper. "Kate Greenaway is the author. Yes, that would be quite useful. Good thinking." I found a few coins and pressed them into his hand, along with the paper. "Go down to Holywell Street, where the booksellers are, and try to find a copy. Then find yourself something to eat. Meet me back at the flat tonight, and we'll do some detective work."

I glanced inside the classroom. Bess was watching us. Why? Why? I gave her a little wave, then turned back to Marcus. He was beaming.

"Right-o, Mr. Holmes. I'll do that that, then."

I smiled back. "Off you go then, Watson. Oh, and Watson?" I said as he walked toward the door. He turned. "Take my key."

The surprise on his face mirrored my surprise at myself. Lazarus would definitely not approve. And yet the past twenty-four hours had given me a new perspective on young Marcus. He hadn't proved himself, not exactly, but his sudden, unexpected interest in books was making me see him in a new light. Perhaps he wasn't only interested in a roof and a meal. Would someone who thirsted for knowledge rob blind the person offering to give it to him? Perhaps it was time to trust him a bit further. We were entrusting Jack with the future of Turnbull House, after all, and I'd known Marcus longer than we'd known Jack.

Standing in the doorway, holding out his hand, Marcus gazed back at me with an expression of true joy.

I threw him the key.

CHAPTER EIGHT

After Marcus left for Holywell Street, Lazarus called the meeting to an official close, and the assembly slowly dispersed—students to chores or vocational assignments, staff to their various tasks, and me, back out into the world. I didn't feel like going home straight away, and I wasn't dressed for the library at St. James's Square. The multiple layers of mismatched clothing in which I'd re-swaddled myself would have raised eyebrows as well as knocked books off shelves. Wilde—my sponsor for membership—wouldn't have forgiven me for either.

The rain had stopped, but I didn't fancy a walk through its aftermath. But when I reached the omnibus and found my pockets empty once more, it occurred to me to pay another visit to Cain Goddard. It was early for supper, but I did owe him news. And he, I realized with a little laugh, owed me a bit of coin for delivering Herr Lothar's flowers.

It was a trek across town to York Street, even cutting through Regent's Park, if one could be said to cut through an area half as large as all of Bethnal Green. But even though the sodden picnic grounds were deserted, and no black-robed governesses pushed their prams along the paths under the glowering skies—even if the geese had abandoned the lake for more clement surroundings—it was still a pleasant journey. As I made my way back toward my old home, I emptied my mind of all of the disturbing events of the past week and concentrated on the squelch of my boots through the grass, the wet green smell so heavy in the air, and the occasional startling roar of the zoo lion in the distance. By the time I walked up Goddard's front steps, I was quite relaxed.

Goddard was in his study when I entered. I waited respectfully for Mrs. Murphy to announce me. His sanctum sanctorum, from which he carried out his most sensitive criminal dealings, had always been off limits, even when I'd been living there. Now that I seemed once again to be on the periphery of those dealings, I thought it best if I not thrust myself immediately into their center. While I removed my outer layers, I watched the rainbow of fish swimming languidly around their enormous bowl. Such beauty: each individual chosen for some specific reason, if I knew Goddard, as well as for its unique contribution to the collection. I could have watched them for hours.

Goddard emerged looking as if he'd just finished a day of satisfying but arduous work. His expression was tired, but his eyes were bright. Perspiration stuck his silk shirt to his chest in places. He had foregone a tie, and his waistcoat hung open. He cracked his knuckles as he greeted me with a fatigued smile.

"Hard at work?" I asked.

"Always."

"Translating the Great Ones, or engaging in a spot of friendly extortion?"

His smile turned enigmatic.

"I came to thank you for the book. It must have been a lot of work," I said.

"A labor of love."

I hoped he was referring to his love of poetry.

He glanced at the grandfather clock and said, "I was just about to have my tea. Care to join me?"

"It's rather chilly out there. Might I bother you for a drop of sherry instead?"

Nodding indulgently, he gestured me toward the morning room—the parlor, as he called it now. I settled myself in one of the Morris chairs, while he poured the sherry into a pair of delicate little glasses with gold trim.

"I have good news," I said, as he took the other chair.

He raised his glass in response. "To good news."

The sherry was expensive, and it burned an elegant trail from my lips to my stomach. I closed my eyes as it went down, the better to appreciate its magnificence. When I opened my eyes, he was watching me with mild curiosity.

"Not only have we come up with an idea for a business that Turnbull House can use to support itself, but we drew up a rough plan earlier today. And I have to tell you, it just may work."

He smiled. "You sound surprised."

"I am, frankly."

He refilled my glass. "It's amazing what one can accomplish with proper motivation."

After a knock on the door, Eileen entered with a three-tiered serving tray stacked high with thin fingers of sandwich—pâté, olive paste, and slivers of roasted meat. The tray also contained wedges of expensive cheese and, on the smallest, tip-top tier, four liquor-filled chocolates.

"Thank you, Mrs. Murphy," Goddard said as she set the tray down on a low table and placed a small plate beside it. "We won't be needing the tea after all, but we could use a second plate."

"Very good, sir," she said, winking at me.

I smiled back, uneasy. The Goddard I remembered didn't believe in high tea or silver-tray frippery.

"Were you expecting someone?" I asked.

"No." He met my eyes. "I figured that if I'm to be alone, at least for the foreseeable future, I should take my pleasures where I can. A fine tea is a definite pleasure. Please, help yourself."

"I can't imagine you wanting for company," I said.

He shrugged. "Many people would be happy to take advantage of what I have to offer. But as time goes on, I find it pays to be discriminating. I may not be as young as I once was, but neither am I so old, nor so hideous, that I'm forced to pay for company. Solitude is the price that one pays for waiting for the right person." He chose one of the elegant sandwiches from the tray and popped it into his mouth. "And you, Ira, are you still waiting for the right person?"

My mouth went dry. "Now there's a direct question."

He brushed the crumbs from his fingertips. "Forgive the intrusion. I'd thought our past intimacies would allow us to be honest with one another. Should I cycle backward to some previous stage of acquaintance? Shall we talk about the weather, perhaps?"

I choked on a sliver of bread. Goddard and I hadn't spoken in such direct terms even when we'd lived under the same roof. Our relationship had been closer to mentor and protégé—rather like that of Marcus and myself, though I'd never called him 'Mr.' once he'd told me to stop. I breathed a sigh of relief when Eileen interrupted again with my plate; however, by the time she left again, my appetite had fled. I couldn't deny that I still thought about Goddard from time to time, and about the life I'd left behind. But I wasn't prepared, I supposed, for the idea that he might have been thinking about it as well.

"I'm the one who should ask forgiveness, Cain," I said after a moment. "The way I left two years ago was cowardly and disrespectful."

He made a dismissive gesture, though the quirk of his lips suggested he appreciated the sentiment. "Completely understandable under the circumstances. No offense taken."

"I'm glad. And no, I haven't found the right person. But then again, I haven't been looking."

He seemed to consider this for a moment—a moment I used to snatch the remaining pâté fingers and a wedge of Stilton. I'd given the rest of my money to Marcus, and if Goddard didn't pay me for the delivery, this would be supper.

"What about the little blond chappie sleeping on your floor?" he asked carefully.

The cheese went down hard. I washed it back with a mouthful of sherry. "Marcus?" How did he know about that? "Marcus is going through a rough patch. I'm giving him a place to stay until he finds work, that's all."

"What does he do? Perhaps I could help."

I set down my glass. The room seemed hotter suddenly, but the fire in the hearth was still burning evenly. It wasn't affront that I felt, not exactly. More like protectiveness.

"That would be contrary to the mission of Turnbull House," I said primly.

He laughed out loud. "Oh, Ira."

"What?"

Mirth sparkled in his deep-brown eyes. "Sometimes irony is even more delicious than an expensive sherry. Don't you think?"

I had to laugh as well—and to recognize that Goddard was probably the only other person who would see the humor in this situation.

Goddard's face had no naturally distinguishing characteristics. Eyes, nose, moustache, lips, bone structure—everything could be described as *medium*. All the better to fade into a crowd. But when he laughed—genuinely laughed—his mirth brought out the healthy glow of his skin, the intelligence in his eyes, and the perfect proportion and arrangement of his features. It made him beautiful.

"Yes, I had noticed the parallels," I said after a moment. "But I'm certainly in no position to help him in any significant way."

"I see."

"And at the same time, I can't turn him out when he's clearly in need."

"And Turnbull House?"

"He's a bit long in the tooth for Turnbull House. The oldest is sixteen, seventeen. That, and I'm not sure Marcus and Lazarus could stay under the same roof for more than five minutes without causing an explosion."

Goddard laughed again. "I see. You are in a pickle." He raised an eyebrow. "Lazarus?"

"Don't ask."

"Aren't you the popular one?"

"It must be my wit and rugged good looks."

"Or it could be that people know quality when they see it."

"Tell that to Lazarus. He thinks I'm the moral equivalent of a dragonfly."

Goddard looked puzzled. "What on earth does he mean by that?"

"No, it wasn't a dragonfly. A butterfly. Moth. He said, 'Ira Adler, you have all the perceptiveness and emotional complexity of a peppered moth.' And this after I saved his ruddy youth shelter. I ask you."

Goddard smiled again, this time gently. "Remind me before you leave, there's something I think you should read." Rising, he took our glasses to the drink cart and set them down beside the decanter. "Now, why don't you tell me exactly how this messenger service of yours is meant to work?"

Grateful to return to shallower waters, I described Jack's plans and exactly how they would enable us to meet the repayment schedule. Nodding approvingly, Goddard took a chocolate from the tray and sat back down.

The curtains were pulled back from the window, and on the other side, Goddard's prizewinning roses weathered the renewed downpour. He'd trimmed the ivies that used to frame the window and filter the light on hot summer days. Behind the roses stood a good-sized greenhouse. The rain drummed against its roof and sides. The mahogany desk in front of the window was clean but unused. From where I sat, I could just make out a patch of slightly darker wood where my Remington typewriter had sat for that year before he'd brought it to me.

"Excellent," he said when I'd finished. "I knew you'd manage, but I didn't think you would do it so quickly."

"Well, the others helped, of course."

"I'd have expected no less. Please write up the details and have your proposal delivered to me as soon as possible."

"Certainly. Oh, and I should mention, we're planning to test the system a week from tomorrow. The more optimistic souls among us believe it possible to take a message from one end of the city to the other in less than an hour."

"I shall look forward to it." He took another chocolate and said, "Thank you, by the way, for making my delivery on time. Did you want me to deduct your payment from the balance of your loan, or would you prefer cash?"

"Cash, I'm afraid. Wilde's still in Paris, and I'm running low."

"That's fair enough."

He took a one-pound coin from his pocket and flipped it to me. The small, solid coin landed in my palm with a soft sound and an instant moral dilemma. I needed the money, badly. But it just wasn't right to accept three weeks' rent for so little work. "It's too much," I said, forcing the unwilling words out. I couldn't quite bring myself to hand back the coin, though I did manage to unclench my fist.

He took my hand in his, closed my fingers around the coin, and guided my hand to my pocket. "I'll be the judge of that."

"But—"

He silenced me with a long, firm kiss. My thoughts fled, and I dropped the coin and tangled my fingers in his neat brown hair, pulling him out of his chair toward me. At this point, one might be tempted to think that I couldn't go out my front door without some man throwing himself at me. Would that it were true. John Thomas had seen more action in the past week than in the previous two years. Goddard gave a small moan. Lowering himself onto the arm of my chair, he took me in his arms—hard muscle beneath soft silk. I remembered how safe and protected I used to feel there. But safety had come at a price—my freedom of conscience and action.

"Stop thinking," Goddard murmured, sliding down to straddle my lap. His breath was hot on my neck, the smell of his desire thick in the air.

"I know, I know…"

But that was the problem, wasn't it? As much as my baser instincts were clamoring for me to charge ahead, damn the consequences, that tiny voice of better judgment was questioning the wisdom of falling back into Goddard's bed. I could feel his pulse pounding, taste the salt on his skin. I could feel how hard he was through his trousers, and I'd no doubt he could feel me. What was I doing? Was I really prepared to involve myself beyond a simple business deal?

"Herr Lothar nearly soiled himself when I handed him those flowers." I gasped, pulling back. "Why? What did they mean?"

He blinked slowly, the fog of lust gradually clearing from his dark eyes. He leaned his forehead against mine and rested his fingers on my cheek. "Ira, you do remember that I'm the Duke of Dorset Street and not the Easter Bunny." I nodded. "And it's not against the law to deliver flowers." I shook my head. "Then let me continue to overpay you for easy, lawful work, and stop asking about matters that don't concern you."

Moment of decision. How weak I am.

"All right," I said. It was reasonable, after all. I needed the money, and I wanted him. I was still in control. I could back out any time I wanted. Goddard smiled, squeezing my torso between his knees, his fingers pulling tightly through my curls. He lowered his face once more to mine. And then, I'm not ashamed to say I abandoned any pretense of rational thought.

❖

Goddard and I ended up in his bedroom. Eventually. Goddard's house has three stories, and we took our time christening each one. It felt a bit like marking my territory. Perhaps at some level I was. When we finally collapsed on the bed we'd shared for two years, it was clear he wanted me to stay the night. I was tempted. But as pleasant as it would have been, my better judgment urged caution. By all appearances, Goddard had recovered from the insult of my abrupt departure. But my reasons for leaving still stood. I wouldn't turn down a good bout of sex for its own sake, but Goddard had stated clearly that he wasn't interested in casual encounters. And unless the Duke of Dorset Street had, in the past two years, suddenly grown a conscience, that was all I could offer.

It all sounds very noble, but leaving was the hardest thing I'd ever done. Feelings of nobility don't go far when the tobacco canister is empty and the floorboards are rotting beneath your feet. Another time I'd have leaped at the chance to give up my newfound independence and tuck myself back beneath Goddard's wing. But one look at the faces of the young people we were helping at Turnbull House—young people Goddard would have been happy to employ in his brothels and other unsavory endeavors—and I knew I'd chosen the right path.

Which is why I had to leave.

For a good fifteen minutes, I lay in his arms, reveling in the clean scent of his musk, the light sheen of perspiration on his skin, and the scratch of his graying chest hair against my cheek. Eventually, his breathing evened out and deepened, and his grip went slack. I eased myself out of bed. Then I went downstairs to search for my clothes.

I returned to my flat after what seemed like hours, to find that Marcus had both let himself in and had the consideration to leave the door on the latch for me. I hung up my coat, wet clothes, and hat, and took off my boots in the dark. Then I crossed the room to my desk to get my lamp. Turning it on very low, I crossed to the bed, where Marcus was curled up, asleep in his clothes. He looked very, very young. I set the lamp on the floor and sat down very carefully, so as not to wake him. In the crook of one arm, he was cradling the book I'd asked him to find, *The Language of Flowers*. I smiled.

As curious as I was about the message Goddard had sent to Herr Lothar, the thought of looking up every last flower made my head pound. It would have been nice if Marcus were able to read. He might have looked up the flowers he hadn't already known. But at least he had found the tool we needed to finish the task. And he hadn't run away with the money. I brushed the blond hair from his forehead. No, I wasn't in any position to take on a protégé, but it was nice to have a friend.

I tried to take the book out of his hand, but he made a discontented noise in his sleep and clutched it tighter to his chest. "All right, then," I whispered indulgently.

Switching off the lamp, I nudged Marcus gently to the side. Then I pulled my feet up onto the bed. My back to the wall, I bunched the lumpy pillow under my head, draped an arm around Marcus's waist, and closed my eyes.

CHAPTER NINE

MONDAY

Monday morning it was my turn to hunt down breakfast. I built a fire in the grate, filled the kettle and set it on the floor near the fireplace, then left Marcus snoring peacefully in the bed. When I returned with bread still warm from the oven, cheese, and butter for a treat, Marcus was awake and washed, and had made the tea. This had all the makings of a pleasant domestic routine, though it would be unwise to get used to it. It was nice to have someone else about for a change, especially someone with a cheerful disposition who was easy on the eyes. But ultimately he would leave, find his own space. And that's what I wanted. Wasn't it?

"Right," I said around a mouthful of warm buttered bread. "We know the first two flowers in Herr Lothar's bouquet—rhododendron for danger and Christmas rose asking for reassurance. Now we have to figure out the significance of thistle and straw."

Leveraging himself up onto his elbows, he retrieved the book from its place under his pillow. He sat on the edge of the bed and began to flip through the pages.

"Fistle," he said, frowning with concentration. "What's it start wiv, *f*?"

"*T-h*," I said.

He rolled his eyes at the vagaries of English spelling and started again at the beginning of the book.

He was wearing the trousers he'd washed the night before while I'd been with Goddard—industrious lad—and dried before the fire. Barefoot, no shirt, his hair clean, combed, and drying in the heat of the coal flame. If it weren't for the bruises and lumps he'd sustained from his tussle on the docks, he would have looked like a choirboy. I felt a stir of guilt but quickly pushed it away. Surely he would soon find a safe, legal way to get back on his feet. Until then, I was doing all I could.

"Fistle," he said. "This it?"

He pointed to a page.

"Well done." I took the book from his hand and read. "Retaliation. That's like revenge."

"Ain't wot I thought it'd be," he muttered.

"What did you think?"

"A fistle looks like sumfin' else, don't it, all fat and *turgid*?"

Laughing, I set down my tea so I wouldn't spill it. "Turgid? Where'd you learn a word like that?"

"Wouldn't you like to know?"

I laughed again. "Good guess, but Herr Lothar didn't look the type."

"Most men don't."

"Maybe, maybe." I tried to picture Herr Lothar splayed out across Goddard's olive-colored divan and nearly choked. "But 'revenge' fits better with the whole meaning of the bouquet. Let's look at the last one—straw."

"That's a *s*, ain't it?" he asked peevishly.

"S-t-r-a-w."

He scanned the pages, diligently looking for the word. He was a quick study, I'd give him that. He might not have been a fluent reader, but at some point in his past, someone had taught him the letters, and he'd not forgotten. After a moment he looked up.

"Just straw, or b-br—"

"Broken?" I asked, looking over his shoulder. "I'll be. There's a special entry for broken straw." I thought back, picturing the bouquet in my hands. The straw hadn't been crumpled; it had been broken cleanly and evenly. Deliberately. "Yes," I said. "Come to think of it, it was broken." I sat down on the bed next to him, crossing my arms so I wouldn't tear the book away in my haste. "Broken straw signifies a broken contract."

"*Danger. Reassure me. A broken contract. Revenge.*" He looked at me, his clear blue eyes wide. "If that Lofar can't give your man the reassurance he needs, somefin' bad's gonna happen to him. Should we try to warn him?"

Probably, I thought. That familiar feeling of conscience-wrestling returned. Goddard's coin weighed heavily in my pocket. The man's revenge was nothing to be trifled with. To say Lothar's life hung in the balance likely wasn't an overstatement. On the other hand, from the look on the sugar baker's face, he'd heard the warning loud and clear. He knew what he'd done, and he'd known, going in, what kind of a man Goddard was. What Herr Lothar chose to do, now that he'd received his warning, was his affair, not mine. And, as Goddard had said, it wasn't illegal to deliver flowers.

"I think he's had his warning," I said, the confidence in my voice belying my growing apprehension. "Whether he heeds it or not is up to him."

Marcus nodded solemnly. Having grown up amid violence and wretchedness, he had a well-developed sense of when it was time to shut his eyes and back away. He closed the book. "More tea?"

"Please."

We finished our breakfast in silence. As I gathered up the dishes, Marcus put on a clean shirt and boots. Glancing in the mirror above my washstand, he gave his collar a final tug.

"Getting an early start?" I asked, as he reached for his coat and my hat. It had been a pleasant two days of idleness. I was glad to see he wasn't looking to make a habit of it.

"The man 'round Holywell Street said if I come back after a few days, when me face is healed up, he might have work for me. Nuffin' fancy, prolly movin' boxes or somefin', but it's a start."

"It certainly is," I said approvingly. With a pang, I realized my new friend might be gone sooner than I'd expected. I slipped a few coins into his coat pocket and gave his shoulder an encouraging pat. "Well, good luck then. See you back tonight."

❖

By and large, Whitechapel's vicious reputation was well deserved. But the area held unexpected delights as well. When I wasn't pressed for time, I often took a different bus to Turnbull House. It took me a bit out of the way and let me out at the very edge of the neighborhood, amid straight, neat streets bordered by meticulously clean shop windows and tidy sidewalks. Early in the morning, the air was redolent with warm baking smells—cinnamon, cooking fruit, toasted poppy seeds, and bread. At night, those safe, clean streets were reborn as a thriving theatre district, where one could stroll, bathed in warm light, listening to lively music in Jewish, Russian, Polish, and, occasionally, English. And on Saturdays, the shops and theatres were locked up tight while their hardworking owners walked to one of the many synagogues, large and small, that dotted the two square miles comprising the Whitechapel ghetto.

As I found myself in front of Levi's Bakery, a cornerstone of the neighborhood, I thought about Jack Flip's remark. *You a Jew, then?* It was something I'd heard before. Both of my names were Jewish, apparently, though I'd never felt a connection to any religion. Not like Bess, whose powerful, peculiarly American faith suffused her life. Not like Lazarus, who I suspect found a way to believe so as to better fit into Bess's world. Though I enjoyed walking through the neighborhood, it wasn't because of any atavistic yearning. The ghetto was clean, safe, pleasant, and more or less on the way to my destination. I was a Londoner, if I could be described as anything at all, and nothing more.

"A gutn morgen!" called a cheerful voice as the bells strung over the door of the bakery signaled my entry. Dark wood shelves lined one wall. Pyramids of baked goods stood, warm and inviting, upon lace-bordered cloths likely made by Mrs. Levi herself.

"Good morning, Mrs. Levi," I called as the proprietress bustled out of the back room.

Mrs. Levi was a wiry, middle-aged woman with angular features and tightly curled black hair much like my own. That day she was wearing a checkered dress and wiping her hands on an apron that had already seen the better part of a day's work. "Oh, it's you, Mr. Adler. *Vi geht es?*"

"I'm fine, Mrs. Levi, thank you."

She cocked an eyebrow. She'd taught me the words to respond, but I could never muster the courage to use them.

"Let me guess. Half a dozen raisin buns for your friends on Raven Row?"

"As always."

While she chose the fattest, roundest pastries and wrapped them in paper, I drank in the warm, sweet air through every pore. It must have been a simple and satisfying life—rising early, making the pastries and selling them, home before supper. Not a lot of moral ambiguity in that. Would I one day enjoy the pleasure of such simplicity?

"You're quiet today. Perhaps you are in love?" Mrs. Levi teased me. My expression must have revealed quite a bit, for she stopped what she was doing and laughed. "That bad? I keep telling you, you want to find a nice girl, you tell me. I find. I know the kind of girl you need."

Politeness wouldn't allow me further comment on the subject.

"Just the raisin buns today, please, Mrs. Levi."

She regarded me for a long moment, then tied off the twine and pushed the package across the counter toward me. "Six buns, and one more for the baby."

"That's very thoughtful. Thank you."

I slid the coins toward her over the counter. Counting them with a glance, she swept them into her pocket. She smiled.

"You tell me, I find," she repeated.

"I'll keep that in mind."

If there was a God, I reflected, he was in the small, unexpected things. Like the warm, sweet-spicy air inside Levi's bakery. Or perhaps at the Sunday soup kitchen five blocks away, where Mrs. Levi took the pastries that hadn't sold that week. He was there watching Pearl tend to the injuries of London's unwanted, or when Lazarus gave up his own lunch so his pregnant wife could have an extra portion. Maybe the luck that brought me up from the gutter to a place where I could help other people out of it—maybe this was the hand of God, I don't know. What I did know was that I felt no kinship to those who blathered on about how people starving in the streets were getting what they deserved, or that they should be happy about it because it was the will of some old man in the sky. It's easy to have faith when your belly is full and your street is safe, well-lit, and evenly paved. And who wouldn't want to think one's luck was due to moral superiority rather than sheer good fortune, which could end at any time?

I had no use for any of it. But I'd nothing against the God of the Raisin Bun.

❖

It was midmorning when I arrived at Turnbull House, Mrs. Levi's parcel under my arm. Bess greeted me distractedly and took the parcel while I hung up my coat and hat, but something was on her mind. She wouldn't meet my eyes.

"Bess?" I asked as she straightened the coats and hats on the rack.

"The meeting's only just started. Come in and find a seat."

I frowned as she turned on her heel and made her way into the classroom. This wasn't like her at all. Then I remembered what had transpired in her husband's office on Thursday. Fuck me, had Lazarus told her about that? He told her about everything else— to his detriment at times, I'd often warned him. No, I thought as I listened to her voice join the conversation in the next room. The woman who thought nothing of wrangling a rowdy band of youths during her second trimester of pregnancy wouldn't hesitate to lay me flat if she thought I was interfering in her marriage somehow.

And yet her discomfort was palpable.

But I quickly forgot my worries when I saw the chaos in the classroom.

"Good God, what happened here?" I asked.

The benches were pushed against the walls and the bookcases, empty, along with them. The books were stacked on the floor next to Bess's desk, and the desk itself was covered with paper—notes, sketches, and a crudely drawn map of Central London. Someone had scrawled another street diagram on the blackboard in chalk. The curtains were open, the fire was lit, and the entire room was crawling with chattering young people. When I walked in, they looked over as one.

"Have you seen Jack?" Lazarus asked. "We were supposed to finalize the plans for the messenger service this morning."

I frowned. "He isn't here?"

Lazarus shook his head.

"He didn't come down for breakfast this morning, and when I checked, his bed was still made," Bess said. "I thought you might have run into him on the way in."

That didn't sound good. Residents weren't supposed to leave without permission. And given that they were treated better here than they ever had been, why would they? I remembered my thought when the constable had brought Jack by—that he would slip away the moment our backs were turned. But it didn't follow. Not today, when he was to reveal the details of his project.

"He was working on the plans all weekend," Bess said, as if reading my mind. "Martha was taking notes." She nodded toward one of our older residents. "She could hardly keep up with him. Why would he leave now?"

"Then let Martha tell us what he had in mind," Tim said. "This is too important. We've got to start making money."

"Did he tell Martha how he intended to get a message from one end of London to another in less than an hour?"

Lazarus grumbled. "Jack can't be the only one who can figure that out."

Perhaps not, but I had no ideas, and I'd grown up on those streets. This was a far cry from paying an urchin a penny to run a love letter down the block.

"I took some notes myself the other day," Lazarus said. "But that was just for the general organization. Today was going to be very important. We were even talking about doing a mock run."

"Well, how hard could it be?" I asked. I glanced at the residents, who had been watching the argument with interest but had suddenly found a new, more compelling interest in the cracks between the floorboards. "What did he say, teams of two? Does anyone know who their partner is?" They stared at me blankly. I looked to Bess and then to Tim, but they were no help at all. "Right. Divide yourselves into pairs, then. Maybe a boy and a girl." While they did so, I went to the map. "Who can read the map? Where are the best places to station yourselves?"

Everyone in the room—Lazarus, Bess, and the older residents—started arguing at once. Ask twenty city dwellers for the best place to do something, or the fastest way to get there, and you'd end up with forty different answers. I had some opinions myself, but it looked like there'd be plenty to go around, if everyone could stop talking for a moment. I couldn't believe it was down to me again. I'd gotten the money and squared things with the landlord. Did I have to do this as well? If so, it was doomed to failure. I didn't know how to run a business, and I'd certainly never supervised anyone. And now I was supposed to take someone else's idea and turn it into seventeen quid a month?

This was how Lazarus must have felt every moment of every day. No wonder his nerves were stretched tighter than a bowstring. I slumped against the desk and helped myself to a raisin bun.

Before I could take the first bite, someone knocked at the front door. I didn't even bother looking for anyone else to answer it. Grateful to leave the commotion for a bit, I trudged out to the corridor.

"Mornin' Mr. Adler." Goddard's man Watkins grinned at me from the doorstep, ginger hair plastered to his head beneath his wet bowler. It was raining again, coming down in sheets behind him and washing yesterday's mud into the gutter. Watkins himself was looking dapper, despite being soaked through. A gold tooth glinted from the recesses of his mouth. He held out another bouquet.

"Candy and flowers from our benefactor?" I asked, gesturing for him to step inside. Watkins handed me the flowers, chuckling under his breath. I felt around my trousers for a tip but, finding my supply of coins dwindling, thought better of it. "Sorry," I said. "Next time. Tell your boss I'll make the delivery by the end of the day."

"Will do." He tipped his hat and turned to leave. Then he stopped and nodded at the pastry in my hand. "That a raisin bun from Levi's?" Sighing, I handed it to him. He grinned again. "Good day, Mr. Adler."

As I shut the door, I looked at the address on the flowers and frowned. The bouquet of almond, buttercup, and...more straw and thistle was bound for an address on Osborn Street, not far away. Another sugar refinery was located in that direction, if I wasn't mistaken. What were the chances? Whitechapel was full of sugarhouses. Of more interest to me was the meaning of this particular arrangement. A broken contract and revenge, clearly. As for the buttercup and almond, I could have used *The Language of Flowers* about then. It would also have been nice to see if Marcus had anything to add.

I glanced once more at the address. So what if it was a refinery? It was Goddard's business, not mine. Probably best I didn't know. Like he'd said, it wasn't illegal to deliver flowers, and he was paying me ever so much more than the job was worth. With that, I swallowed my objections. Whatever trouble Goddard was dealing out, Turnbull House would benefit. And that was all that mattered.

"I'm going for a walk," I called, sticking my head back into the doorway of the classroom.

Lazarus looked up from his discussion with two of the older residents. I held up the flowers. He scowled.

"Don't look at me that way. It'll be that much less to pay back. And like you said, Jack can't be the only one who can figure out how to get a message from one end of London to the other. You'll do a fine job."

Lazarus opened his mouth, but before he could come up with some rejoinder, I grabbed my coat and hat from the rack and ducked out the door.

I splashed southward from Raven Row, through the narrow streets with gutters now running ankle-deep in freezing water. The path wound through corridors flanked by noisy warehouses and factories, vast tenements and narrow little shops. As I crossed Flower and Dean Street, a commotion caught my attention. The rain was pouring down—whatever was happening down the street had to be important to attract a crowd that size and hold it there. Angling my umbrella into the downpour, I trudged over to get a closer look.

My stomach sank when I saw what remained of the sugar refinery where I'd delivered Herr Lothar's flowers last Thursday. One of the smokestacks and a good part of the left outer wall had been reduced to a pile of charred planks and bricks. Even through the moisture-heavy air, the smell of burning wood was still clear.

There was a tug at my sleeve.

"You hear about the explosion, sir?" A grimy street-paper seller no older than eight or nine grinned up at me, unabashedly excited at the prospect of the death and mayhem detailed in the pages he clutched to his chest. "Read for yourself, only a penny."

"There's a ha'penny for you if you give me the highlights."

His greedy little eyes glittered. "Of course, sir. Heard it meself, I did. Woke me up. I were sleepin' right over there." He nodded toward a nearby alley. "There were a big boom, an' then the air went all hot. There were a queer smell, too—like grass an' boiled sweets all at once."

Yes, come to think of it, I could still detect traces of those smells in the air. Standing on tiptoes, I peered through the sea of hats and sideburns. In addition to the explosion, the left side of the building had suffered significant fire damage as well. Between that and the buckets of rain now assailing the structure, I doubted the factory would be resuming operations any time soon.

"Did you see anyone go in or out?" I asked the boy.

He shook his head. "Like I said, it woke me up. Didn't see nuffin' before, but after, there were a great rush of fire from the hole, straight up into the air. That's when I run for the fire brigade."

"What time was that?" I asked.

"Dunno. It weren't light yet, but almost."

I squinted through the crowd again. Suddenly the people began to stir. "Make way!" someone shouted. Others took up the cry. The crowd slowly parted as two burly men dragged a third out of the building and toward the street.

"Who is it?" someone asked.

"Is he dead?"

"My God!" I cried as they passed me, dragging the third man who was most undeniably dead. "Stop!"

The two men, dressed in the dark jackets, tall boots, and smoke helmets of the fire brigade, turned and stared, their eyes unseen behind dark protective lenses.

"Do you know this man?" one of the firemen asked, his voice muffled by his breathing tube.

"It's Rudolf Lothar, the factory manager." I frowned. There was no blood, and, aside from the dirt, his body was intact. He looked almost peaceful. "This man doesn't look like he died in an explosion."

"Succumbed to fumes is my guess. Same as the first two firemen who answered the call. They thought it was just another boiler explosion, but something was down there. We had to wait for it to clear before we went back in for him." He nodded toward Lothar's corpse.

As they dragged Lothar's body away, my heart began to pound. Three days earlier, I'd delivered Goddard's threat to this man, and now he was dead.

"Did you know him?" the boy asked, tugging again at my sleeve. I shook my head. "Too bad. I coulda made another ha'penny sellin' his story to the paper." He stuck out his hand pointedly. Numbly, I pressed the promised coin into it. "But you knew his name, though. Are you sure he weren't your friend?"

The air suddenly felt hot and thick. The crowd seemed to close in around me. Pulling at my scarf I staggered back out into the street. The little paper-seller followed me for a bit, but soon found an eager audience in those who remained.

"Said the man's name is Lothar...he were the manager there..."

Had Goddard killed that man? It certainly didn't have his tidy signature. An explosion was a very indiscreet way of disposing of someone. And sugarhouse fires were not exactly rare. At the same time, Herr Lothar had crossed the Duke of Dorset Street. And from the look on his face the last time I'd seen him, his death probably hadn't come as a surprise. But what had the fireman said about fumes—fumes no one had anticipated at the site of a refinery explosion? What had been going on inside that factory? I glanced at the flowers I was clutching and shivered. I couldn't very well track down Watkins and give them back. Turnbull House needed the money, and so did I. But even if the explosion had been a coincidence—and I dearly hoped it had been—this would be the last delivery I'd make. Pulling my coat tighter around my chest, I set off for the address on Osborn Street.

The intersection of Osborn Street and Whitechapel Road had been the site of one of a series of grisly murders that had begun the year after I'd taken up residence with Goddard. Emma Smith hadn't been one of the Ripper's victims, but her brutal death at the hands of a gang of youths had caused the police to start looking more closely at murders in the area and to draw the parallels between certain cases that would eventually identify the Ripper's handiwork—as much good as that had done anyone forced to squeeze a living from the night.

But it wasn't this fact that made me suck in my breath when I turned the corner. Farther down that crowded, muddy lane bordered on both sides by walls of brick and windows, lay another sugarhouse. It was smaller than the one on Flower and Dean Street, but had a similar brick-and-wood construction, with smokestacks on either side. Even through the rain, the wet air was still heavy with the same mixture of sweet and chemical scents. As I made my reluctant way forward, I knew even before I checked the address that I'd find the second recipient there.

The noon whistle blew as I approached. The front door opened, and workers began to trickle outside. Steeling myself, I picked an innocuous-looking man standing against the wall, shielding his pipe and matches from the rain with his shoulder. Taking a deep breath, I forced myself forward.

"Excuse me," I said as I approached. The man took a long pull on his pipe and met my eyes. "I have a delivery for..." I glanced at the card tucked into the flowers. "Herr Backer. Erich Backer."

The man took the address card from me and frowned, his sparse eyebrows coming together across a fine brow. He was probably in his mid-thirties and built like a gazelle. He tipped his cloth cap back over thin, light hair. "Today is his day off." He took a pencil from behind his ear and scribbled an address on the back of the card and handed it back to me. "This is where you can find him."

"Thank you."

The address led me to a tenement not far away, on one of the many poorly marked residential roads that twisted through Whitechapel. The building wasn't wide, but it was tall, with soot-encrusted windows facing the street and clotheslines weighted down with dripping clothes, running from the wall below them to just beneath the windows of the adjacent building. I squeezed my way through the front door, which hung unevenly on rusted hinges.

The dark hallways echoed with familiar sounds—the shouts, bangs, clatters, and wailing babies could have been transplanted from my own building. The staircase was narrow and ill maintained. I squinted again at the card. Second floor. Careful not to rest my hand on the decrepit-looking banister, I made my way carefully up the stairs.

As I stepped out onto the second-floor landing, the air was warmer and thick with the odor of burning coal. Two voices echoed in the corridor: one higher—a woman or a child—and the other the unmistakable voice of a very angry man. I didn't understand the German words interspersed with the English, but argument sounds the same in every language. I winced as someone landed a blow. One might think that having grown up surrounded by similar sounds, it would have been easy to ignore them. But cruelty is never easy to ignore. On these streets, though, choosing your battles wisely can mean the difference between life and death.

Unfortunately, some battles choose you.

Glancing again at the address card, I cursed under my breath. I considered setting the flowers against the door, knocking, and running. But before I could consider it any further, something heavy landed against it with a wall-shaking thud.

"Herr Backer?" I called. When there was no response, I pounded the door with my fist. "Mr. Erich Backer?"

"Help me!" the higher voice shouted. "Please!"

"You came back to take it! Admit it!"

"No!"

"Delivery for Mr. Erich Backer!" I shouted back, hammering on the door. Two flats down, a hard-featured man in a stained shirt popped his head out. He was in his forties, built like an ox, and something cunning lurked behind his flinty eyes. "Do you know—" I said. The man shook his head quickly and slammed his door, engaging the lock behind him. Clearly he had a stronger survival instinct than I.

"I'll teach you a lesson, thief!" came the man's voice from behind the door. "Where is it, you little minx?"

"Somebody help me!"

The child's voice sounded familiar, but I couldn't quite place it. It didn't matter. Anyone with any survival sense would have left then. But survival wasn't the only code I lived by these days. Two years ago, my friend Nate had sacrificed his life to help the original residents of Turnbull House. Lazarus and Pearl routinely put themselves in danger from all manner of disease. Daring rescues really weren't my style, but I was already there. If I just skulked away, the guilt would be worse than any beating I might incur.

The door opened onto a dismal flat—a warped dining table, a single chair, and a makeshift privy consisting of a chamber pot hidden by a stained curtain hanging in a corner. When I stepped inside, a man and a child of about twelve blinked back at me through sallow paraffin light. The man was standing over the youth, one arm poised to deliver a blow with a wide leather belt. His other arm pinned the boy to the ground, the child's trouser-clad legs scuffling ineffectively against the floorboards.

I swallowed. "Mr. Erich Backer?"

He was a burly, thickly bearded fellow, with forearms as round and hard as bowling pins. At the sound of his name he looked over sharply.

"What the devil do you want?"

The child continued to wiggle beneath his grip. Between the welts on the boy's face and his ripped trousers, it was hard to tell anything other than his gender. And it turned out that I was even mistaken about that, when the child gave a violent twist and ripped the man's shirt she was wearing in a way that left no doubts.

"Ah..." I said, not at all certain what I'd interrupted. She was probably closer to fifteen, I thought, as I watched her scramble to cover herself. Was this a paid assignation? No. Despite the intimacy of their posture, and its violence, closer examination told me there was nothing sexual about it. A beating, and a vicious one, but no more or less.

But why was she wearing trousers?

"Go away," Backer growled.

That was probably the most prudent course. He was taller than me, broad chested, and well muscled from labor. But I wasn't going to leave the girl in that situation. Were they father and daughter? Uncle and niece? It didn't matter. No one deserved that. The girl had twisted around to face me directly, and she was looking at me in the strangest way. Not as if she wished me away, and not as if she held any hope for me as a savior.

She was looking at me as if she knew me.

I cleared my throat. "Delivery for Mr. Erich Backer."

I held out the flowers. When it was clear I wasn't going to leave him to his fun, he sighed and straightened, his belt-arm dropping to his side. "What's this, then?"

The girl shot to her feet the moment he stepped away. I forced myself not to back away as Backer lumbered toward me and snatched the bouquet from my hands. It was difficult to hide my satisfaction at the fear that crept over his features while he read the card. A strange, silent moment passed between us, and then he looked at me plaintively.

"It ain't what it looks like," he said. He glanced back at the girl. "She's a thief. And a pervert. You see how she dresses herself. Not like a proper girl..."

Oh yes, I thought. *She brung it on herself.* That's what they all say. The young woman touched her swelling cheek gingerly while clutching her ruined blouse closed. When I turned back to Backer, he'd lost his aggressive posture and his expression was pleading.

"Tell him I didn't mean it. I just run out of time, that's all. Tell him I just need more time."

Not my business, better judgment told me. *Not my business at all. Just deliver the flowers and be off.*

Backer swallowed "He'll kill me, you know."

"That's not my concern."

Backer's eyes followed mine as I looked back at the young woman. He licked his lips and gave me a sickly smile.

"My daughter. You like her? You can have a go with her if you want. Go on. I'll step out. Just tell your boss I need more time."

The young woman didn't regard me with the fright I'd have expected. Curious. I didn't shout my preferences from the rooftops like Wilde did, so something else about me must have told her I posed no danger to her virtue. She frowned again, and I could read it in her face. She recognized me from somewhere.

"I'll tell him," I said, pulling away from the young woman's unnerving gaze. "But she's coming with me."

What I was going to do with her once we left the building, I couldn't imagine. She was almost an adult—it wasn't as if she had to leave with me in the first place, though she was probably grateful for the chance to escape. But I couldn't just leave her there after what I'd witnessed, even if Goddard's justice was about to catch up with her father.

"Of course." Backer laughed, a cringing little sound. "Take her back to the alley. Or wherever you like. Bring her back later. Or don't. Whatever you like, sir."

Backer continued his nasty patter as I took his coat and hat—rather too nice a hat, I thought, considering the state of the rest of the man's possessions—from the hook near the front door and held them out to the young woman.

"Come on, Miss," I said, as if speaking to a frightened animal. "Anywhere's better than here, right?"

Exhaling with relief, she crossed toward me. I held the coat up as she shrugged into it. It reached nearly to the floor and could have wrapped around her thin frame twice. Her light-brown hair barely reached her shoulders—unusual for a girl. Perhaps she'd been shorn for lice a few years back. She turned and gave me a quick, knowing smile. She seemed so familiar, and clearly she knew me. But from where? She wasn't one of Goddard's, at least none of his associates that I'd ever met. She was too young to have been on the streets when I'd been there. And I hadn't met her through Wilde. I scratched my head.

I spotted a jolly nice pair of men's boots by the door. New, and much better made than I'd have expected from someone living in a dump like that. I snatched them up to give to her later. If she didn't want to wear them, she could sell them. And then I ushered her out the door before her father snapped out of his panic and changed his mind.

"Are you all right?" I asked we hurried down the hall.

"I'm fine, now."

We walked to the stairs in silence. We would part company the minute we exited the building. I'd helped her escape her father's wrath for the moment; the rest was up to her. Lazarus would strangle me if I returned with another stray. We'd moved two of the youngest into one bed to accommodate Jack—wherever he might be—and Lazarus certainly wouldn't ask a young lady to sleep on the floor.

The gray London skies seemed like a bright, sunny day after the darkness inside the tenement. While I squinted, trying to make my eyes adjust, a carriage splashed past through a puddle, spraying my trousers with black water.

"You'll be all right, now, Miss," I said, hoping I was right. I handed her the boots. "Here. These may be too big, but they're better than the ones you're wearing. Do you have somewhere to go?"

The young woman stared at me for a moment, and I experienced another frisson as I tried to place her battered, swollen face. Then she threw her arms around my neck and buried her face in my shoulder. "Oh, Mr. Adler!" she cried, the rest of her words lost, swallowed up by sobs of relief.

CHAPTER TEN

A cold drizzle fell as we stood on that busy street corner, she wailing loudly into my shoulder, and I wondering where on earth we might have met. Gradually, she pulled herself together. With a loud sniff, she wiped the sleeve of the coat across her swollen eyes and stepped back. "Sorry about that," she said gravely.

Her arms were lost in the voluminous sleeves of the coat. The hat covered her ears. I thought of Marcus the night of his arrival.

"Does he beat you often?" I asked.

"Not since I left."

"When was that?"

The sky was darkening again. A crack of thunder shook the air. Then the clouds opened up for real. I held out my elbow, and she took my arm. She shuffled alongside me but managed to keep my pace, despite the ungainly garment. It might have been my imagination, but she seemed to know which direction we were going without my saying a word.

"A year ago July," she said. "He were never wot you'd call *warm*, but when me mum died, that's when it got bad."

I nodded. It was a common story. One I'd seen a thousand times and might even have lived, had circumstances been different. "Why'd you go back?" I asked.

"Had to get somefin', didn't I? Thought he'd be at work."

"His day off," I said, remembering what the man at the sugar refinery had said. The young woman nodded. The rain was really coming down now. It was hard to tell where her sopping hat ended and the hair plastered to her neck began. "What did you need to retrieve?"

"Railway map," she said.

"What?"

I stopped, pulling us into the shelter of a doorway. Surely I hadn't heard that correctly. People streamed past, hurrying to get out of the rain. Paper crackled as she reached into the pocket of the coat and pulled out the sheet she'd been holding when I'd arrived at her door.

"You put your life at risk for a—a—a *map?*" I'd been about to tell her about Turnbull House, but it was clear I should have been heading for a lunatic asylum instead. "Is that what he was ranting about?"

"Thought the map could help," she said.

"With what?"

She frowned at me as if I were the one who was daft. "The messenger service, Mr. Adler. If we use the new underground lines we can get the messages across town twice as fast, and for pennies." Her face fell. "But I s'pose the meeting's already over, ain't it?"

"The—"

Shit. Oh, shit.

"Jack?" It took me a moment, but when I concentrated on the face, and not on what I had seen in the flat—the torn blouse, her undeniable anatomy, and Erich Backer calling her "daughter"—it all became clear.

He—she—he gave the cheeky smirk I'd come to know so well. "Wot'd you fink?"

I crossed my arms over my chest and rocked back on my heels. "I'll be damned."

"No, you won't. That's twice you saved me, Mr. Adler. God don't forget fings like that. That's wot Mrs. Lazarus says."

"You believe in God?" I asked.

"Nah, but the missus does, and she can't be wrong about everyfing."

I shook my head, looking hard at this thin, wet creature wrapped in a coat twice as big as she—as he—as she was. "But...

you…why?" It wasn't as if I hadn't seen any number of men dressed as women. It just didn't seem to happen so much the other way around. Or perhaps I just never noticed. "Do you like dressing that way?" I finally sputtered.

"In me da's coat? Not really."

"You know what I mean."

Stuffing the map back into her coat pocket, she pushed her hat down determinedly and ducked back out into the rain. I followed her as she wove in and out of the crowd, cursing myself for having left my umbrella back at the shelter. When I caught up with her at the corner, she turned to face me.

"It's just easier this way. Don't you fink?"

"Well…"

The traffic stopped, and we crossed with a large group of people, stepping carefully around broken stones and puddles of black water. When we reached the other side, she threaded her arm through my elbow.

"Mr. Adler, me da tried to buy you off with me favors. It ain't the first time, neither. If every man you knew was like that, would you go about in a dress? Besides, it's a lot easier to run from an angry coster if you're wearin' trousers, ain't it?" She elbowed me playfully.

"I s'pose," I said.

Raven Row was just around the corner. Jack—or whatever her name was—sensed it, too. As Turnbull House came into sight, she stopped and regarded me very seriously.

"Listen, would any of you have taken my delivery idea seriously if I'd been wearin' a dress? No. 'Cause you'd have packed me off with the girls to learn sewin' and needlework." She spat in a most unladylike fashion, as if to emphasize her point.

It embarrassed me to admit it, but it was true. Not out of any evil intent, but still. "But Mrs. Lazarus—" I said.

"The missus does what she finks is best for us. But sometimes what folks fink is right ain't the right fing at all. The world don't need another seamstress, but Turnbull House could jolly well use a delivery service."

"Well, we're not going to have one without you. When I left, they were still arguing about what actually constituted Central London."

"But I—"

"Left without sharing the information that would actually make your idea work," I said.

"I meant to come back."

"And now you have, which is all that matters. Come on. The meeting is probably over, but everyone will be very happy to see you."

He—she—looked relieved at that.

"But before we do," I said, "what should I...how do you want me to...er..."

"I'm Jack," she said. "Just Jack. Forget about the rest of it, yeah?" He stuffed his hair back up beneath the hat. "I ain't never been much good at bein' a girl, and it's just better for everyone this way. All right?" He stuck out his hand.

"All right," I said, taking it. "But don't think someone won't figure it out sooner or later."

❖

A few moments later we hauled our waterlogged selves out of the cold and into the comparatively stuffy coal-heated vestibule of Turnbull House. The classroom was empty, the furniture having been returned to its rightful configuration. Bess was sitting at her desk, examining her students' scrawlings, while Tim poked the coals in the fireplace.

"Look who I found," I called by way of greeting.

Lazarus glanced over as we wiped our feet on the mat and hung up our coats. "It's about time you returned, Adler," he said as he hurried out to join us. He squinted at Jack, and I was relieved that Lazarus was having the same trouble I'd had recognizing our little entrepreneur through the bruises and dirt. "Mr. Flip," he finally pronounced. "Where have you been?"

"And what happened to your face?" Mrs. Lazarus cried, close on her husband's heels. She swooped down on Jack like a very angry angel, turning his head this way and that, frowning at the welts and bruises. Drawing away, she frowned at the boots under his arm. "Those are nice."

"Didn't steal 'em, if that's wot you're finkin'," Jack muttered.

"Just a spot of bother," I explained. "Boy stuff. Nothing to worry about."

Lazarus gave us both a quick once-over and agreed. "Cuts and bruises. A fight, I'd wager. You'll live. Though you won't live here for long if you don't leave your battles at the door, young man."

"Yes, Doctor."

"Fighting!" Bess exclaimed. Then the fire in her eyes mellowed to concern. "You go downstairs right now and wash yourself off. Dr. Lazarus will be down in a moment with some dry clothing."

"No, Missus!" Jack cried out in terror. This time I understood why he'd consistently refused to bathe or change clothing. Though Tim and Bess would hardly turn him away for preferring trousers, they probably wouldn't allow him to continue his masquerade. He'd chosen to stay with us until now. If he ran away, where would he end up?

Bess turned to Lazarus, exasperated. "See what I mean? He won't take a bath or even change clothes. I know you men don't mind dirt, but he was filthy when he came here, and now, well, just look at him!"

"I'll take the clothes down," I said. "And I'll see that he bathes. As for the bruises, you heard what Tim said. It looks worse than it is. Really. He's a tough little runt."

Bess gave me a hard stare. She knew I was hiding something. She was also likely evaluating whether it would be worth arguing over at that moment. Slowly she nodded. "All right, then."

Jack looked at me gratefully. "Thanks, Mr. Adler."

Bess crossed her arms and watched Jack disappear down the basement stairs. Then she turned to me. "Is there something you'd like to tell us, Ira?"

Oh, I'd like to share so many things. But I stuck to the topic at hand.

"I met Jack's father today."

"Really?" Lazarus asked.

I hadn't wanted to embarrass Jack by relating the events in front of him. I still wasn't about to reveal his secret, but after all the exceptions Tim and Bess had made for Jack, they did deserve at least a partial explanation for his odd behavior.

"The man is quite a piece of work, and the thrashing he gave his son is the least of it. When the constable brought Jack here the other day, I didn't think Turnbull House was the best place for him. But after what I saw this morning, and what Jack told me, I've changed my mind. He asked me not to talk about it. But let me just say, we'll get a lot farther with the issue of hygiene if we grant him a little extra privacy."

Bess narrowed her eyes. "I'm sure he appreciates your discretion, Ira."

"If we respect that, I'm certain he'll show more respect for our rules as well."

She nodded, though I could see from her expression that she wasn't completely convinced. "I'll bring some fresh clothes from upstairs."

Lazarus's eyes followed her up the stairs toward the dormitories. "Well, that's one problem solved, in a way. Did he say why he ran away like that?"

"He didn't run away. He went back to his father's flat to get a railroad map. He thought we could use the new underground trains for deliveries. Unfortunately, when he got back to the flat, he found his father at home, rather than at work. The man took exception to the theft and used a belt on Jack. Otherwise, Jack would have been back before anyone noticed he was missing."

"And you just happened to turn up there?" Bess asked from the head of the stairs. The wood creaked as she began her slow, careful descent. She was carrying a bundle of clean clothing beneath one arm—trousers, a shirt, small clothes, and socks—and when she reached us, she thrust them into my hands.

"I...well..." They knew I'd gone out to make Goddard's delivery. I'd no reason to hide it. But given Herr Lothar's death and Goddard's very likely connection to it, I didn't want to draw any more attention to their scheme than was necessary. "I was on my way back from the delivery, when I heard someone crying for help. I followed the noise and, well, as you can see I brought him back."

"Quite the hero," Lazarus said.

"It's what we do."

"Indeed," Bess said. The sounds of splashing came from below stairs, and an expression of contentment settled over her face. "Well, now that we've got that sorted, I'll get back to tomorrow's lessons. Gentlemen."

She gave Lazarus a meaningful nod—meaningful for him, at least, from his expression—then returned to her desk in the classroom. When I turned back to Lazarus, he was examining a chip in the paint, pretending he didn't have something else on his mind. And of course he did. It would have been kind of me to address our unresolved business at that point. But quite frankly, he was the one who had accosted me, and I wanted him to do it.

"Could we speak in my office?" he finally asked.

"Just let me leave these for Jack."

"Certainly."

I felt his eyes on my back as I made my way to the back stairs. Then I started down, the clean clothing under my arm. The splashing sounds stopped as my footsteps echoed in the narrow stairwell. Jack had put the screen around the copper tub, but I could feel his nervousness from across the room.

"It's just me," I called, turning completely around so that when I reached the bottom, my back was to Jack and I was facing up the stairs. "I'm leaving the clothing on the bottom step."

Jack's relief was palpable. "Thanks, Mr. Adler."

"Stay out of trouble."

Lazarus was waiting when I emerged. I followed him into his little office and waited while he turned on the lamp. He had organized the place since I'd last seen it, and though the room was still cramped, one no longer felt the imminent danger of having toppling paper piles crush him.

"Am I in trouble?" I asked.

Shaking his head, he sat down on the edge of his desk and raked his fingers through his hair. He took a moment to compose himself, then said, "I'm sorry. I wasn't myself the other day."

"No, you weren't. What's wrong?"

He shrugged. "I could use some sleep, among other things."

His desk was clear for once—in contrast with his rumpled shirt and waistcoat.

"You could use a holiday," I said.

He laughed. "A holiday. That's good."

In addition to sitting at the helm of Turnbull House, Lazarus had his clinic. He also saw private patients from time to time and lectured on different subjects at the London Hospital to bring in extra income. He was stretched very, very thin, and I was amazed he hadn't yet had a mental breakdown.

"We could mange. Just get away for a few days. Walk in the park. Read a book."

He cocked an eyebrow. "When would you suggest I do that?"

"Before the baby comes, I should think."

"Oh, God."

And that's when I understood. Lazarus, who carried us all on his shoulders—on whose strength we had all come to depend—was terrified. It was one thing to run a youth shelter, but quite another to bring a completely new person into the world—a person for whom he would be wholly responsible from the beginning—for its success...or its failure. My involvement with Turnbull House was as close as I'd ever wanted to come to fatherhood, but Lazarus had jumped in feet first. And with the future of Turnbull House not quite as secure as he'd thought, he must have been questioning the kind of future he could provide for his own offspring.

"Adler, what was I thinking?" He began to pace around the tiny office, even though he had to push me aside to do it. "I can't bring a new life into this world."

"You were thinking that you love Bess and now that you're married, a baby is the next logical step. Right?"

"I don't know. I don't know anything anymore."

And there it was. A bushel of burden, a pint of nostalgia, and a good dollop of sexual indecision. Mix well and let fester for a few months. No wonder he thought I had it easy. I might have envied my life, too, from where he was standing. I might have looked back fondly to simpler times and mistaken the desire for simplicity for... well...desire itself.

I wasn't surprised when I felt his arms slip around my waist from behind, his chest pressing against my back, his face nuzzling my hair. I wasn't angry anymore, either. But understanding, now, I couldn't let it go any farther than this.

I unpeeled his arms and turned. "Tim, I really don't think—"

"Shut up." He backed me up against the desk and kissed me long and deep. It was good. I won't lie. And I didn't stop him when he did it again.

My body responded predictably as he unbuckled my belt. I moaned as his tongue thrust aggressively, searchingly around my mouth. He didn't possess Marcus's professional expertise or Goddard's heart-stopping will to dominate, but it was good, and I wanted him.

But the longer he pinned me against that desk, the louder that little voice at the back of my mind became. It wasn't just about what Tim or I wanted anymore. Only a thin door stood between that quiet back room and Bess. At one time his home life would have been of no interest to me. But things had changed. I had changed. As his fingers fluttered over my trouser buttons, images of peppered moths filled my mind's eye. When Lazarus had made the comparison, he'd meant to say I was flighty, with superficial emotions that changed direction with the wind. But while that might once have been true, it was no longer the case. I was no longer that young man who had exchanged sex for money and betrayed friendship for a higher class of customer.

And I was surely too good to let a friend make the biggest mistake of his life. Not only did the thought of what Bess would do to us both make me shiver. But Lazarus—once he'd regained control of body and spirit—would never forgive himself.

"You need to get hold of yourself," I said, pulling away.

The moths in my mind's eye rose together as a great cloud—white, speckled, and black. Then they dispersed in all directions, vanishing into the darkness.

Lazarus stepped back quickly, blinking as if only just realizing where he was and what he'd been doing. "Quite. You're quite right, Adler. God forgive me."

While I refastened my trousers and belt, he ran his hands through his hair. The dim light betrayed a mist of perspiration across his face and neck. He was breathing hard, and I could hear his heart pounding against his breastbone. I watched him force himself to regain composure, as if he were once again taking up a heavy mantle.

"My apologies, Adler. It won't happen again."

"Get some rest, Tim. The world can turn without you for a few days."

He nodded, his expression a mixture of resignation and embarrassment. "Please don't tell Bess."

"Do I look suicidal?"

He smiled grimly.

I tucked my shirt back into my trousers and smoothed down my hair. Taking a deep breath to calm the blood, I crossed to the door.

As I opened it, he said, "You're a good friend, Ira."

I didn't know how to respond to that. I hoped I was. I tried. Glancing back at him, I nodded. Then I stepped out into the corridor to leave him with his thoughts.

❖

"More boy stuff?" Bess asked, appearing suddenly in the doorway of the classroom as I hurried down the hall.

"Pardon me, Bess." My heart raced. How much had she heard? "I have somewhere to be."

She walked with me, right at my heels, her swollen belly swaying with each step. I walked faster, but she easily kept pace.

"Ira? Is everything all right?"

"Now that Jack's returned, it should be," I said, hoping my bright tone would disguise my deliberate redirection. I reached for my coat, flinching as she took it by the shoulders and helped me into it. I put my hand on the front doorknob. She covered it with her own.

"I meant with my husband."

"Er…"

The students had cleared off some time ago to their vocational lessons. Jack was still downstairs. We were alone. While I fumbled with my coat buttons, she took my elbow and led me back into the empty classroom.

"May I confide in you?" she asked.

"Er..."

"I'm worried." She began with her usual confidence and directness. But in her voice lurked a vulnerability I'd never heard before. Letting go my arm, she sighed and looked away. "It sounds so crazy I can hardly bring myself to say the words. But the more I think about it, the more I think that there can't possibly be any other explanation. Ira," she said, turning and meeting my eyes with her deep, intelligent brown ones, "is Tim seeing someone? Is there another woman?"

Good God. I'd stopped Lazarus before things had gone very far, but I'd enjoyed those things far too much. And most likely I hadn't been as quiet, or as discreet, as I should have been. I could still smell Lazarus's cologne on my shirt, feel his muscular arse beneath my hands.

"No." I almost choked on the denial.

She narrowed her piercing gaze and impaled me with it. "Is there anyone who...is not a woman?"

She didn't put her suspicion into exact words, but we both knew what she meant. Lazarus had told her about our past, and they had agreed not to revisit the issue. She had decided to trust him, and he had been grateful. But I could tell, from the tone of her voice and from the look on her face, that if that trust were broken now, it would never be mended.

"Lazarus is under a lot of pressure, as I'm sure you're aware," I said carefully.

She nodded, but her expression was dubious.

"He loves you," I said.

"I'm sure." She was too intelligent to be fobbed off like that but, even in her current state, too kind to remind me of the fact.

"He's overworked, he hasn't slept well, and if he doesn't get away from this place for a few days, he's going to drop dead from the strain of it. Take him home. It's what he wants, even if he won't admit it."

"Is that all it is? Stress and strain?" Her grip on my elbow tightened. "I'm asking you as a friend, Ira."

I wasn't going to lie to her. But what good would the entire sordid truth do anyone? I took her hands in mine. Square, callused hands—like Tim's own—rough from work, but clean, strong, and gentle. Were there ever any two people more clearly made for each other than Tim and Bess Lazarus?

No, I wouldn't lie if she asked me what had happened in that back room. But volunteering the details would do more harm than good.

"As a friend, I'm telling you, there's no one else. Not in his heart and not in his arms."

It was the truth. It was *a* truth. And that was where I planned to leave it.

How ironic that Lazarus's own influence—his scruples, which I had somehow absorbed through working so closely with the man for these past few years—had caused me to put the brakes on what might have been a very pleasant interlude. Or perhaps the seeds of conscience had always been there, and they just needed the right environment to flourish. Either way, gazing at Bess now—how the worry drained from her face, how her shoulders relaxed—I knew I had done the right thing. What's more, Lazarus knew, and I was pretty certain the incident had scared him back to good sense.

Bess searched my face then nodded, apparently deciding to believe me. It was a sacred trust, a precious second chance. I wouldn't throw it away.

"Thank you, Ira," she said, a grateful if shaky smile spreading over her face. She might not have been ready to write off all of Lazarus's eccentricities to stress and strain, but she would accept my word. And I would make good on that word. "Well, I suppose I should let you go to wherever it was you need to go," she said.

I smoothed her dark curls with my hand, then bent down to kiss her cheek. How soft, how smooth, and how different it was from that of a man.

"Look after yourself, Bess," I said.

"I will." She waited until I was on the doorstep to say, "And Ira, Tim's right. You *are* a good friend."

CHAPTER ELEVEN

I returned to my flat near suppertime in need of a drink. Marcus was still out—moving boxes for the bookseller, I assumed. I fished my picklocks out of my pocket. After I'd given Marcus my key, I'd taken to carrying the picks again. The lock gave way with disappointing ease, and it occurred to me that I might do well to exchange it for something more robust.

I switched on my desk lamp then crossed the room to lay a fire. As flame engulfed the kindling and settled onto the coal, an uncomfortable feeling prickled across my back. It was hard to put a finger on it, except that something was wrong. Off-center somehow. The funny thing about having someone else in your space is that things don't always stay where you left them. My water glass, for example, still with the residue of the wine Marcus had brought— was sitting on the floor near my bed, rather than by the basin where I washed dishes. He hadn't managed to make the bed, either—a small irritation, as most of the time I didn't manage it myself. But still, somehow it rankled to see that my guest wasn't taking more care with my things.

But the feeling was too strong for mere items out of place. I looked about for signs of a larger disturbance—what was I expecting, a trail of blood, perhaps?—but found none. Sighing, I hung up my coat and hat and lined my boots up on the folded towel beneath them.

The Language of Flowers lay on the bed, partially covered by the wadded-up blanket. I shook it free of the covers and picked it up. Marcus loved that book. Reminded him of his sister, no doubt, as well as the new direction his life was taking. I was surprised he hadn't taken it with him. I was about to set the book on the bookshelf, when I remembered the second bouquet—the one I'd delivered to Jack's father. Almond, wasn't it? And buttercup. Rather late in the year for both of those, though Goddard could accomplish just about anything, given his ambition and his fancy new greenhouse.

Pushing the covers aside, I sat down on the bed and opened the book on my lap. Almond—ah, there it was. Stupidity—in particular, some sort of indiscretion. Buttercup symbolized ingratitude. And then, of course, the broken straw and thistle. After I'd spirited Jack away to safety, I had wished his father nothing but ill. All the same, the message of the flowers made my blood run cold. If I was reading this correctly, Jack's father had broken a contract with Goddard, been spectacularly indiscreet about it, not to mention ungrateful, and would be dealt revenge forthwith. Another explosion, perhaps? Or something worse?

Once again, I wondered what Goddard was up to. Whatever it was, the plan had involved a manager of one sugar refinery and a foreman from another. Both German. I tried to remember what little I'd known about Goddard's criminal enterprises. He'd made much of his fortune in opium—specifically from exporting it to China, though Goddard also supplied opium dens here in London. He maintained a few of what might be called disorderly houses, could anything Goddard touched be even remotely "disorderly." But he was hardly a panderer. He limited his involvement to collecting rent from the young men and women who used the rooms and a share of their profits. I was sure he was involved in other schemes, but what sugar production had to do with any of it, I couldn't begin to guess.

That tingling feeling returned to the spot between my shoulder blades. Something was wrong, out of place. I glanced around my room. I'd put the screen back in its spot near the commode, and it hadn't moved since. The bathing tub stood on end, leaning against the wall next to the cold fireplace. My desk appeared undisturbed. My typewriting machine—the most valuable thing I owned—sat in its usual place amid the piles of work that had gone as cold as the fireplace coals while I waited for Wilde to return from Paris. It looked as if Marcus had gone through the few books I owned, but they were all on their shelf as well.

Actually, it made me happy to think he'd perused my books. It meant that his show of interest in learning wasn't merely for my benefit. Standing, I crossed to my desk to give the stacks of paper lying on it a much-needed tidying. Thumbing through each one, I removed notes no longer needed, discarded them into the bin, and gave each stack a sound tap on the desk to straighten it.

Usually, about this point, my favorite pen would roll out from some hiding place and clatter to the floor. But this time it didn't. Frowning, I lifted up the other stacks one by one and looked again. I checked under the desk and in the drawers. Where was that thing? The pen wasn't gold, or even silver, but it was well made. It had been one of my first purchases when I'd started working for Wilde, and I liked it.

Had Marcus taken it?

It's a horrible thing to be suspicious, but when one has grown up in doorways and workhouses, where every possession emits an invitation to steal it, suspicion comes naturally. The pen wouldn't have brought much from a pawnbroker, but it would have brought something. And in the eyes of someone who had nothing, it might have been enough. Had Marcus reconsidered the new life he was building? Had he thought about the easy money he'd made before he'd gone down and compared it to the honest pittance for which he'd have to work harder than he'd ever worked before? Looking at it that way, I couldn't rightly blame him if he'd snatched a handful of my possessions and bolted.

Disappointment joined suspicion in the pit of my stomach. Certainly, I'd been too quick to trust him. He wasn't even a week out of prison. Before that, he'd lived in a brothel and, before that, some squalid cellar on Drury Lane. How could I have been so blind as to think that a love of books would transform him, over the course of a few days, into a sterling citizen? And on top of everything else, I'd gone and given him the key. If the first theft was successful, he'd be back—probably with friends. I should have known. I should have *known,* sod it all!

Sitting back down, I forced myself to take a deep breath. Perhaps I was overreacting. If Marcus were to steal from me and disappear, wouldn't he have taken the typewriter? It was a Remington keyboard machine, one of the first of its kind. It cost as much as Goddard's overpaid butler had made in a year, and it would have been easy to lift and easier to sell. He could have lived off the profits for quite a while.

But the typewriter still sat, unmolested, in its place. Of course it did. Because I was letting my imagination run away with me.

Gradually, my suspicion began to subside. Marcus was down on Holywell Street working, most likely. He'd be back. And the pen would turn up. Sooner or later it would.

Something else that was definitely turning up, I thought, absently scratching my chin, was unwanted facial hair. A complicated beard looks smashing when it's well maintained. It's an inexpensive fashion to follow, which makes it ideal for someone like me, who has to mind his budget. The only problem was that my hair grows very dark and very fast. I hadn't had the time lately to pay it proper attention.

Standing, I crossed to the washbasin and glanced at my reflection in the mirror above it. Not bad, actually, even coming up on thirty. My skin was a tannish color, though it hadn't seen enough sun to become weathered or wrinkled. My moustache and the sections of beard along my chin were thick and dark. The hair was meant to be cut close to the skin, but it had grown out over the past few days, and the shaven parts were filling up with an unseemly stubble. Before flower-coded messages and possible pen-theft had distracted me, I'd been toying with the idea of muttonchops. A Franz Joseph style beard—a continuous line of hair from one ear to the other, rising in a graceful arc to form a moustache—might also have suited me, but I'd have felt naked without a bit of chin cover. I narrowed my eyes and examined my face from different angles. And then it came to me. I would thin out the moustache, shave my cheeks clean, and keep two thin lines of hair coming down from my ears, across the jaw, to meet in the middle of my chin.

It was a bold move, but in the matter of fashion, boldness covers a multitude of sins.

I poured water into the basin and brought out my razor, soap, and brush. Then I reached for my scissors.

Which weren't there.

Now that was a problem. It wasn't like the pen, where at any given time I had a vague idea where it was. The scissors were silver—a gift from Wilde—and I always kept them in the drawer of the washstand, along with my razor and brush. I always cleaned them carefully and put them away when I was done. I felt around in the drawer. Then I bent down and looked. The razor and brush had been there. But not the scissors.

What the devil?

Just then the key turned in the lock. I looked up to see Marcus backing inside, cradling two bottles and a paper-wrapped package in one elbow.

"Where are my shaving scissors?" I asked. The words came out sharper than I'd intended, and I immediately regretted them when I saw his face fall. "Let me rephrase that. I've had a very difficult day and was looking forward to giving my beard a much-needed trim. My silver scissors are missing from the drawer where I keep them. They were a gift, and I should very much hate for them to be lost. Have you, perchance, used them and put them away somewhere different?"

Of course he hadn't. His face was as hairless as a babe's. I'd watched him use the razor, once, the day after he arrived. But scissors hadn't figured into the equation.

"I brung supper," he said weakly.

I sighed.

While he shed his coat and boots, I cleared a spot on my desk and pulled out the chair for him by way of apology. Repositioning his load, he crossed the room and laid the bottles and the package down amid the stacks of papers. The wrapping was stained with grease and radiated warmth. It smelled heavenly. While he removed the paper, I brought over my plate and handed him my bowl. I really did need to acquire an extra table setting. Perhaps even a table.

I handed him a fork, and he gave me the larger of two gorgeous meat pies. The pastries were all golden brown with thick dribbles of juice bubbling out between the seams. Suddenly the entire flat was redolent with onion and beef.

"You're welcome," he said, as I greedily tucked in.

"Thanks," I said, savoring a mouthful of flaky pastry and piping-hot meat. By God, it was delicious.

"Thought you might fancy a treat." He flopped down in my chair and gave me a crooked smile. Which made it all the harder to ask the question nagging at my mind.

"Ah, Marcus?"

"Mmm?" he asked, his mouth full.

"Where did you get the money for this feast?"

His face went stony. "You fink I stole them scissors."

"The thought had crossed my mind." He scowled. "But then I realized how silly that was, when I'd gone to such lengths to help you."

While he chewed on this bit of information, I added a few more pieces of coal to the fire. Soon, the warmth rose and spread. When I turned back to Marcus, his full belly seemed to have overcome his irritation, and he looked over with a thoughtful expression.

"I got paid today."

"Really? That place on Holywell Street, where you found the book?"

He licked a crumb from a fingertip. "You askin' so's you can check?"

"I'm trying to make conversation. You had work today. That's excellent. Thank you for the pie."

He looked slightly mollified. Popping the last bite of his supper into his mouth, he said, "I did do some work for Mr. Samuels today at that book shop, but it weren't much. On me way out, he introduced me to another man wot had some other work to do. And that," he said, wiping his fingers clean on his trousers, "is where them pies come from. Now, do you want one of the beers I brung, or is you going to interrogate me some more?"

That's exactly what I wanted to do. *Who was that other man? I wanted to ask. What manner of work did he hire you to do? And where the devil are my shaving scissors?* But Marcus wasn't my ward, or my employee, and he had brought supper, and the scissors would turn up—or they wouldn't. At any rate, the last thing I wanted right then was an argument. I reached for a bottle of beer.

"I delivered more flowers today," I said.

He looked up, interest lighting his face. "Wot kind?"

"Almond, buttercup, more straw and thistle."

He frowned. "That ain't good." He tipped his head back and took a long swig from his bottle.

"Not entirely bad, either, though," I said.

I gave him an abbreviated account of Jack's story, leaving out, of course, Jack's name and true gender.

"Bastard," Marcus said, wiping his mouth on his sleeve. "Better to have no father at all than someone like that."

Having myself grown up without a father, I could only agree. "If his boiler explodes, I won't lose any sleep over it." I picked up the plate and bowl and carried them to the basin. "On the other hand, it would be very awkward indeed, if two men turned up dead right after I'd delivered threatening messages to them—in front of witnesses, no less."

His expression turned wary. "Who'd you say you's workin' for?"

"I didn't, and I don't intend to. I was grateful for the money at first, but, quite frankly, the sooner this is over and done with, the better."

But would it ever be completely finished? The Turnbull House messenger service was off to a shaky start. I owed Goddard an unspeakable sum, and right then it didn't seem inconceivable that I might end up working as Goddard's delivery boy for the rest of my life. The thought would keep me pacing the floor all night if I let it. I picked up my bottle and sucked it dry.

"So," I said, suppressing a belch. "Tell me more about this man you met through the bookseller."

Marcus shrugged. "Ain't much to tell."

"Rich man? Poor man? Teacher? Tradesman?"

He cocked his head. "He weren't no toff, not really. But he spoke good. Dressed rich. Not fancy-like, but his togs was quality, an' his shoes cost a bundle, I'd wager. His hair were cut recent, an' he didn't have no beard. Nice cologne."

"Old man? Young?"

"Older'n you, I fink. Some gray, not much."

"What sort of work did he want you to do?"

What I feared must have been evident in my voice. Marcus snorted a laugh. "Nuffin' like that, Mr. Ira. Actually," he said, stretching languidly as the heat from the fire spread throughout the room, revealing the lithe form beneath the worn shirt and trousers. "He just wanted me to run a few messages."

"What sort of messages?" I asked suspiciously. Another overreaction, to be sure. At any given moment hundreds of messages were making their way across London in this manner. Turnbull House was banking on it. But between Goddard's little bouquets and all of my other current troubles regarding messengers and messenger services, the coincidence gave me pause.

"You fink *I* read it?" Marcus asked, laughing. "You fink I would, even if I could?"

"No, no, of course not."

"I don't know wot you want from me, Mr. Ira," he said, frowning suddenly and sitting up. His features clouded and his voice rose, as if he was coming to an unpleasant realization. "If I don't work, you fink I'm some kind of scrounger, and if I do, well, I must be up to no good."

"I'm sorry. That's not what I meant. I just—"

He shot to his feet. "You don't want me to pay for me room an' board the only way I know how, but when I finds a new way, it ain't good enough—"

"I didn't say that. I'm sorry!"

He stalked across the room and jammed his feet into his boots, his fingers stumbling over the laces as if they couldn't move fast enough.

"Where are you going?" I asked. How had I offended him so deeply in such a small stretch of time? Clearly I wasn't the only one who was overreacting.

"Out. Glad you liked your supper," he mumbled as he finally gained control of the laces and pulled them tight. "And the beer."

"It was just an innocent question!" I cried. Then, more calmly, I said, "You don't have to do this."

"You don't want me here," he said, pulling on his coat and hat.

"I never said—"

"You didn't have to. I'll be goin', now."

As if on cue, a great clap of thunder shook the walls, and the rain began again, coming down in sheets, by the sound of it. "In this weather?" I asked.

"You fink I should wait for springtime?"

Surely he wasn't leaving just because of a few awkward questions. We'd been getting on so well, and he'd really been making progress. I thought back to the lively conversations about the meanings of Goddard's flowers and the easy routine we'd fallen into. Was he willing to throw away everything we'd shared—everything I was trying to do for him—over some imagined offense? I might have been a little less suspicious, I suppose. But then I'd thought we were beyond that tentative phase of initial acquaintance. I'd thought we were friends.

"Will you be back?" I asked. If not I'd best ask for the key.

He shrugged.

"Marcus, I'm sorry."

He met my eyes, his own more sorrowful than angry now. "Me, too. Here." He took the key from his trouser pocket and tossed it to me. "Maybe you'll find them scissors after I'm gone."

I opened my mouth to speak, but he was already out the door, pulling it closed—loudly and dramatically—behind him.

Well. Nothing like a spirited argument to liven up an otherwise dull evening, I thought, as a wave of chill air spread from the door across my small room. Sighing, I crossed to the shelf where I kept my books and took down my bottle of carefully rationed Scotch. It was excellent whiskey, which I'd bought when I'd had too much employment rather than too little. I wiped my water glass clean and poured myself a drop. The fire was cheery and warm, while outside was as miserable a night as I'd ever seen. Marcus was out in that. By his own choice, but still. I went over the argument in my mind, but as hard as I tried, I couldn't find anything I might have said differently. Marcus was being remarkably thin-skinned about my inquiries. He hadn't seemed the volatile type. Ah well, just like the scissors, he'd be back or he wouldn't. But at least I had my key now.

I sat down on the bed. The cover of *The Language of Flowers* poked my arse. I tossed it toward the desk with the vain hope that it would land there. It fell nearby on the floor. Not optimal, but the whiskey was burning pleasantly in my gullet, and I wasn't in any hurry to rush over and pick up the sole remaining trace of my strange young acquaintance. I reached to switch off the lamp, but before I could douse the light, I heard a wooden clatter as my missing pen fell from the desk and rolled across the floor toward me.

CHAPTER TWELVE

I woke to a sharp rapping at the door. I'd drawn the curtains, and the inside of my flat was as dark as pitch. The fire in the fireplace had died, and on top of everything else, it was cold as hell. I reached out my arm to steady Marcus, and my fingers brushed the cool, smooth plaster of the wall instead. He was gone, and I was alone.

"Mr. Adler?" called a gruff man's voice. It wasn't Marcus crawling back after his snit. It wasn't any voice I recognized, but he knew my name—a fact that, given its urgency, did not comfort me. "It's the police. Open the door!"

The police? My first thought was that a neighbor had overheard something he shouldn't have and reported me and my mysterious male friend. No evidence was required to convict a man of gross indecency—nor indeed any actual indecent occurrence. Even "attempted" indecency carried a penalty of two years at hard labor. How fortunate Marcus had chosen the previous evening to absent himself.

My next thought was that something had happened to Marcus. Or to Lazarus, or even to Bess.

"Coming!" I called. Scrambling out of bed, I pulled on my trousers and grabbed the lamp off my desk. When I opened the door, the dim light revealed a pair of constables dripping black rain onto the floorboards of my corridor. They looked as happy to be there in the middle of the night as I was to receive them.

"Come in, Officers. How can I help you?"

The first man, short and stout, with a ruddy face and a thick, dark moustache, shuffled inside. His boots were shiny, his whiskers well groomed, and he had the whiff of a military man about him. His partner—a taller blond man who was clearly the subordinate—followed closely, shut the door behind him, and stood against it, as if to emphasize that I wasn't going anywhere.

"Mr. Adler, we need to ask you a few questions," the first one said.

"Why? What's happened?"

"You're living here alone, is that correct?" He glanced about as if expecting me to lie about it.

"Yes. As you can see, I have barely room enough for one."

Behind him, the second constable took out a small pad of paper and began to scribble notes. "And you work for Turnbull House on Raven Row?"

"That's right. Are you familiar with our work?"

"A number of officers give to the Christmas fund every year. Your Mrs. Lazarus can be quite convincing. But that's neither here nor there. The reason we're here, Mr. Adler, is that we're searching for a young woman last seen in your company. A Miss Kathe Backer."

He watched my face closely with his sharp blue eyes, but the only response I was able to offer was confusion.

"I...I've never heard that name," I said. Though something about it was familiar. Backer...Backer...Oh.

"One of Erich Backer's neighbors reported someone of your description paying a visit yesterday to the flat he shares with his daughter."

"Kathe Backer," I said, trying—and failing—to reconcile this new name with the young man we all knew as Jack Flip. The taller constable continued to move his pencil silently across his little pad. "I was there yesterday."

"In connection to your work at Turnbull House?"

"Ah—" I wasn't sure how to respond to that inquiry. If I said yes, then whatever trouble Jack was in would follow him to

Turnbull House. If I said no, then I'd have to explain why I was delivering flowers to Erich Backer, which would bring the trouble to Goddard's door.

"Let me be blunt. Witnesses reported seeing you at Backer's flat and hearing a commotion. Then, they say, you and Miss Backer were seen fleeing the premises. Sometime after that, Backer was found dead."

"Dead?" My pulse began to race. Dead like Herr Lothar, after receiving a floral-coded threat hand-delivered by Yours Sincerely? "How?"

"Perhaps you could tell us."

I swallowed. They thought I did it? Why? And who could possibly have identified me?

"How do you know Miss Backer, Mr. Adler?" the constable asked while his partner began to poke about my flat. Looking for a murder weapon, no doubt. When I didn't answer, he said, "Let me offer you a theory. You and Miss Backer were having a little *affair de coeur*. You go to take the young lady flowers and find her old man giving her one beating too many. You whisk her away to safety. So far so good. But later, you sneak back, and—"

"No!" I cried. "That's not how it happened!"

The constable's bushy brows came together in a thoughtful point. "Then why don't you tell us how it did happen, Mr. Adler?"

"I-I don't know how the man died. I didn't do it. I had no reason to. I'd never even met him before yesterday."

"What were you doing at his flat?"

"I was delivering the flowers to him, not to her. I sometimes make deliveries for a little extra money. You know how it is."

"Go on."

"And his daughter was there. At least I assumed she was his daughter. That's what he said. I'd never met her either." Which was technically true, I supposed. "And yes, he was beating her—with a thick leather belt, I might add."

"So you decided to be a hero. Rescue a young lady in distress."

"Yes—no—well...He had to let her go in order to accept the delivery. While he was reading the message, I took her out of there. I did. But he was alive when I left. I swear, constable."

"And Miss Backer?"

"She left with me."

"She's not your sweetheart, then?"

"Sweet—no! I'd never met the girl. Besides, she's a...a bit young for me, don't you think?"

"I see. But you did interfere with Mr. Backer's disciplining of his daughter. You did argue with him."

"He'd have beaten her to death!"

Something glinted in his eyes, as if he had found a missing puzzle piece.

"Would you say, Mr. Adler, that it's not immoral to kill in defense of someone else?"

"What?" My pulse raced. "No! I didn't do it!"

"Where's the girl now?"

"Gone," I said, meeting his eye. "Long gone." It was the truth, in a sense. Kathe Backer had been Jack Flip for long enough to convince everyone around her—even Bess Lazarus, and fooling Bess wasn't easy. One might well say the young woman she'd been *was* long gone.

"One might say, Mr. Adler, that if Miss Backer were completely innocent, she wouldn't have a reason to run."

I frowned. Could Jack have done it? I was sure he'd wished his father dead more than once. And yet considering how large Backer was, and how slight was Jack, it hardly seemed likely.

"Then you must know *I* had nothing to do with it. I was exactly where you expected to find me."

"Or, you thought that if both of you disappeared, it would appear suspicious. Perhaps you're planning to rendezvous with your young lady after we leave."

"What? No! I already told you..."

The other constable slipped his pad and pencil into the pocket of his overcoat. I had a sneaking suspicion that it was because he'd heard everything he needed to. The moustached officer narrowed his eyes.

"Tell me more about your work, Mr. Adler. Aside from being a convenient way to mix with the criminal classes."

I drew a long breath. A sharp tongue was my natural reaction to pressure. It rarely made the situation better. "I sit on the board of directors at Turnbull House," I said. "Sometimes I help in the classroom. As for my vocation, I'm a secretary."

"Is that so?"

"There's my typewriting machine." I nodded toward the desk. "How many people do you know who can use something like that?"

He strode over to my desk to inspect the machine. I had to force myself to keep silent while he played with the keys. It was a delicate piece of equipment, and expensive. He flipped through the manuscripts and notes piled on the desk. Temporarily satisfied—but not for long, I imagined—he turned back to me.

"Where do you conduct your business, Mr. Adler?"

"Out of my clients' homes, or from here, depending on the client's needs."

"Do many people in Whitechapel need secretarial services?"

"You'd be surprised."

"I'll need a list of your clients, then."

Another question that I needed to handle gingerly. Wilde had not yet been taken to task for his peccadilloes, but with the way he carried on, it was only a matter of time. Briefly, I wondered whether the constable had noticed Wilde's name while going through my papers.

"I'm between clients, at the moment," I said. "That's why I'm making deliveries."

The constable smoothed the sausage-like halves of his moustache with his fingertips. "Show me your hands."

I balanced my lamp in the crook of my arm and held my hands out. I hadn't worked for Wilde for almost a month, so I didn't have any ink stains to speak of. On the other hand, my knuckles weren't cut or callused, like one might expect from a hired bruiser. He frowned. Disappointed again, I imagined.

"Spatulate fingertips consistent with work as a typist," he said, looking over his shoulder at his partner. "Just like that lady in *A Case of Identity*. You like Sherlock Holmes, Mr. Adler?"

"Not particularly."

He let my hands drop. "Skin is smooth and fine, also like a lady. You make any other 'deliveries' lately?"

Yes, I had. To another employee of another sugar refinery, who had also turned up dead. A death that was being treated as an accident, if the reports in the papers were anything to go by. But, having experience with police more interested in closing a case quickly than in closing it well, I sensed it was in my best interest to not give him any further ammunition.

"I don't like what you're implying. And as edifying as this has been, I don't think I want you here anymore."

"Is that so?" The constable's voice turned triumphant. He glanced at his partner, who was inspecting the few knickknacks on my imitation mantel. The men exchanged a nod. "And I think, Mr. Adler," he said, producing a set of manacles from beneath his overcoat, "you're acting very suspicious. I think London would sleep a lot better with you under lock and key until we get this all figured out."

CHAPTER THIRTEEN

I wasn't unfamiliar with the inside of a Black Maria. The windowless police wagon painted black on the outside; the splintering benches that ran around the perimeter inside, with iron rings on the walls to which especially dangerous prisoners were shackled. Two years earlier, Marcus and I had been caught up in a raid at the former Fitzroy Street brothel. It was in the bowels of a Maria much like this one where we'd exchanged names and I'd promised to help him once we'd both served our time. Lazarus and his employer, Andrew St. Andrews, had intervened on my behalf, sparing me a week or two in a holding cell under Bow Street. Marcus hadn't been so lucky—two-and-a-half weeks underground waiting for the judge, then two years at hard labor at Pentonville. And now I was looking at the same—or worse.

Well, I couldn't very well drag old Tim into it this time, could I? As the police wagon lurched over uneven cobblestones toward New Scotland Yard, I could almost hear his words: *If you wish to enter into an ill-advised, legally binding agreement with a known criminal, that's your business.* He'd say I'd brought it on myself, and he'd be right. Not to mention that he had, hopefully, taken my advice and made himself unavailable for the next week or so. Involving Bess was out of the question as well. And Goddard?

It wasn't the first time working for Goddard had put me in a compromising position. I had a sinking feeling it wouldn't be the last, either. The question was, how long until the police connected

Erich Backer's murder with the refinery explosion that had killed Rudolf Lothar? It might take some time for them to abandon their theory that Backer's daughter and I had done Backer in as part of some lovers' pact. And perhaps the police were too busy to interview Lothar's co-workers and discover that I'd delivered flowers to Lothar as well, though I doubted it. Five years ago, the small number of police officers might have ensured that the idea of a connection between the two deaths never even came up.

But we weren't just dealing with a few overworked Peelers anymore. Over the past few years, the Metropolitan Police had grown from a thousand harried officers to more than ten times that. They'd outgrown their original digs and moved into a vast complex right in the heart of Westminster. They now had space and staff and all manner of fancy new equipment that would allow them to leave no theory unexplored.

And as the man who had personally delivered threats to both Lothar and Backer, I found the connection between their deaths obvious—as obvious as the fact that Goddard's hand had been behind both incidents. The thought made me queasy. It was one thing to understand intellectually that Goddard was the head of a large criminal empire. One doesn't get ahead, he'd often reminded me, by playing at Father Christmas. Once again, I was reminded why he'd tried to shield me from the more brutal aspects of his business. It's hard to enjoy the touch of bloodstained hands.

Even if those hands belonged to someone I could, once again, love.

Or could I?

It was disconcerting how easily York Street was beginning to feel like home again. The more time I spent there, the more difficult it was to leave. Goddard seemed content to ply me with food, wine, and sex. But he'd stated at the very beginning that he would rather be alone than waste his time with casual encounters. The contract I'd signed would keep me tied to him for at least two years—by which point, if I allowed things to continue in the same direction, I might well be living back at York Street.

And I knew that this would be disastrous for everyone.

The wagon bounced over a rough patch, jostling my head against the hard wooden wall and scattering my thoughts.

Goddard could get me out of this mess. But sending for him would risk calling attention to what he had done. Or had he? Some part of me desperately wanted to believe in coincidence—that the explosion had been an accident and Backer's killing had been unrelated. Either way, though, calling on Goddard would greatly diminish his trust in me—the trust upon which his saving loan had been based. Good God.

The pavement grew even beneath the wheels of the Maria as we pulled to a stop before the new police headquarters on the Victoria Embankment. The door opened, and gaslight flooded the vehicle, along with the stink of the Thames. The moustached officer took the chain between my wrist-shackles and led me out onto the walk. All was still but for the lapping of the river against the embankment walls and the twinkling lights of distant boats.

My legs began to tremble. I've a horror of enclosed spaces. Though New Scotland Yard was vast compared to its predecessor, I'd no doubt the holding cells were still windowless and cramped, with only a letterbox-sized hole in a solid iron door for ventilation. More likely than not they were also underground, just like the ones at Bow Street had been. A cold drop of sweat ran down my back. The moustached officer looked at me curiously. Could there have been a guiltier-looking man than I, right then, in all of London?

"This way, Mr. Adler," he said.

I had no choice but to follow, though my legs felt like jelly. The second officer walked behind me, his presence making it clear that resistance would make things worse for everyone and the delay of the inevitable would be but momentary. They led me through the front doors of the building—three stories of new brown brick interspersed with stripes of white—where I was booked with dispassion and efficiency. It was surprisingly quiet, given the time of night—more like a clerk's office than a bustling police station. The procedures, carried out in civil, measured tones, had distracted me enough to keep panic at bay. However, once the last "i" was dotted, I felt that familiar anxiety rise.

"Are you unwell, sir?" asked the young officer tasked with conducting me to my cell. I opened my mouth to speak, when another voice interrupted us.

"Excuse me!" I turned to see a ginger-haired officer bustling toward us. I felt a rush of relief as I recognized the constable who had delivered Jack to the door of Turnbull House.

"Segeant Masters!" I cried.

"That's Mathers," the sergeant said. He turned back to the constable. "I asked you a question, Constable. Where are you taking that man?"

"He were brung in for questioning about a murder, Sergeant."

"Murder?" The sergeant's face grew serious.

"I didn't do it," I said.

"Yes, yes, the prisons are filled with innocent men," Mathers said dismissively. "All the same, I find it hard to believe someone who works for Dr. and Mrs. Lazarus would be involved in any sort of criminal activity, never mind murder."

"It's all in the paperwork, sir," the constable said. "And the paperwork's been filed. Even if we wanted to let him go—"

"Nobody said anything about *letting anyone go*, man. Still." He looked at me regretfully. "How is the young man I brought you last week?"

"W-well. He's doing well." *Aside from really being a girl. And being wanted for questioning in this very same murder.*

Mathers nodded. "A clever lad like that—terrible thing for him to end up here. And he would have, too, sooner or later. Mark my words."

"I don't doubt it." Even worse, I wanted to say, was for someone like *me* to end up there, but I didn't want to test the sergeant's tentative sympathies.

"Yes, well. Grateful and all, but like Harris, here, said, we can't just turn you loose. Who'd you say brought him in?" he asked the constable.

"Dixon and Jeffries, sir."

"Good men, good men both. Sure they had their reasons." He thoughtfully stroked his whiskers. "Still, one good turn deserves another. Is there someone you'd like me to contact?" he asked me. "Someone who might be able to clear up any possible misunderstandings?"

Goddard was my first thought. Possibly Lazarus. But I wasn't at all sure that either of those names wouldn't make things worse. It was only when the constable put a hand on my shoulder to lead me toward the cells that I remembered a third name. Yes, by God! If he couldn't help, no one could!

What's more, he owed me.

"A pen and paper, please," I said. The sergeant already had them waiting. I scribbled a name and address, folded the paper over, and handed it to him.

"A friend?" he asked.

"Of sorts." As the constable led me away, I silently added, *At least I hope he sees it that way.*

❖

By some small mercy, I was directed not to some dark, subterranean horror chamber, but to an open room down the hallway from where I'd been processed. The room comprised three solid walls and was separated from the corridor by a fourth wall of metal bars. It was as inescapable as the dungeon rooms beneath Bow Street, but the space between the bars gave the illusion of openness, saving me the indignity of being reduced to a gibbering idiot. I didn't even mind the stark wooden bench that would serve as my bed or the chamber pot beneath it—though I was grateful to have been apprehended with an empty bladder.

I must have eventually fallen asleep, for when the constable came to fetch me, I was lying on my back on the bench, my coat bunched under my head.

"Mr. Adler?"

I started at his voice, then slowly pulled myself up, stretching out the kinks in my neck and shoulders. The shifts must have changed while I slept, for it was a different constable from the one who had brought me to the cell—a young, sandy-haired chap who hadn't been long enough on the job to dull his enthusiasm. "They told me to tell you you're free to go, and Sergeant Mathers personally apologizes for any inconvenience."

"I can leave?"

"Mr. St. Andrews came to collect you. He explained everything. Sergeant Mathers said he knew all along there were some sort of misunderstanding, and he hopes you won't take it personal."

Well, how about that? The man had actually come.

It had only been out of desperation that I'd asked the sergeant to notify Lazarus's former employer, Andrew St. Andrews, of my situation. For while it was true that he would be indebted to me for the rest of his life for dealing with a blackmailer some years ago, our history was complicated. Not to put too fine a point on it, Andrew St. Andrews, amateur detective, and Cain Goddard, Duke of Dorset Street, had been bitter enemies for almost two decades. And though sending for Goddard would have been the worst of all wrong choices, I wasn't convinced that sending for St. Andrews would be that much better in the long run. Nonetheless, the man had pulled my crumpet out of the fire, and I was grateful.

The constable unlocked the door. Sighing with relief, I followed him into the corridor. As we emerged into the main chamber, I squinted at the daylight streaming in through the windows. New Scotland Yard was a completely different place midmorning—a place of rustling papers and slamming doors, of raised voices and heavy bobby bootsteps on the new floorboards.

"Mr. Adler!" St. Andrews's voice carried sharp and clear through the crowded room. He looked much the same as the last time I'd seen him. Over six feet tall and scarecrow-thin, he still wore the plaid Inverness cape he so favored, a deerstalker cap perched on his head. The easy smile into which his features naturally configured themselves grew wider as I approached, and he stuck out his hand.

"Still playing detective, St. Andrews?" I said as we shook hands. He was completely besotted with the Sherlock Holmes stories, and, as his family's money ensured he'd never need to work, he ran a consulting detective business for amusement.

"Always. And you, Mr. Adler? Up to your usual mischief? No brothels this time, I trust." He smirked, no doubt remembering the last time he'd found himself summoned to the Yard on my behalf. "It's good to see you." I was surprised at how true that was. The first time I'd met him he'd reminded me of a puppy. He still did, but only in the sense that, despite having bailed me out of jail for the second time in two years, he was greeting me like a long-lost friend.

"Thank you for coming."

Still smiling, he turned, and we walked together through the crowd toward the front door.

"After what you and Dr. Lazarus did for me, it was the least I could do. Besides, what good are money and connections if one can't use them to help his friends?"

I was touched, really, that he would refer to me as a friend. When we'd first met, I'd treated him with all the contempt I'd thought his due, given Goddard's low opinion of the man. But his actions had spoken louder than Goddard's words. He'd shown himself to be just, fair, and a canny ally, if a bit overzealous. All in all, a good man to have in one's corner, even if his unabashed worship of a certain fictional detective made him appear slightly ridiculous at times.

"But I do hope you don't intend to make a habit of this."

"I'll try," I said.

A carriage rattled past us as we stepped through the gates onto the embankment. London could be dark, dirty, and dangerous, but it was likewise filled with wonders of engineering and imagination. The walkway was already crowded with pedestrians. We strolled along it, leisurely, watching the boats traveling up and down the Thames. Like the new home of the Metropolitan Police, the Victoria Embankment was a recent addition, and a boon to the city. Not only did it provide a picturesque place to walk and gather one's thoughts—the elegant electric streetlamps were the first in the city, and though some found their light harsh, I appreciated the novelty. The embankment road also eased traffic congestion in surrounding areas, and the entire construction gave the sewers much-needed support.

"I don't suppose you'll tell me how you came to find yourself dragged off by the police in the middle of the night," St. Andrews said, swinging his long arms as we strode along the riverside.

"I didn't kill that man."

St. Andrews turned to me, his eyes gleaming. "Oh, this *does* sound promising. Perhaps I'll get my money's worth after all."

A sharp response rose to my lips, but his childlike enthusiasm squashed it. Laughing, I shook my head. "I suppose I at least owe you a good story."

"Make it a very good story, and you can tell it over a late breakfast at the Criterion."

We turned north onto a side street, where St. Andrews gestured toward a modest two-seater. I raised an eyebrow.

"No velvet-lined brougham?" I asked, remembering the overdecorated monstrosity he'd brought the last time he'd sprung me.

He laughed. "Believe it or not, I sometimes prefer not to make a spectacle of myself."

The hansom might have been small, but the freshly painted wood creaked as he opened the door, and the interior smelled of new leather. As I sank onto the well-padded bench, I felt almost optimistic.

"I really must apologize for the way I treated you the last time we met," I said.

He waved away my concerns. "I can't say my feelings about you were entirely charitable, either. But that's in the past. Now," he said, rubbing his hands together with relish, "why don't you tell me why those nice officers were so convinced you had something to do with some sugar baker's murder?"

❖

"Goddard put you up to it, didn't he?" St. Andrews said once I'd finished my tale.

I'd held back the incriminating details, including Goddard's involvement, the refinery explosion, and my suspicions about both. But St. Andrews was disarmingly easy to talk to, and the good food and lush surroundings of the Criterion restaurant had put me at ease. There in the warm shimmer of the gold-leaf-covered walls, surrounded by polished wood, silver, and clean linen, I found myself telling him quite a bit more than I should have. Moreover, he appeared to have a frightening gift for inference. Perhaps he wasn't such a miserable investigator after all.

"He paid me to make the delivery." I dodged his question. "Anything else is speculation."

"Then why didn't you send for him when you found yourself in custody?" He took an enthusiastic bite of buttered roll. The ensuing silence must have revealed more than any words of mine could have. "I see," he said after a moment. "You're in a very delicate position, Mr. Adler. I appreciate that, and though I've never approved of Dr. Goddard's activities, out of respect for what you did for me, I won't make your position any more difficult by pursuing this topic of conversation further."

"Thank you," I said sheepishly.

"At least for now."

I speared a last bite of kipper, popped it into my mouth, and laid my knife and fork across my plate.

"By the way," he said. "Now that I've helped you, perhaps you could be of some assistance to me. You see, I'm in desperate need of a secretary. Someone to organize my case files, handle correspondence, that sort of thing. I've gone through at least eight since Lazarus left. I'm afraid his competence spoiled me utterly."

To my credit, I didn't laugh. Nor did I mock him for being so obvious. St. Andrews wasn't one of Wilde's intimates, but the Piccadilly set, of which both men were members, are relentless gossips. No doubt word had gotten about that Wilde had left me in a tight spot. It was decent of St. Andrews to offer me what would no doubt be interesting and easy work. Moreover, St. Andrews would make a congenial employer. At the same time, my life was complicated enough as it was. More to the point, Goddard held the future of Turnbull House in his hands. If I went to work for his nemesis—even if said nemesis appeared to have given up his side of the grudge—things would bode ill for everyone who was dear to me.

"Thank you," I said. "But my hands are rather full at present."

He smiled. "I understand."

"But perhaps there's another way I could help."

I gave a brief description of our nascent messenger service. He listened politely, but I could tell it wasn't really what he'd had in mind.

"The problem is, I don't send that many messages. What I need is someone to bring order out of chaos."

"How many cases are you currently working?" I asked.

"Well...none at the moment. But my office is a mess."

"Then you don't need a secretary. You need someone who can help you find customers."

"You mean, like a Watson?" His eyes lit up at the prospect.

"Not exactly." I poured the remaining tea into my cup and signaled the waiter to bring a fresh pot. Then it came to me. Oh, yes, it was perfect. Moreover, it could help us both. "More like...who were those urchins Holmes had scouring the streets looking for clues?"

"The Baker Street Irregulars? You think I need Irregulars?"

"Definitely. You need people pounding the pavement for you. When they're not looking for clues, they can look for customers. The Turnbull House kids know the East End like no one else. They can roam the streets unnoticed, gather information without raising suspicion, and disappear into the shadows when the job is done. You, by contrast, would get your arse kicked up between your ears if you went skulking about Dorset Street listening at keyholes."

"That's so true!" Then he frowned. "How many do you think I'd need?"

"Why not start with two?"

"Just two? Holmes has at least five."

"If you need more, we'll send more, but why not start with a more manageable number until you're sure it's what you want?"

He leaned back in his chair, crossing his long arms behind his head. I polished off my lukewarm tea and glanced about to see if I could salvage anything from the remains of our excellent breakfast.

"Will they work for a shilling a day?" St. Andrews asked. "The Baker Street Irregulars work for a shilling a day, plus expenses."

I did a few quick sums in my head. A shilling a day worked out to a pound and a half a month—quite a bit less than they'd make running messages on the streets under Jack's original calculations.

"May I borrow a pen?" He handed me one, then took a small notebook from his front pocket, tore out a sheet, and handed me that as well. "Two pounds," I pronounced after a moment. "Surely it's not too much to pay someone to bring you custom."

He frowned. "For two Irregulars?"

"For each. Paid in advance on the first of each month."

"Holmes doesn't pay in advance."

"Holmes's Irregulars aren't answerable to Bess Lazarus."

"That's true."

"They'd have to begin work after luncheon, though. They have lessons in the morning."

"I suppose they'd want Sundays off as well." He sniffed.

I laughed. "I'm sure they'd rather be stirring up trouble on the East End than sitting in church, but Bess may insist on it."

"Right."

His interest was waning. It probably wasn't the money— St. Andrews likely threw away more than four quid a month on cigarettes alone. But my proposal had brought us a long way from his original offer.

The waiter replaced our spent teapot with a fresh, steaming one. The clean, earthy scent of the Criterion house blend mingled with the traces of the rich breakfast we'd enjoyed. I recharged St. Andrews's cup and then my own. The last of the late diners had cleared out, and the dining room was silent, save for the hissing of the gas sconces and the distant kitchen clanks and clatter.

"I'll think about it," he said. From his tone, I knew it was the best I was going to get. "I'll send word to Turnbull House in the next few days."

I nodded, adding a slice of lemon to my tea. I hoped my disappointment didn't show. We really could have used that money.

"But you have helped me already, in a way, Mr. Adler," he said, raising his teacup in a salute.

"Oh?"

"You've given me something to investigate—the identity of Herr Backer's real killer."

My mouth went dry. "You don't have to do that."

"Oh, but I do." His eyes gleamed with renewed enthusiasm. "We both know that *you* didn't do it. You might kill someone, accidentally, in a blind panic, if the threat were great enough. But anyone can tell you're not one for cold-blooded murder. So that leaves the question of who actually did kill the sugar baker. And why?"

"Aren't the police investigating that?"

He shrugged. "The police have hundreds of cases. I just have the one—thanks to you."

Thanks to me. The Criterion house blend turned to dishwater in my mouth. Thanks to me—and possibly the pair of Dorset Street Irregulars that I would provide—St. Andrews would be poking his beak into an execution. It wouldn't take him long, with his well-hidden deductive gifts, to see Goddard's hand behind it. And though he'd promised not to make *my* situation any more difficult, I'd no doubt that he'd relish the opportunity to do exactly that to his old enemy.

"And I *do* thank you, Mr. Adler," he said cheerily, though his grin no longer seemed innocuous. He tossed a handful of coins onto the table. "Now, we're a ways from Aldersgate Street. May I offer you a ride home?"

"No, thank you," I said, trying to keep the quaver out of my voice. "I believe I'll walk."

CHAPTER FOURTEEN

W hat an idiot I was!
I cursed the pride that had kept me from sending for Goddard in the first place. He'd have surely been unhappy to have the attention of the police for the brief time it would have taken to broker my release. On the other hand, it was attention he could have deflected with charm and coin—unlike the dogged pursuit of Andrew St. Andrews, consulting detective.

A gray sky glowered down over the tall, white buildings and gracefully arched windows of Regent Street. The tang of coming rain was sharp in the air. I turned up the collar of my coat and ducked my head as a gust of wind blustered down the wide, white corridor. I could have hopped a bus home, but I had to clear my head. Moreover, I was, once again, out of pocket. Home was forty-five minutes away on foot. Not a daunting prospect, given my full belly and the fact I'd nothing better to do with the rest of the morning. At the same time, the thought of returning immediately to my dank little flat— especially now that Marcus had taken his leave—depressed me. As I came up to the spot where Shaftesbury Avenue forked off from Regent Street, a thought occurred to me. Rather than following the familiar route home through the wilds of Soho—where the things that came out at night would still be sleeping it off—I turned right onto Haymarket Street and headed for the Strand.

The Lyceum Theatre, where Wilde's friend Stoker worked, was located on Wellington Street, not far away. It was a stately building, with a dramatic entryway flanked by tall Corinthian columns. The theatre was owned by Sir Henry Irving, who had found international acclaim bringing Shakespeare's greatest roles to life. Stoker had worked there as the business manager for some twelve years. I felt a little trepidation as I walked up to the building. It had been days since I'd sent Watkins to Stoker with Wilde's lewd little note. It didn't bode well for his response. Still, one never knew until one tried.

The front door was unlocked. I let myself in. The freshly painted corridor stretched out in both directions from an open double door. Thick carpeting swallowed my footsteps as I crossed toward the auditorium. The inside of the theatre was vast, comprising several sections of twelve rows each on the floor and three stories of balconies adorned with sweeping velvet curtains and gold-touched curlicues. The stage was enormous, the orchestra pit immense. A fitting home for the most famous actor of our time. I hoped Sir Henry appreciated every spectacular inch of it.

"May I help you, sir?" I jumped at the sound of a London-tempered Irish brogue. I'd thought myself quite alone. When I turned, Stoker smiled back. "Mr. Adler, isn't it? We met, I believe, at one of Oscar's suppers. Forgive me for not responding to your message. Between our current production and preparing for next year, I've been quite busy."

"Which play is currently gracing the Lyceum, Mr. Stoker?" I asked as we shook hands.

"Merivale's *Ravenswood*. It's a shame the critics haven't been as pleased with it as we'd hoped. But we'll be putting on *Henry VIII* and *Lear* in the New Year. I've always felt Mr. Irving is at his best doing Shakespeare."

"So I've heard."

"Please, step into my office."

I followed him back into the corridor to a small but bright room. The mahogany desk and matching chairs were well made and recently polished. They were also covered in papers. Bookshelves crammed with playbills, music scores, and books lined one wall, while the opposite wall was taken up with the window that provided most of the room's light. Stoker cleared a stack of papers from a chair, motioned me toward it, then took his own seat behind the desk.

"Cigarette?" he asked, taking an engraved silver case from the top drawer of his desk.

"No, thank you."

I waited while he lit one for himself. He was a bear of a man in his mid-forties, with a full beard, encroaching belly, and appraising eyes. He looked every inch the business manager but had a refinement about him that betrayed an artistic soul. Wilde had once predicted that facilitating Sir Henry Irving's career would prove to be Stoker's greatest contribution to the artistic world. However, I'd read his novel, *The Snake's Pass*, and wouldn't have been at all surprised to see Bram Stoker one day make a name for himself in literature.

"So, Oscar sent you to me to collect the money he owes you." He gave a hearty burst of laughter and shook his head. "I won't ask for proof. It's exactly the sort of thing Oscar would do. Moreover, he's the only one I know who would dare." He sighed heavily, loosing a long plume of smoke. "Unfortunately, young man, I'm not in a position to make good on our mutual friend's debts."

"Of course. It was presumptuous of me to assume—"

"If you were the only one, perhaps, but..."

I straightened. "There are others?"

He looked at me ruefully. "Our friend has always been generous to a fault, but until recently he's been able to keep ahead of his obligations. I'm usually not one to speak out of turn, but I think his current embarrassment can be traced to a certain recent acquaintance with whom we're both familiar."

Bosie, I thought uncharitably. I'd met Wilde's new favorite, the third son of the Marquess of Queensbury, some months before. He'd struck me as reckless and rude, and had demanded Wilde sack me because he'd aesthetic objections to my supposedly Hebraic name. Wilde had laughed off the slight—it wasn't a slight against him, after all. After that, young Lord Alfred Douglas and I had been spared the sight of one another.

Of course now that I think about it, it was after that unfortunate supper that my once-reliable flow of income had suddenly dried up.

Stoker continued. "That young man is richer than Croesus but expects Oscar to indulge his every whim. And Oscar is happy to do so. In Oscar's eyes, he can do no wrong. But I've a terrible suspicion that one day that young man is going to bring a world of trouble down on our friend's head."

I, too, had entertained that suspicion. But I'd figured it stemmed from our mutual dislike. I hoped it would turn out to be wrong. I had liked Wilde, even if he wasn't the most responsible employer.

"What a shame that would be." I stood and offered my hand. "Mr. Stoker, I'm sorry I wasted your time. I'll take my leave, now."

He stood and clasped my hand between his meaty paws. "Nonsense. I'm sorry I couldn't help you. And I do apologize for not writing back immediately and sparing you the trip. I hardly have time to breathe, no less flag down a messenger."

"Wait," I said. "What if I told you I could ease that particular burden?"

"Messengers, you mean? I'm listening."

We sat back down. As I described Jack's plan, Stoker nodded thoughtfully. He seemed especially keen on the idea of paying one lump sum to have a messenger at his constant disposal and didn't balk at the idea of the workday starting after luncheon.

"It's only me here in the mornings anyway," he said. "Things really don't start moving until late afternoon. Send me two of the older ones who wouldn't mind working into the night. I'll have someone drive them back after the performances—if you would find that acceptable, that is."

"Thank you, Mr. Stoker." I pumped his hand enthusiastically. "I'll discuss it with Dr. and Mrs. Lazarus. I'm certain we'll find an arrangement that will suit everyone."

As I stood again, a third man appeared in the doorway.

"Oh, I'm terribly sorry. Didn't mean to interrupt."

"Nonsense, Arthur. We were just finishing. May I introduce you to Mr. Adler?"

Arthur Conan Doyle was perhaps ten years younger than Stoker and had a robust sportsman's build. His tweed suit was well cut but not outrageously expensive, and his hair was short and tidily pomaded. His most distinguishing feature, however, aside from his rich Scottish burr, was a thick moustache that he'd waxed and fastidiously twisted at the ends. He assessed me with intelligent eyes as we shook hands.

"Very pleased to meet you, Mr. Adler."

"And you, sir. I've enjoyed your stories in *The Strand*."

He chuckled. "It's kind of you to say so."

My pulse began to race. I'd read the stories, of course. But more importantly, so had St. Andrews. St. Andrews had built his entire identity around them. He would probably give his eyeteeth to meet his hero's creator. Perhaps it might even be enough to persuade him to back off from an investigation, if it came to that.

"Mr. Adler works with Dr. and Mrs. Lazarus at Turnbull House," Stoker said.

Conan Doyle's face lit up. "I've heard of their work. London needs more places like that. And more people like them."

"May I pass that on?" I asked. "They'll be thrilled to hear it."

"Certainly." He withdrew a leather case from an inner pocket and handed me a card. "I'm staying at the Langham Hotel. Do call on me at any time. And, if I can help your organization's efforts in any way, please don't hesitate to let me know."

"Thank you, sir." I couldn't suppress what must have seemed inordinate enthusiasm. "I will indeed."

❖

I emerged from the Lyceum shortly after lunchtime, my head spinning with conflicting emotions. A number of problems had sorted themselves out. Our messenger service now had an all-but-guaranteed income of four easy quid a month—eight, if one counted St. Andrews's "Irregulars," though I was rather hoping St. Andrews would forget about that. I was no longer wanted, either by the police or by Tim Lazarus. Jack was safely returned to Turnbull House, and I had a possible bargaining chip—an introduction to Arthur Conan Doyle—with which I might be able to tempt St. Andrews if he started to sniff around Goddard's business too closely.

However, just as quickly, new problems were rising to take their place. Erich Backer had been murdered. Rudolf Lothar was also dead, and though the police still thought the explosion had been an accident, I was sure that it hadn't. What did seem a certainty was that Goddard's hand was behind both deaths—an idea that would make it impossible to resume a relationship with the man—something my rational mind had no intention of doing, but that some deeper part of me had never stopped wanting.

And then there was Marcus. At some level, I was relieved he had gone. My room was too small for the both of us, and my finances were spread too thin as it was. On the other hand, he'd been good company. I'd rather enjoyed having a protégé. And, if one must tell the truth, I felt responsible for driving him away. No doubt where he'd ended up sleeping had been infinitely more wretched than where I'd spent the night—and I'd spent the night in jail. Yes, I felt very guilty about everything that had happened between Marcus and myself the other night. Even though at the back of my mind I still suspected he had nicked my shaving scissors.

But fortunately, at that point, I hadn't the luxury of stewing in self-recrimination. The sun was making a brief appearance—through a blanket of clouds, of course—and the rain, for once, was nowhere to be seen. Tugging my hat to a rakish angle, I headed east on Fleet Street, back toward Raven Row. No sooner had I crossed the threshold of Turnbull House and hung up my coat and hat, than Bess Lazarus was upon me.

"Ira, where have you been? Tim," she called over her shoulder. "He's here!"

"What are you doing here?" I asked as Tim, looking tired, but happy, emerged from the classroom. The residents milled about us, the younger ones happy to be released from lessons and the older ones preparing to go out to their vocational placements. I turned to Bess. "Didn't you tell him to stay home and rest?"

"I slept late this morning and had breakfast in bed. It was wonderful. But that's neither here nor—what did you get up to last night?" he asked, suddenly frowning. "You look like you slept in your clothes."

A night behind bars never did much for anyone's appearance, but what Tim and his wife didn't know wouldn't hurt them—at least, not at this point.

"That reminds me," Bess said, taking the direct path while I prevaricated. "Two constables came by earlier, asking about you. Are you in some kind of trouble?"

"Er, not as such."

At least I hoped not. But perhaps I'd been naïve in thinking that St. Andrews had merely cleared up the officers' misapprehension of the situation out of the goodness of his heart. Perhaps he'd taken the opportunity to plant more destructive seeds in their minds. Perhaps he wasn't as inept as he seemed but rather was weaving me into some larger web with which he hoped to ensnare Goddard after all these years. Good God.

"They were also asking after a young woman name Kathe Backer. Of course I told them no such person had ever passed through here."

"Ah…I have some good news and some bad news," I said.

"St. Andrews, we know!" Tim exclaimed. "You just missed him. He said you drove a hard bargain but ultimately agreed to take on two messengers. Don't know why I didn't think of him before. It's not charity, after all. It's business. Business that'll be worth four pounds a month, if it works out."

"Yes," I said, with somewhat less enthusiasm.

Something soft brushed across the back of my neck—spiderwebs, I imagined. Stifling a shudder, I discreetly tried to swipe them away. Oh, God, the thought of St. Andrews sending my charges to find evidence of Goddard's guilt! No. No, it was useless to panic until I had more concrete information. Besides, if I spoke to the future "Irregulars" before they embarked upon their new career, perhaps they'd turn up so much new business St. Andrews would be forced to back off Goddard and let Scotland Yard bungle their way through the case.

Then I remembered Stoker and smiled. "Of course it's not just four pounds, it's eight. I just came from the Lyceum Theatre. They also agreed to take on two runners at a monthly rate."

"That's fantastic!" Tim cried.

Bess frowned. "The theatre? I'm not sure that's an appropriate place for children."

"Ordinarily I'd agree with you," I said. "But the manager is one of Wilde's friends and a family man himself."

"That's hardly a recommendation," Tim grumbled.

"May I remind you it was you who introduced me to Wilde in the first place? Come to think of it, perhaps I should ask you to make good on what he owes me."

"What?"

"Never mind. We can send Stoker two of the older residents. They'll be working inside the theatre the entire time, and a driver will bring them back every night."

Bess cocked her head, one hand absently stroking her round belly. "I suppose that would be all right."

"All right? That's nearly half the monthly obligation solved in one day!"

Tim nodded slowly, a smile pulling at the edges of his lips.

"Wot's all the good news, then?" Jack asked, coming down the hallway toward us. My heart sank as I remembered the bad news it was my duty to impart along with the good. He seemed to have recovered well from his father's beating, but would he recover from the news of the man's death?

"I need a word with you alone," I said. "Excuse us, Bess, Tim."

Jack's face sobered. He followed me to the classroom, where a warm coal fire was burning. I pulled one of the classroom benches up to the hearth and motioned for him to do the same. With his skin clean and hair slicked back beneath the cap, the swelling gone down around his cheekbone, I could see the barest hints of the girl, Kathe Backer.

"Wot's happened, Mr. Adler?"

I ran a fingernail over the splintering corner of the little bench. No one had told me when my mother died. I'd no idea how to do this. And though the only time I'd seen Jack and his father together had been when I'd interrupted a beating, one could never tell how the news would affect him. The man must have had some redeeming qualities; otherwise Jack would have left before he did.

"Your father was found dead last night," I said.

Jack's jaw dropped. His eyes widened. For a moment the only sound was the soft *pitter-pat* of rain against the window.

"How?" he finally managed.

"The police didn't say, but they were fairly certain he was murdered."

He seemed to consider this for a moment, different emotions playing across his face. Finally, he asked, "They fink I done it?"

"They want to question you, perhaps to find out if you knew of anyone who might have reason to do your father harm. But last night they seemed more interested in me as a suspect."

He frowned. "You?"

"A neighbor said he saw us leaving together yesterday afternoon. The police surmised that you and I are sweethearts and that we'd done him in and run away together. I told them if that were the case it didn't make sense that they'd find me at home, alone, the night it happened. But I spent the night in jail anyway. You didn't do it, did you?"

His expression turned from horror to outrage, and he sprang up from his bench. "I were right here! You brung me here yourself! I ain't left the house since then—you ask the missus!"

"Mrs. Lazarus knows Jack Flip was here, but she told the constables she's never heard of Kathe Backer."

A great weight seemed to settle on his shoulders, and he sat back down on the bench, exhaling heavily. He ran a hand back over his forehead, tipping his cloth cap back at a precipitous angle. A few seconds later it fell off, though he didn't seem to notice.

"I'm gonna have to tell her," he said.

I picked up the cap and handed it to him. "Probably."

"They still fink you done it?"

I shrugged. "They seem to be considering other possibilities at this point, but your neighbor was, apparently, very specific about what he saw."

"They say which neighbor?"

I shook my head. "I ran into someone in the hall on my way in, but…"

"Shovel-faced bloke, built like a cart horse?" Jack asked. I nodded. "That'd be Mr. Geary. He an' me da work together at the sugar house. Or used to, leastways. He's always lurkin' about, now. Only fing is, how'd the coppers know it were you? Mr. Geary don't know your name."

"I don't know," I said. Though at the back of my mind, a terrible thought was forming. As far as I knew, only Goddard and Watkins were aware I had made a delivery to Erich Backer. Watkins had instructed me to deliver it to the sugarhouse, but it was likely only Goddard would know where Backer lived.

Could Goddard be setting me up?

Stone-cold revenge wasn't his style, but the way I'd left him two years ago had been insulting, bold, and unprecedented. Enough so, perhaps, for him to deviate from his usual tactics just this once. Was it possible that he was feigning his interest, luring me back in order to spring some elaborate trap? Did he intend to punish me by seeing me hang for a crime I didn't commit?

If so, it had almost worked.

And because it hadn't, the question remained—what would Goddard do once he learned I was no longer in police custody?

"You all right, Mr. Adler?" Jack asked.

I swallowed. "I'm not sure."

"You fink I should go to the police?"

"No." I'd seen too much in my own dealings with the police over the years to trust that they wouldn't take any likely suspect as a bird in the hand, especially in a case like this—the murder of no one important, the resolution of which was just another notch on some constable's baton. Jack didn't have an Andrew St. Andrews to make suspicions disappear.

At the same time, the truth would come out at some point, and when it did, I couldn't let it look as if Tim and Bess had been hiding a murder suspect.

"You need to leave," I said.

"Where?"

"I don't know, but you can't stay here."

"You're just gonna turn me out wiv' nowhere to go? An' me da...*murdered* an' all?"

I sighed.

"No, no, of course not," I muttered. I stood and began to pace. Jack couldn't go back to my flat, he couldn't stay at Turnbull House, and I certainly wasn't about to ask Goddard for advice. A thought occurred to me—perhaps Jack could lie low at Stoker's theatre. He could stay out of sight and earn his keep without ever leaving the Lyceum. And eventually the police would find the real killer and stop looking for Kathe Backer. One hoped.

But I couldn't ask that of Stoker. I'd only met the man twice, and he was already doing us an enormous favor. I couldn't ask him to put himself, his family, and the theatre at such risk.

I slumped back down onto the bench. Jack should leave, just disappear into the shadows and back alleys until the police found someone to blame. But he was right. I couldn't just send him out there. Not in this weather, and not knowing what was waiting for him on those streets.

Perhaps the police would find the actual murderer on their own, I thought. Perhaps St. Andrews would put that formidable brain of his to work and absolve Jack without implicating Goddard.

And perhaps one day the streets would be clogged with horseless carriages, and great flying ships would take people from London to New York in a matter of hours instead of weeks.

"Right. Don't say anything for now," I told him. "It'll do more harm than good. I know you didn't kill him, so we're not actually hiding anything from Dr. and Mrs. Lazarus." I wished my words sounded more confident than I felt. And I hoped that if it came to it, the police would see it the same way. "Just...keep quiet until we figure out something better."

"Wot 'bout you?"

"I can take care of myself."

The coals glowed in the fireplace. Heat rose from them in shimmering waves, but I was chilled to the bone. The rain was coming down hard, now, battering the roof and windows, and washing the cobblestones clean. Marcus was out there, too, a little voice reminded me. Just in case I'd forgotten. And St. Andrews and Goddard. And before I dealt with any of them, I'd have to pass by

Tim and Bess, who wouldn't let me leave Turnbull House until they were satisfied that all was well with their charge.

When I glanced back at Jack, he was twisting his cap in his hands and his eyes were brimming with tears. "He weren't all bad, you know, Mr. Adler." He swallowed hard. "Before me mum died, he used to bring me sweeties sometimes..."

Oh, God.

His shoulders started to shake. I slid over to his bench and put an arm around him, pulling him close while he wept like the child he was. My own throat went tight. We were both orphans, now. Not uncommon, especially on these streets. But I remembered how I felt when I'd learned about my own mother's death. I hadn't seen her in years, hadn't even thought about her. But until I'd learned she was truly, irretrievably gone, I'd always thought I might again one day.

"I ain't got no one, now," Jack whispered into my shoulder.

"You have us."

"They gonna catch the one wot done it?"

"I don't know."

We both jumped as someone rapped sharply on the door.

"Is everything all right in there?" Bess called.

"One moment," I called back. "We should tell them you've had some bad news, at least. They're kind people. And you know they'll keep asking."

Jack nodded, swiping a sleeve across his eyes. Giving his shoulder a squeeze, I crossed to the door. After a quiet word with Tim and Bess, I returned.

"She said to take as long as you need. She'll bring you a cup of tea and something to eat in a little while. Would you like me to stay for a bit?"

He looked up, eyes shining. "Will you read to me? The missus sometimes reads us Jules Verne if we work hard at our lessons."

Jules Verne? I smiled to myself. And here I'd thought the woman read Deuteronomy for pleasure. "Be happy to."

Jack sighed, settling his bench against the wall by the fire, while I searched Bess's desk until I found a well-thumbed copy of *A Journey to the Centre of the Earth*.

CHAPTER FIFTEEN

I returned to my flat on Aldersgate Street as the waning sunlight gave up its struggle against the clouds. Dark skies turned my thoughts to dark subjects as I ascended the stairs. Which would be worse, Goddard setting me up to take the blame for a murder—or two—or Goddard being innocent of wrongdoing toward me, but still being implicated in the deaths of Backer and Lothar? Once, I might have been able to turn a blind eye to the latter, but the past few years had changed me. And now I knew myself too well to think that the knowledge would sit comfortably for even a moment.

Worse than either of these possibilities was the idea of Jack going to the gallows as a patricide. I believed him when he said hadn't left Turnbull House since I dropped him there. Pearl kept the premises locked up tighter than a vault at night. If anyone had been out of bed, all of London would have heard about it. But the police were the ones who needed convincing, and fast. Society's attitude toward punishment had been moving steadily away from the cruelties of the past, but Her Majesty had no compunction about hanging murderers. And being somewhere between fourteen and sixteen years of age, Jack would hardly be the youngest to swing for his supposed crimes.

I was so lost in thought I didn't see the incongruously dapper man lurking in my hallway until he stepped out of the shadows near my door. My heart stopped. Dressed in sharply creased black trousers, a well-cut overcoat, a silk topper, and a white silk scarf, Cain Goddard looked out of place, to say the very least.

"Oh, my," he said with a self-deprecating smile. "I do seem to be startling you quite a bit these days."

"You could say that."

What was he doing there? I felt a sudden flush of guilt, then fear, and hoped my morbid suspicious weren't showing on my face. Goddard hadn't deigned to visit my flat since we renewed our acquaintance. Showing up unannounced was out of character as well. I glanced at his silk gloves, imagining the steely grip they hid.

"I have theatre tickets for tonight."

I'm ashamed to admit I flinched when he reached beneath his coat. Looking at me quizzically, he brought forth a large, soft package.

"It's one of the suits of evening clothes I had made for you before you left." He winked. "As far as I've seen, your dimensions haven't changed appreciably since then. Neither have men's evening fashions. There's quite a bit of time before the performance begins. Get dressed. We'll have dinner at the Wellington first."

"W-what's the performance?" I asked stupidly as I took the carefully wrapped bundle from his hand.

"*Ravenswood* at the Lyceum."

I nearly dropped the package.

He laughed. "Come, now, the reviews weren't that bad."

"Sorry. I have a few things on my mind at present." I took a deep breath and felt around my pocket for the key. Fingers shaking only partially because of the cold, I let us inside.

"Your flat hasn't changed," he said, looking around while I opened the package and carefully unfolded the clothing. The last time he'd been here was Christmas 1890, to deliver the typewriting machine he'd bought for me a year and a half before. He was surveying the room in much the same way he had at that time. When his sharp eyes lit on the machine, which was obviously in active use, he smiled. "Glad to see the Remington has proven useful."

"Quite." I stammered. I carefully hung the trousers, jacket, and shirt over the screen and admired them. "These are exquisite, by the way. Thank you."

I glanced at the cold fireplace and rubbed my hands together. The chill had seeped in from outside and settled in the flat. If I was going to lay a fire, now was the time. On the other hand, if Goddard ultimately convinced me to go to the theatre, a portion of my remaining coal would be wasted. Unaware of my dilemma, Goddard continued his inspection, noting the copper bathtub leaning against the wall next to the fireplace, the unmade bed, and, finally, the book hiding amid the covers.

"*The Language of Flowers?*"

I mumbled something about wanting to have a look at his greenhouse one of these days.

"Ah. I thought perhaps you were trying to figure out the meaning of the bouquets you delivered for me." I turned. He'd leaned his umbrella against my desk and was regarding me over the glove-covered tips of his steepled fingers. "I can see from your face that you did figure it out. I do wish you hadn't."

Oh, God. This was it. The police hadn't been able to hold me, and now he was here to finish the job.

He took a step forward. I lunged for the fireplace poker.

"My word, Ira," he said, stopping short. "Do you think I mean to harm you?" He attempted a little laugh. "If I did, I certainly wouldn't do it in my theatre clothes." I gripped the handle harder. "And if you mean to harm me—though I can't imagine why you would—surely the poker is a better choice than a fireplace brush, hmm?"

I glanced at the little long-handled broom in my hand and set it down, cursing under my breath. He took another step forward, speaking in the conciliatory tone generally reserved for lunatics and rabid dogs.

"Clearly something is bothering you. Shall we discuss it like gentlemen, or have you completely reverted to your feral East End ways?"

I looked from him to the door. He was stronger and faster than I and could probably kill me in eight different ways before I reached the hallway—even if I hadn't put down the fireplace brush. Yet, though his appearing on my doorstep was unprecedented, he'd given no indication that he'd come for any other reason than to take me to the theatre. And it wasn't like him to be coy.

I was being ridiculous. I had to take myself in hand.

"You're the guest," I said, trying to calm my racing pulse. I gestured back toward the desk. "You can take the chair."

"You're not going to whisk me to death the moment I turn to retrieve it?"

"I promise."

While he brought the chair, I smoothed down my bed covers and sat, feeling more foolish now than afraid. Closing *The Language of Flowers*, I laid it on the pillow next to me.

"So, let me guess what the trouble is." Goddard set the chair down facing me, close enough to speak quietly but well out of poker range. "You delivered my threats to two men, and now they're dead. You think I killed them. And now you think I've come to silence you."

A line from a children's book went through my mind: *What a clear way you have of putting things!* I stretched out my legs in front of me, perhaps subconsciously putting more distance between us.

"I know you didn't kill them personally, Cain. At least not in your theatre clothes." That earned a slight twitch of his lips. "But if they betrayed you as badly as those flowers suggested, then I can't imagine you'd give a second thought to punishing them."

"Punishing, yes, but having them killed?" He frowned. "You must know I consider that a waste and an unnecessary risk except under the direst circumstances. Moreover, if I'd intended to kill them, why increase the risk of failure by warning them in advance?"

He did have a point. Goddard was the ultimate pragmatist. He answered to no gods but risk and reward. Come to think of it, flowery gestures themselves—pun quite intended—were well out of his usual repertoire.

"Why the flowers, then? It doesn't seem like you. And those men certainly didn't seem the type to spend their time studying *The Language of Flowers*."

"Precisely the reason I've been using a limited version of that particular code to communicate with certain of my associates. If anyone is less likely to be versed in Miss Greenaway's floral vocabulary than sugarhouse workers, it's your average London bobby. I could have sent five orange pips, I suppose, if I'd thought any of you had read *The Strand* this month. Forgive me for wanting to show off a bit, as well."

I blinked. "Show off? To me?"

He shook his head. "I should have just sent Watkins with a shillelagh."

The image made me want to laugh, and that was probably the intent. But as much as I wanted to believe his facile explanations, everything I'd experienced in the past few days indicated otherwise.

"You can't tell me the flower arrangements were random. I know what I read."

"Oh, yes. You read correctly. But I didn't kill them." He caught my eyes. "Lothar and Backer were helping me with a sensitive project. They were a little too free with their words, but not so much that I'd have had to abandon the project altogether. *Then* I would have killed them. As it stands, though, their deaths have cost rather than benefitted the project. I really needed their expertise."

"Are you saying the explosion was an accident?"

"Happens all the time."

It did, actually. Sugar refineries were hot, filthy places filled with explosive chemicals and flammable residues. It was a wonder, really, that they didn't go up more often. That didn't make the coincidence any less convenient, though, or Goddard's involvement any less suspicious.

"You're not going to tell me what the project is, are you?" I asked.

"You wouldn't approve."

"Probably not."

He sighed, pulling at the fingertips of his gloves as if preparing to remove them. Then, checking his watch, he smoothed the gloves back into place and folded his hands in his lap. "As for coming to silence you or to punish you for some imagined infraction, the answer is no. It's ridiculous. Why would you think such a thing?"

Oh, where to begin?

"You really don't know where I spent last night?" I asked.

"Well, you didn't spend it in my bed. Apart from that, no, I have no idea."

Briefly, I outlined my adventures over the past day and a half, omitting, of course, the involvement of Andrew St. Andrews. All the while I wondered how much of the story he already knew—knew, because he had set the events in motion himself. I watched his face carefully, but his expression never wavered from that of appropriate concern.

"Dear boy," he said, laying a hand over mine once I'd finished. "Why ever didn't you send for me?"

"I thought I was protecting you. If you were behind Backer's death, I didn't want the police anywhere near you, and I didn't want them to connect you to the explosion, either."

"That's very thoughtful." His fingers closed around mine, silk and steel.

"Later, of course, I started to wonder if you'd meant for me to take the blame."

The warmth in his expression dissolved, and he pulled his hand away. "I'm sorry you think I'd do that."

I didn't know what to think. Drawn-out revenge games had never been Goddard's style. He'd always preferred his justice quick, clean, and to the point. On the other hand, the past two years had changed me in fundamental ways. Perhaps they'd changed him as well. Yet as much as my better judgment screamed at me not to trust him, part of me—the part that was desperate to forget every moment of the last two horrendous days—suggested the oblivion I sought would best be found in a night on the town with an old friend.

Goddard put on a forced smile and stood. "Well, no matter. Shall we try to banish this unpleasantness with a good show and an expensive dinner?"

As I took in his familiar features—his neat moustache, fresh haircut, and the intelligent brown eyes that hid dark depths—I wanted nothing more in all the world. Or, rather, I wanted to want it. But until I could allay my suspicions, I'd be miserable...and miserable company.

"I'm sorry," I said. "I'm otherwise engaged this evening."

"Oh?" he demanded sharply.

"Not...not with someone else. With...work. Yes. I'm quite busy with work."

"Don't be ridiculous. Your only work in weeks has been for me. It would be crass to harp on the substantial debt you've incurred. But if you've any intention of repaying it, you'd do well not to alienate your only employer."

His meaning was clear. Wilde was gone and would likely never pay me what he owed. I'd no other clients, and my funds were running out. Once again, I found myself dependent upon Goddard's pleasure—a position I swore I'd do anything to avoid. How had this happened? Fury bubbled and burned in my chest—at his manipulation, at my own stupidity, at the unfairness of it all.

"Fine," I said through clenched teeth. "But only dinner."

"As you wish. The Wellington always has plenty of tables."

I stalked over to the screen. Positioning myself pointedly behind it, I changed into the evening clothes he'd brought me. A white silk shirt, black wool trousers and jacket—it all fit magnificently and felt like a full-body caress.

"Very handsome," he said as I emerged.

"Just dinner," I said again. "And Backer was my last delivery. You'll have to find someone else."

Without waiting for his response, I grabbed my coat and hat and pushed past him through the door. I heard him shut it and follow me down the stairs. The street was deserted, except for a familiar black hansom sitting sentinel in front of my building. My pulse raced. As the driver tipped his hat and climbed down from his perch to open the door, something told me, very distinctly, not to get in the car.

"If I meant you ill, Ira, you wouldn't still be standing here worrying about it."

That makes me feel so much better, I thought. We stood there for what felt like a week, Goddard waiting for me to enter, and I paralyzed with indecision and straining to hear the voice of my better judgment over my pounding heart. I still had time to change my mind, to dash back into my flat and lock the door. Goddard's fingers closed around my elbow.

"It's only dinner, damn you," he said. "You have all the time in the world to eat stale bread all alone in your dank little flat. You've had a miserable few days. Let me do this for you."

Was I being ungrateful? Goddard clearly thought so. But as much as I resented his manipulation, some part of me wondered if the evening might not still be salvageable. It wasn't every day that one was invited to dine at the Wellington, after all. Not only were its kitchens the stuff of legend, but for Goddard to agree to dine with another man in Piccadilly—an area very dear to Wilde and his set—demonstrated just how far he was willing to bend to please me. If that was indeed where we were headed.

At the same time, my trespasses against Goddard were many, especially recently, and I'd spent the past hour insulting him with my suspicions. I could either take a chance and find out what he had in mind for our evening, or I could insult him further by refusing— and drive myself insane waiting for the consequences.

Swallowing hard, I climbed into the hansom.

"I'm sorry, Cain," I said as he slid in beside me and the driver closed the door in front of our knees. "I don't know what came over me."

"I suppose it's understandable."

The driver climbed back to his seat above and flicked the reins over the horse's back. The moist air, redolent with the metallic smell of rain, pushed against our faces as the hansom began to roll. For several tense moments, the only sound was the *clip-clop* of the horse's hooves on the cobblestones. The carriage's headlamp swayed back and forth on its hook, animating the open cabin with moving shadows. As we turned onto Newgate Street, which was already crowded with evening traffic, Goddard relaxed enough to let his knee rest against mine.

The last time I'd been so frightened of the man had been the day he'd invited me to take up residence at his home on York Street nearly five years earlier. He'd been a client before that. A regular. That night—the night of our standing appointment—I'd found myself on the wrong side of a sadistic constable and turned up at our lamppost looking as if I'd been run over by a team of horses. Any of my other clients would have kept walking. Goddard took me back to his home, sewed me up—personally—and asked me to stay.

That was when I began to suspect he was something more than the lonely academic he'd portrayed. He was a little too comfortable with the blood, for one, and decidedly too handy with a surgical needle. To this day, I'm certain Goddard was behind the constable's gruesome murder later that night. Admitting nothing, he spoke affably of the details before the story broke in the papers. The body was found near our lamppost.

I'd accepted his offer not only because it was generous, but also because I'd feared his reaction should I offend him by turning it down.

But as frightened as I'd been, I'd also been exhilarated.

There's something intoxicating about walking out under the devil's wing. I felt invulnerable. Protected. I'd never felt any of those things before—not in the workhouse, and certainly not in the alleys and back rooms of Whitechapel. He had treated me well—provided I kept to the rules. And why wouldn't I? His offer was everything I'd ever hoped for...at the time, anyway.

And he was, then as now, a forceful and thorough lover. I could feel the heat of his thigh through his trousers and mine, and smell that heady combination of jasmine, bergamot, expensive tobacco, and power that was uniquely and utterly his. I shivered beneath the clothes in which he'd dressed me—half from fear and half from memories steeped in desire. As if reading my thoughts, Goddard glanced at me out of the corner of his eye. Saying nothing, he set a hand on my thigh.

"Shall I tell the driver to take us home?"

Home, he'd said—not *my home* or *York Street*. The thought of those hands peeling off my clothes, clutching at my flesh, pushing me down on the bed—or his desk or the floor—*possessing* me—made me shiver again. Despite my suspicions—or perhaps because of them—I suddenly wanted him more than words could say. Words became immaterial when he moved his hand beneath my coat flap and cupped his fingers around my body's answer. A smile flickered over his lips.

"Just say the word," he murmured.

I closed my eyes. Took a breath. Good sense prevailed. "I think we should just go to dinner."

He removed his hand. "As you wish."

The new chill in his voice made me want to take back my words. My indecision must have made him wonder if I were playing some kind of game. But there was no game. The easy way in which we'd fallen back together had given me false confidence about our situation. Being dragged off to New Scotland Yard in the middle of the night had reminded me just what a dangerous individual Cain Goddard was, how dirty were his hands, and—worst of all—that he had both the means and the motivation to cause me great harm.

Perversely, it made some part of me want him all the more.

It had been a long time since I'd felt the thrill of that kind of danger and uncertainty. Long enough that I'd thought I'd left those desires behind. But as much as it terrified me, it touched me at some undeniable, primal level, teasing back to life a hunger that would be the death of me if I didn't get it under control again.

I couldn't trust him, but I wanted him. It had been correct to refuse his advances—correct, though, glancing at the stony set of his features, probably not wise. And certainly not what, at the basest depths of my soul, I most desired.

The driver turned onto Fleet Street, and as the carved stone buildings rose around us like canyon walls, a bit of my apprehension drained away. The Wellington was straight ahead, and if Goddard had other plans, he wouldn't have bothered with subterfuge once he had me in the hansom. The street was crowded with vehicles and cheerful with light from the lively parade of restaurants and taverns. I forced my mind in the direction of the Wellington's renowned wine selection. I wondered what would be on the set menu that night. Another point in favor of the establishment: its several spacious dining rooms and rotating menus ensured that even at the drop of a hat a man could still be assured a seat and a splendid meal.

"Stop here." Goddard's voice jarred me out of my thoughts.

I said, "But we haven't arrived."

The driver slowed and pulled to the curb. My heart began to pound again. I craned my neck, peering out of the open front of the hansom. It was a public-enough place. He wouldn't attempt anything here. But the Wellington was still some distance ahead. What was he doing?

"Get out of the carriage, Ira."

"Where are we going?"

Not bothering to answer, he stepped down. I followed mutely, heart thumping in my ears. Briefly it occurred to me to run. It wouldn't have been hard to disappear in that crowd, and he wouldn't chase me. But he would catch up with me at some point. Or delegate the task to one of his employees.

He clamped an iron hand over my shoulder and guided me through the crowd toward the mouth of an alley. Goddard was a fighting-arts master. I'd seen him batter his hands bloody against wood wrapped in rope. I'd seen those hands break bricks. Those hands had also mended my wounds with breathtaking tenderness, brought my body to new heights of pleasure, and cradled me during long, cold nights.

I'd no idea what to expect when the shadows of the alley finally closed around us, but I doubted it would involve cradling or tenderness.

There would be some sort of punishment—this much was becoming clear. I'd known him to deal out justice to people who had crossed him—I'd just never crossed him before now. I'd been too distracted by my new life of luxury, too grateful for his generosity, and too enthralled by the hint of danger that never materialized to even think of defying him. But recently I'd done nothing *but* defy him. I supposed I should have seen it coming. The only question was degree. Would I be punished for prying too deeply into the matter of the flowers, or—and my knees almost buckled at the thought—did Goddard know I'd brought St. Andrews into it?

I should have run. If I moved quickly enough, I might have slipped away and made it back to the street before he caught me. But like a cow toward the slaughterhouse hammer, my legs propelled me forward step by step, even as escape fantasies flashed through my mind.

"Turn here."

The noises of the street faded. The alley—sharp, windowless walls—narrowed. He splashed me through a puddle, then turned me left into a cramped tunnel barely wider than a man. Then, just as instinct took over and I tried to twist out of his grip, he caught my left arm in a lock and pushed me into the wall so roughly the impact jarred my teeth and knocked my hat to the ground.

"I really don't know what to think, Ira." He pressed me to the brick. "I have so much to give you. I keep trying, but it seems you don't want any of it."

What?

"Shh." His one hand still pinned me. He ran the other one through my hair with firm, deliberate strokes. As one might calm a ruined horse before shooting it, I imagined. The bricks were rough against my cheek and black with soot. I struggled, but he gave my arm a cruel twist that shattered all thoughts of escape.

His other hand slid down my cheek and settled, feather-light, around my throat. "I could give you everything, damn you. Why won't you let me?"

I stifled a cry as his fingers tightened. I squeezed my eyes shut, my pulse pounding hot against the cold bricks.

"Frightened? You're smart."

His hand left my throat and moved to my chest, tugging open my coat buttons one by one. He chuckled mirthlessly as I shuddered out an involuntary sigh of relief.

He rested his forehead against the back of my skull, his breath a series of short, hot bursts against my neck. He'd shaved. His cologne mingled with the smell of sweat, soot, and rain. His hand tugged my shirt out of my waistband, then addressed the buttons of the exquisite trousers he'd brought me.

"But you like it," he said. "You like not knowing the lengths to which I'd go."

I did like it. Something told me I shouldn't. But now that his hand had left my throat, my cock rose to meet him all the same. Rising with relief, along with the rest of my body, though the threat was far from over. It had merely changed shape.

"I could hurt you," he whispered into my ear. He worked my cock with short, efficient strokes. "I could hurt you like you hurt me. I could hurt you so much worse."

He leaned into my back. God, but he was hard. His strokes were tight, punishing enough to convey his anger but not enough to cause actual damage. In some ways it was worse than having that hand at my throat.

In some ways it was better than anything I could have imagined.

Dancing on that razor edge of uncertainty made me nauseous with fear. It also made me feel alive. He could have done anything to me at that moment. I was powerless. In his hands, literally and figuratively. And part of me did like—very, very much—not knowing how far he'd go or whether he'd be there to catch me once he'd pushed me off the edge.

He yanked my trousers down.

I heard him spit onto his fingers, felt him prepare himself with a few practiced flicks of his wrist. I would have come the moment he thrust into me, but he clamped his fingers down hard over the end of my cock.

"No," he said. And that was all he said until it was over.

It was a hot, harsh, all-too-fast fuck. When he let me go, I came as if on command, thinking, ironically enough, of poor, damned Dorian Gray.

The strangest thoughts and sensations coursed through me as I felt him pull away. The usual bodily release—intensified by simple relief at still being alive. There was also a sense of cleansing. I'd paid for my offenses and survived. Having put me in my place, he was offering to start again. But I didn't want to start from that place of unquestioning obedience. I'd moved on from there two years ago, when I'd left York Street. I wanted more from life, now, than material comfort and consciousness-shattering sex. I needed purpose, responsibility, and a sense of doing right in the world.

Part of me really wished I didn't.

I felt dizzy and light. Released, but also weighted down by the choice ahead of me. I wasn't ready to go back on his terms. And if that fuck had been anything, it had been a reiteration of his terms.

"Here," he said, holding out a handkerchief. It was silk—expensive, and as soft as his hand had been hard. He had his back to me, but the skin at the back of his neck was flushed and he was sweating. His voice sounded breathless. Weary, as well. Perhaps a bit disgusted.

I felt disgusted as well, and not just at the idea of using such an exquisite piece of silk for that particular task. Once I'd cleaned myself up, I tossed the handkerchief into a corner and pulled up my trousers. I tucked my shirt back in and buttoned up my coat.

When I turned, Goddard was staring back out into the alley. From the slump of his shoulders, I could tell he regretted it. To him it had been an unpleasant duty.

Like disciplining an employee.

Or shooting a horse.

Who did he think he was?

But that was exactly the point. He knew who he was, and he thought he knew who I was.

But he was wrong. God damn him.

Anger burned in my chest. God damn him to hell—not only for what had just taken place, but for everything I'd been through since I'd stupidly reinserted myself into his life. For putting me in the position of having to trust him, knowing he couldn't be trusted. For treating me like some problematic functionary—a part of the machine to be fixed—an unruly animal to be bludgeoned into submission.

For making me see things about myself I never wanted to see.

I'm still not sure what happened at that point. Everything went terribly silent and slow. Blood roared in my ears like an approaching locomotive. A red fog clouded my vision, and I felt on fire from the inside out. Goddard turned, his mouth open to speak. The fingers of my left hand slowly clenched together as if of their own accord.

The next thing I knew, he was on his arse in the dirt, trying to pop his jaw back into place. His bottom lip was split. The moon had come out, and the blood running down his chin glittered black in its light. My left hand, still upraised, throbbed so hard my entire body pulsed with its rhythm. I lowered my fist as Goddard cautiously stood.

"I deserved that," he said, wincing as he dabbed at his lip with his sleeve.

"Yes, you did."

I'd hit him. Good God, I'd hit him. He could have taken me apart in the blink of an eye, but he hadn't. Instead, he brushed off his coat, eyeing me warily.

My teeth were chattering. The heat had drained away, and I was suddenly chilled to the quick. A cold drop of rain fell on my cheek. Then another. Soon we were standing there, regarding one another through a light rain.

Moving slowly, he bent down to retrieve my hat. I snatched it from his hand.

When next he opened his mouth, I expected a rebuke, or at least some attempt to justify whatever the hell it was that had just happened. Instead, he said, "Why isn't all that I have enough?"

I shook my head, wondering if I'd heard correctly. Because I could not have heard correctly.

"A gracious home, fine things. Once it was more than enough."

"Let me try to understand this," I said, pushing back a burble of grossly inappropriate laughter. "All of this was because *your feelings are hurt?* Are you joking?"

"Once it was all you ever wanted. What changed?"

"I found out the human cost of all those evenings out. I learned how much blood it took to buy Italian shoes and Egyptian tobacco. I discovered—"

"Don't be melodramatic." He scoffed. "I suppose that's why you're spending all your time playing with Bess Lazarus's orphans. Trying to save your soul, are you?"

"They're not orphans. They're throwaways. People no one wanted. Like I was."

"I wanted you."

"As an ornament. Something for your collection. You certainly didn't want someone who thought for himself, or who…who would challenge the ethics of your ambitions."

There was a long pause after that. Rain pattering on the crown of my hat, on the rooftops, on the muddy ground at our feet. The murmur of the evening traffic on Fleet Street that was so close, but seemed miles away. Then he said, "It was your idea to come back."

The words hit like a slap. But he was right. I could have turned down his advances. I could have laughed the entire idea away before I ever reached York Street and avoided all of this nonsense to begin with. But I hadn't. Part of me had very much wanted to pick up where we'd left off two years ago. But that was impossible. I'd changed. He hadn't. And at the time, I hadn't the sense to realize it.

"Ira, what do you want?"

Standing there in the rain, the anger and tension slowly draining away, I felt as if something had broken. A wall had toppled, and for the first time, through its dust and over the piles of its rubble, we were truly seeing one another. My entire body was shivering, now, and my chattering teeth could likely be heard all the way to the street. I was disgusted with him, with myself, and with this entire accursed evening.

I said, "I want my goddamned dinner."

I stalked out of the alley with Goddard's steps echoing behind me. I was a wreck. Angry as hell. Nauseous. Exhausted. I'd never seen Goddard stripped so bare. Part of me was curious what might come of that. Part of me wanted to hit him again. When we emerged onto Fleet Street, the crowds were still thick and the hansom was standing where we'd left it.

"Just tell me one thing," I said, turning so abruptly in the mouth of the alley that he nearly walked into me. "Did you set me up?"

"On my life, I did not." His eyes were clear, his voice frank. I nodded, feeling not exactly reassured but grimly satisfied with the answer. "Shall I have my driver take you back to your flat?"

"No. We're going to the Wellington."

"Ira..."

"Don't dare tell me I haven't earned it."

I started through the crowd toward the restaurant, leaving Goddard staring after me. It would have taken melon-sized testicles to follow me at that point. But even if Goddard's nerve faltered, his credit at the Wellington—where he had been a patron of long standing—would not. As I strode down Fleet Street, the crowd parted as I approached, as if before an angry god, then closed silently behind me.

CHAPTER SIXTEEN

B y the time I arrived at the restaurant, my hands had stopped shaking, and I'd managed, with great effort, to collect my thoughts enough to decide in favor of the English set dinner. My nausea had receded and left me with an enormous appetite that the French kitchen's less substantial fare would not satisfy. I needed flesh—bloody rare and paired with a deep-red wine. I stopped briefly before the doorway to brush off the soot and rain. By the time I rid myself of my coat and hat, my voice had recovered enough that the maître d'hôtel didn't look up from his fat book in alarm when I addressed him, but greeted me like an expected guest and inquired after my needs. We negotiated a table, at which point he nodded and said, "This way, please."

Vast dining rooms sprawled across the Wellington's ground and first floors, each seating close to two hundred. The décor was too fussy for my taste, but the patrons were a lively mix that night— mostly upper-middle-class types and theatregoers, with a sprinkling of lower aristocrats and a few Piccadilly folk thrown in for color. Goddard hadn't followed me as far as the restaurant. At least I saw no sign of him at that moment. My feelings about that were mixed.

I followed my host through a sea of laughing, well-dressed people, crisp table linens, and tinkling silver, toward a table near the kitchen doors. Objectively it wasn't the most desirable perch, but the air was warm and thick with the smell of well-cooked meat and hot buttered vegetables. I liked it. Soon a ten-shilling bottle of

Clos de Vougeot and a roasted quarter of lamb were in front of me. At least the evening wasn't a complete loss. I ate like a starving man. One might think such events would kill an appetite, but anger had stoked the fire within until it threatened to consume me. Anger at Goddard, of course, but also at myself. What had I been thinking, going back there? While the past two years had turned my own life inside out, he'd continued along his merry path untouched. I'd begun as his employee—his whore, let's be honest—and that was still how he thought of me. Why had I thought that would somehow have changed? Because I had a proper vocation, now—such as it was, with no clients and payments in arrears? Because I spent my spare time with disadvantaged youths? God, I was pathetic. By the time I surfaced from my thoughts, the wine was gone, and the lamb had been reduced to a pile of clean and gleaming bones.

"Mind if I sit down?" Goddard asked, appearing suddenly across the table. He'd cleaned his face, though his lower lip was swollen and a lovely bruise was forming below it.

"Suit yourself. You always do."

The silence that followed was excruciating, but I wasn't about to cede my territory due to mere discomfort. I'd a feeling he felt the same way. My meal was suddenly very heavy in my stomach, and the wine was rising to my head. I was about to signal the waiter for another bottle when Goddard nodded toward the center of the dining room.

"Isn't that your little friend?" he asked.

Good God, it was Marcus. The pleasant, alcoholic cushion between reality and my head evaporated. Marcus was sitting alone at a table set for two. His own wine had arrived, but the meal had not. His pomaded hair, combed back over his skull, was translucent in the gaslight, and he wore a suit much like my own. At least someone was doing well for himself, I thought sourly.

"He's not 'my' anything. But yes, I know him."

"But I assume from your tone, you don't hate him enough to wish him bobbing in the Thames with his throat slit."

Now I turned toward him. Beyond bruises and scabs, not a trace remained on Goddard's face of our earlier encounter, and he did not appear to be joking. "That's Rupert Sudworth's table," he said.

"Good God."

The financier wasn't a criminal in the technical sense, though his business dealings must have skated along the edges of a hundred different laws. He made enough money for enough influential people that he likely employed an entire army for the sole purpose of scrubbing away any appearance of wrongdoing. In other circles, he was known for his taste for fine things and beautiful men, which he seemed to go through like handkerchiefs. And there were rumors. None that had been investigated—the police had better things to do than look into the disappearance of every gutter-bred rent boy. But though nothing had ever been proved, I'd known a few young men who'd come to a bad end after falling in with Rupert Sudworth.

I should warn Marcus. But crossing Sudworth was ever-so-slightly more dangerous than sleeping with him. The same could be said for Cain Goddard, come to think of it. I glanced at Goddard and wondered just how close I'd come to a bad end that evening.

As if conjured by my thoughts, Sudworth's hawkish face appeared in the crowd. He was handsome enough—in his late thirties, dark, well-formed, and impeccably dressed—but something cruel and predatory flickered beneath those smooth patrician features. Even halfway across the dining room I could see it. I wondered if Marcus had seen it too, or if he was too dazzled by Sudworth's money to look closer.

"Won't you excuse me?" Goddard said, rising. Good Lord, I'd forgotten he was even there. "I've been concerned about some of my investments lately. I do believe Mr. Sudworth is just the one to advise me."

Before I had time to ponder that, he was moving purposefully across the busy dining room. I saw him and Sudworth greet one another with a smile and a handshake and then watched as Goddard guided the financier back across the room toward the bar.

One might be tempted to think Goddard was creating this opportunity for my sake. But the truth was, he seldom did anything if it didn't serve more than one purpose. I'd never seen him act out of sheer good will. Besides, I didn't want his good will. If he'd offered me wine, I'd have tossed it back in his face.

But this wasn't wine. It was the life of a friend. I could consider the implications later, once I'd at least pointed Marcus in the direction of safety. I stood.

My erstwhile protégé must have seen me coming, for when I arrived at his table, he looked up with a poor imitation of surprise.

"Why, Mr. Adler, as I live and breathe."

"Marcus."

Sudworth had dressed Marcus up as Goddard had dressed me: to be seen by those who saw and to pass for a junior acquaintance by those who did not. His suit was tailored, his shirt silk, and I'd have wagered the feet he was resting on a chair were sore from the pinch of new leather shoes. Did Sudworth know Marcus had a sister who'd taught him the names of all the flowers? Did he know he could read a man's history in a framed bit of newsprint on the mantel? My heart stopped. At that moment I dearly hoped Marcus hadn't shown off his surprising perspicacity to his new benefactor. Suddenly the issue of the silver scissors seemed rather petty.

"Wot's the matter?" He glanced into the depths of his empty wineglass, then glanced at the bottle. "You look like you seen a ghost."

"I think you should come with me."

He snorted. "Why?"

Goddard and Sudworth were sitting at the bar, their backs to us, deep in conversation, criminal to criminal. It made me a little queasy to realize they probably had a lot in common, though I'd never known Goddard to dispose of his paramours once he'd become bored with them. Still, it seemed rather convenient for them to turn up in the same place at the same time. The more I thought about it, the more likely it seemed that Goddard had arranged the meeting before even thinking to invite me. If he were attempting to start some large-scale project, Sudworth would know exactly how to fiddle the books in order to make everything appear aboveboard.

"I'll tell you later," I said to Marcus. "We need to leave. Right now."

Lazily, he turned the stem of the glass in his fingers. A single drop of red traced a path along the inside of the bulb. "Oh, I see. Now you seen I can do better, you want me back. Well, I ain't goin' back." He looked up. "Not to nasty coal fires and drinkin' wine out of water glasses in some filthy, cold room on Aldersgate Street."

That stung. I hated that flat, but it was all I had, and I'd shared it with him. Still, that wasn't the point. "Marcus, what do you really know about Rupert Sudworth?"

He snorted again. "Wot're you, me da?"

It did feel a bit that way right then, but I didn't let the unpleasant image push me off the track. "Where did you meet him?"

"At the bookseller's. He were the one wot give me the money for that food I brung you. You know, when you said I stole them scissors. You still fink I done it."

I did. It was true. "I'm sorry about that. But you had work. You had somewhere to live. You were building a new life. Why did you want to go back to—"

He met my eyes, and the petulance was replaced by hurt. Very, very briefly, I saw a flash of the young man who had so eagerly leafed through *The Language of Flowers*, stumbling over himself to help me.

"Don't you get it, Mr. Adler? You was kind to me. I had to give you somefin' for it. Pay you back, like. I got me pride, you know."

Well, wasn't I a right shit, then? Driving him back into that life in order to repay the kindness I'd forced on him. But instead of saying that, I pushed his feet off the chair where he'd been resting them and sat down.

"Don't you know Sudworth's reputation?" I asked, leaning in to spare the neighboring tables the details.

"Them's just rumors." He didn't sound convinced.

"Are you staying with him?"

"Ain't your business, is it? But...if you must know, it were just that once. And tonight."

"Where *are* you staying?"

He preened a bit. "Wiv' Mr. Samuels, the bookseller. He let me sleep in the back, so's I can keep an eye on the shop at night."

"Do you think Mr. Samuels would appreciate your leaving the store unguarded while you sell yourself for dinner and a fancy set of clothes?"

His eyes flashed. "Wot I don't 'preciate is you tryin' to ruin me fun."

A group of men had gathered at the bar, obscuring my view of Goddard and Sudworth, but straining, I could just make out bits and snatches of Goddard's side of the conversation. *Factory. Centrifuge. Chloroform.* My instincts had been right. Goddard and Sudworth were discussing more than investments. My mind flashed back to the refinery explosion. Did they use centrifuges in sugar production? What about chloroform? Suddenly Sudworth's head rose above the crowd—he was standing up! As his head swung toward us, I leaned away, trying to blend in with the boisterous party at the next table. When Sudworth sat back down, I grabbed Marcus's arm.

"Hey!"

"Two friends," I hissed. "Of mine. At the bottom of the Thames. Stand *up*, damn you!" Taking his wrist in what looked like no more than a friendly handshake, I leveraged him to his feet. A couple of people glanced over from the next table. I gave them a simpering smile. "Hate me if you like, but you'll thank me when you're warm and safe in your corner of the bookstore." Still subtly twisting his arm, I pushed him into the crowd. "Sudworth is a bad man. And even if you did steal my damned scissors, I'd never forgive myself if something happened to you."

His arm relaxed, and he stopped struggling. "You mean that?" The lifelong loneliness in those three words hit me like a hammer. It was entirely possible, I realized, that Marcus had gone through much of his life without so much as a single friend. "Ain't no one cared wot happen to me since me sis."

"I care." We reached the perimeter of the room, separated from Sudworth by at least fifty people. I let go Marcus's arm, a twinge in my own reminding me—to my shame—that not an hour ago I'd been on the receiving end of a nasty joint lock myself. We both straightened out our clothes. "Now look, did you order food yet?"

"Jus' the wine. Why?"

I did some quick calculations. Marcus wouldn't know claret from vinegar—a fact Sudworth would surely have apprehended within five minutes of meeting him. Which meant Sudworth wouldn't have spent more than two shillings on wine for the both of them. If Marcus left now, Sudworth might be irritated, but he probably wouldn't feel that Marcus owed him a debt worth pursuing. Marcus could send the clothes back in the morning.

"Good. It means you can get away unscathed. If you want to, that is."

"Two friends of yours?" he asked.

"Throats slit. Dumped in the river. Marcus, you've spent as much time out there as anyone. Do you really not see it?"

He looked away. "I seen it. Only I was finkin'..."

That he would be the exception? That wishful thinking would make the danger go away? That he could ride the luxury train a little farther before danger forced him to jump off?

Glancing toward the bar, I saw Sudworth clap Goddard's shoulder, both men laughing as if Goddard had said something terribly amusing. It bothered me that Goddard could enjoy a drink with Sudworth, knowing what he was. But I was also grateful. As much as Goddard's fluid morality made him untrustworthy, it had also made it possible for him to give me this opportunity to spirit Marcus away. Even if the opportunity was only an incidental bone thrown to an unjustly kicked dog.

"Let's go, then," I said.

Keeping to the perimeter, we made our way to the door. I spared Goddard one last glance and met his equivocal stare. He dipped his chin in subtle acknowledgement—approval, perhaps—then quickly returned his attention to Sudworth. I exhaled with relief.

Goddard's hansom was parked a block and a half away. We walked quickly toward it, not turning around. When we reached it, I gave the vehicle a tap. The driver looked down, recognized me, and tipped his hat.

"Please take my friend to Holywell Street," I said. "By the time you return, Dr. Goddard will no doubt have finished his dinner."

"Very good, sir."

He descended and opened the door. Once Marcus was settled inside, I said, "I wish you all the best. But if you're ever in a spot, you can always come to me. At the very least you can tell me your troubles over a water glass full of wine."

He smiled sheepishly. "Thanks, Mr. Adler." He wanted to say more, it was clear, but there really was nothing more to be said. I had a sudden, strong feeling that this was the last time our paths would cross—at least in the foreseeable future. We'd given each other what we had to give, and there was nothing more to be done for it. I raised a hand in farewell.

The driver flicked the reins over the horse's back and turned the vehicle into the flow of traffic. I watched it slowly merge into the river of carriages and disappear. Then I turned around and started back up the Strand toward home.

CHAPTER SEVENTEEN

Aldersgate Street was a long walk home in the rain—very long indeed without my umbrella. But I was still alive, I was home before dawn, and I had enough whiskey in the cupboard to make the last few hours go away for a while. All things considered, the situation was a lot better than it could have been.

At the foot of the staircase, I shook off the rain. Peace had settled over the building. The wailing babies and incessant arguments were silent for once. The only sound was the patter of rain on the pavement outside. I trudged up the stairs, soaked, frozen to the bone, and wincing every now and then as sharp, burning lances of pain shot upward through my core—a reminder of Goddard's discipline. I anticipated no more satisfying sound in all the world than the clack I'd hear when I drew the front-door bolt behind me. I had enough coal in the scuttle for a jolly good blaze, and once the ice in my veins had thawed, I'd drift off to sleep with my bottle in one hand and a good book in the other. And I wouldn't wake until I was damn well ready.

I should have known it wouldn't be that simple. Especially when I found a Turnbull girl on my doorstep.

Ruth Gray, age sixteen—hatless, dripping wet, coat unbuttoned, and panting as if she'd run the whole way. She must have arrived just before I did.

"It's the missus, Mr. Adler. Come quick!"

In the dim light from the lamp at the end of the corridor, I saw her wide eyes, her trembling lip. Irritation drained away, and my pulse began to race. "What happened?"

"She fell. Jack's gone for the doctor. He sent me to fetch you."

"And the baby?"

"I don't know, Mr. Adler. We heard a great thump on the stairs, an' then she were callin' for help. She weren't bleedin' or nuffin', if that's what you're askin', but she were scared to stand up and didn't nobody want to move her. You've got to come right away!"

Rain glistened on her asymmetrical face and plastered her hair to her head. She was as thoroughly soaked as I was. I watched my dreams of a well-earned rest fade back into a reality of mud, crisis, and freezing rain.

"Yes, yes, of course. Just...give me a moment."

Numbly, I teased the front-door lock open. I lit the lamp on my desk, then went for my bottle. I'm not normally one to drown my sorrows, but that night I'd have drawn and quartered them if I'd had the energy. While I felt around the upper shelf, Ruth padded in behind me on tentative feet. My fingers met glass at last. Glancing furtively over my shoulder, I quickly unscrewed the cap and took a belt, sighing as it went down. Now burning at both ends, I tucked the bottle under my arm and turned.

Ruth looked up guiltily from her perch on the corner of my bed, blinking over the pages of *The Language of Flowers*, which had been sitting nearby on the floor.

"Sorry," she said, scrambling up from the bed. "So sorry, Mr. Adler. I didn't mean...I...I don't much like books, but I do like this one, ever so much."

Ruth was a good worker: reliable, industrious, and handy with a needle. But she struggled with her lessons. It touched me, somehow, that she should take to that little volume—just like Marcus had. But Marcus was gone now, and he wasn't coming back.

"Why don't you keep it, then?" I said.

"You sure?"

"For your trouble. I won't be needing it anymore. Come on, let's go."

Dousing the lamp, I walked us back out and locked the door behind me. We hurried down the stairs and out onto an empty street lit only by a flickering gas lamp. The rain had stopped—thank heaven for small favors—but the clouds hung low and heavy above the city, and the street shimmered with puddles. I didn't need to check my watch to know that neither bus nor cab would be coming through this part of town any time soon.

"You came on foot, I suppose."

"'Course I did. I ain't scared."

Ruth had lived on the Whitechapel streets during that awful spate of murders a few years ago and had come out none the worse. She probably thought if she could evade the Ripper, she could escape any other danger that might present itself. She probably could have run the entire mile and a half to Turnbull House. It was me, ultimately, who had to slow down once we turned onto Bishopsgate Street.

"Sorry." I panted, stumbling to a stop and wondering whether I'd somehow forgotten impaling my backside on a flaming thorn bush. I leaned against the wall and took a long draught from my bottle, breathing deeply until the sensation subsided a bit. One way or another, Cain Goddard would pay.

"You limpin'?" Ruth asked as I started out again, slowly, gingerly.

"Just…not as young as I used to be." I drew in deep breaths of piercing-cold air, sighing relief as the whiskey blunted the evening's edges.

"You ain't as old as the doctor."

That was true. Though with Bess waiting, Lazarus could probably have run twice the distance without a thought. The streetlamp that marked the beginning of Raven Row wasn't far away, though, so turning the corner we picked up our pace. As we splashed through the water that had pooled between the uneven cobblestones, Ruth took a crumpled piece of paper from her coat pocket and handed it to me.

"It's from Mr. St. Andrews. He wanted me to leave it for you, but as long as you're here…"

"You're working for St. Andrews?" I asked.

She nodded. "Me an' Daisy Tucker." Her words were white puffs in the darkness. "I thought it were odd for a bachelor to take girls, but I overheard the missus say she wouldn't give him no boys. Didn't want no scandal, she said."

I stifled a snort. It was good to be cautious, of course, though St. Andrews would never make that kind of trouble for Lazarus. What's more, St. Andrews's tastes ran older rather than younger.

The envelope had been sealed with glue. I worked my finger beneath the flap and freed the letter inside.

Have come across some promising leads in our case. Messrs. Dixon and Jeffries have proved quite helpful. Anticipate a satisfying resolution for all concerned. Shall we meet to discuss it?

Good God. I pictured the two constables in my mind's eye—the lean and daft paired with the stout and suspicious. Imagine those two proving useful for anything besides fitting my neck for a noose! Promising leads indeed! One could only hope that by "promising," he didn't mean "implicating Cain Goddard." Not that I feared it would disrupt our newly rekindled affair—Goddard had put a tidy end to that on his own. All the same, St. Andrews and I certainly would discuss it, and the sooner the better. I shoved the missive into my coat pocket.

Ruth and I jogged the last few blocks to Turnbull House. Lights were blazing on both floors as we came up the front stairs. When I opened the door, Bess was sitting near the bottom of the stairs, surrounded by a number of young people who looked eager to help but not convinced they wouldn't do more harm than good. I could sympathize.

"Ira," she said weakly. "You didn't need to come, really. Tim should be here soon."

"Nonsense." I handed my coat and hat to Ruth. Reluctantly, I handed her the bottle as well. The huddle of young people parted as I approached. Gingerly, I lowered myself next to her on the bottom stair. "Are you injured? Anything broken?"

She shook her head, then winced. "It really was the stupidest thing. I'd just finished the one o'clock bed check and was coming down the stairs when I slipped."

"Does it hurt? Are you bleeding?"

"There's no blood, at least not so far. And it doesn't hurt, exactly. But when I tried to get up, it felt like something...shifted. It's hard to explain. I'm afraid to stand up, at least until Tim gets here."

"That's probably wise. Is there anything I can do right now?"

She adjusted herself on the stair. Given her proportions and their unaccustomed distribution, the wooden step couldn't have been very comfortable. I was suddenly very aware of the twelve sets of eyes fixed on us.

"The children need their rest," she said pointedly.

I looked around at them. "You heard the missus. Go on, then. Quietly, now."

It was a measure of their concern that they filed back upstairs with only a token show of protest. Once they had gone, she said, "Tim keeps an instrument in his office. A fetoscope. It looks like an ear trumpet at the end of a rubber tube. It should be in his desk somewhere."

"I'll get it."

Marcus had given me back my key when he left, but I'd grown re-accustomed to carrying my picks—and a good thing it was, too. The lock gave way easily and I tucked the picks back into my pocket. The lamp was on Tim's desk where he'd left it. I switched it on low, and a soft glow filled the room. It was disorienting to be back in that room, rummaging around in the man's desk, considering what had taken place between us the last time I'd been there. Pushing those particular images away, I picked my way through the odds and ends in the flat middle drawer to no avail. The top side drawer held only neat stacks of paper organized with clips. Then, finally, in the bottom drawer I found it. When I emerged, Lazarus and Jack had arrived, to my relief.

"I should have been here instead," Lazarus was saying. He was sitting on the stair next to her, holding her hand. She was still pale, but looked relieved. "You should have been at home."

"I could have slipped at home just as easily, only there wouldn't have been anyone around to help."

"Then I should have asked Nurse Brandt to do tonight's watch instead. It was fine in the beginning, but you're too far along. You shouldn't be working."

Something that might have been anger flickered in her eyes, but she looked at his face and her expression softened. She set a hand on his arm. "Pearl needs to keep the clinic open. Stop blaming yourself. Jack, thank you for bringing him. You should go on up to bed, now. I'll be fine."

"Yes, Missus."

As Jack disappeared up the stairs, I emerged with the fetoscope. "Is this what you wanted, Bess?" I asked, holding it up.

"Ah, Adler, thank you for coming." Tim stood and, taking the instrument with one hand, clasped my fingers with his other. His eyes were tired, but his handshake was confident and strong. "Darling, do you mind? Bess shook her head. "This is an instrument for listening to the baby's heartbeat," he told me. He placed the large end of the horn on Bess's abdomen and inserted the end of the rubber tube into his ear. Bess and I held our breaths. After a few seconds, Lazarus gave a smile that was more than half relief and removed the tube. "The heartbeat is regular and strong. It doesn't mean the worry is over, but it's a good sign. Would you like to listen?" he asked Bess. She nodded, and he handed her the tube. While she positioned the instrument, he stood and walked me a few steps down the hall.

"Thank you again for coming, Ira. I know I've been behaving abominably recently, but I really am very grateful—for everything. I'm ashamed I never thanked you properly for taking on the obligation of the leasehold. It's not how I'd have done it, but..."

"You did ask us for solutions, no matter how unorthodox."

He opened his mouth as if to protest, but smiled wryly instead. "That I did. In any case, thank you. And regarding my recent, well, irrationality, I do apologize." He glanced back toward Bess, who was still listening intently with the fetoscope. "Sometimes it takes a crisis to make one see what's really important. You're my closest friend, Ira, but..." He met my eyes, and in his I saw the same soppy expression that had been there the day he first told me of his intent to marry.

"I'm happy for you, Tim," I said. "I'm happy for you both, and I wouldn't have it any other way."

Relieved, he clapped my shoulder soundly. "Now." He looked around, newly energized by his role as rescuer and provider. "I'd really prefer for her not to have to go upstairs, especially since the fireplace is on this floor. On the other hand, it'll be a lot easier to help her to the bedroom than to move the bed and everything else she needs down here. Right. It's settled, then." He strode back down the corridor to Bess. "There's nothing for it, old girl. Up you go. Carefully, now. Lean on me. Adler, will you help us?"

"Are you sure, Tim?" Bess asked.

"Sure I'd rather throw my back out carrying you up than carrying down that iron monstrosity you call a bed? Absolutely."

The words were said with such affection that not even the most churlish person in the world could have taken offense. Beaming up at him, Bess held on to his right arm, while he supported her from behind with his left. I walked just behind them in case either of them slipped. Slowly we made our way upstairs to the small bedroom between the boys' and girls' dormitories that had been set up for whoever was doing the night watch. While Tim turned down the covers of the single bed, Bess leaned against the wall, exhausted from her ordeal.

"Will you be all right, Ira?" she asked, rubbing a hand over the swell of her abdomen.

"Absolutely. If I can take one of those pillows, I'll stretch out on one of the classroom benches. Thanks," I said as Tim tossed a pillow in my general direction. As I turned to go, I suddenly remembered St. Andrews's message. "Do you have a pen?" I asked. Tim nodded toward the side table, which was cluttered with books and papers. I took what I needed, then left them to their business, closing the door quietly behind me. Then, balancing the paper against the wall, I dashed off a quick response.

The girls' dormitory was dark and silent, but I was pretty certain no one would be drifting off to sleep any time soon. "Ruth,"

I whispered. Covers rustled, and a moment later she appeared, rubbing her eyes. "Are you working for St. Andrews tomorrow?"

"He's sendin' a hansom after luncheon," she said sleepily.

"Give him this, please." If St. Andrews wanted to buy me supper tomorrow night to discuss his findings, I wouldn't object. The American Bar at the Criterion should do nicely. I folded the paper over twice and handed it to her. She nodded, yawned, and then, taking the note, disappeared back into the darkness.

As I made my way toward the stairs, I heard Bess and Lazarus speaking quietly. I couldn't make out their words, but their voices were calm, affectionate—as if they were the only ones in the world. It was a strange little moment, and it left me feeling at once wistful and warm. For the first time I realized what was truly meant by that passage I remembered from their marriage ceremony—the one about two people becoming one. For the first time, I wondered whether there would ever be someone with whom I would become one. At one time—recently—I'd thought Goddard was that person. But he himself had shown me the error of that line of thinking.

"Do you need anything else, Adler?" Lazarus asked.

"No," I said, embarrassed that he'd somehow sensed me standing there. "I'll just be on my way downstairs. Good night."

CHAPTER EIGHTEEN

WEDNESDAY

The rest of the night passed as peacefully as one might expect when one passes it on a hard bench in an empty classroom with a damp coat for a blanket. Still, I'd slept soundly enough that the students' morning preparations hadn't disturbed me. When I opened my eyes, the sun was peeking around the edges of the curtains, and I could hear everyone downstairs making their breakfast. Soon they'd be filing in to start their lessons. Slowly, painfully, I pulled myself up, stood, and stretched. After a knock at the door, it cracked open and Lazarus's face appeared in the breach.

"All right, Adler?"

"I'll be out of your way soon," I replied. "How's Bess?"

"Still sleeping. I'll be doing the lessons today."

"Really?" Lazarus had always struck me as too impatient to enjoy teaching. And it wasn't something one could do effectively if one didn't enjoy it. "Try to relax," I advised him. "If they smell fear they'll eat you alive."

"The only thing they're going to smell is your feet. Put your shoes on, will you?"

I grinned. He was going to be fine.

"Actually," he said, "women are a lot stronger than we give them credit for. I'll probably have more trouble keeping her in bed than dealing with the schoolroom."

"If you have trouble keeping your wife in bed, you're doing something wrong." I pulled the drapes back from the window, letting the anemic morning light stream in through the grimy window.

He laughed. "I've left her a stack of books. That should keep her busy for a while. It's not her I'm worried about, though."

"Oh?"

He shut the door behind himself and leaned against it. The muted light accentuated the dark rings beneath his eyes and the wrinkles at their edges. He held a large envelope in his hand. "She had some pain last night, a little bleeding."

I didn't know the precise implications of this, but from his expression, it didn't sound good.

"I'm sorry, Tim."

He shook his head. "I've seen worse, but I've also seen what appeared to be nothing turn very serious very quickly. I just hope she doesn't try to take on too much in order to compensate. She's so competent, and she'd rather drop dead from exhaustion than risk people thinking her weak."

"Sound familiar?" I asked.

He laughed again—a soft, tired sound. "I just want everything to be all right. Can't things go smoothly and quietly for more than five minutes at a time?"

"Smooth and quiet would bore you to tears, and you know it." I stretched again, wincing at the sharp pain that shot up my spine.

"Are you injured?" Lazarus asked.

I sighed. "Forget it."

I swept the ashes out of the fireplace and tore yesterday's newspaper into strips. Crumpling the strips into balls, I arranged them in the grate, along with some sticks and bits of wood the residents had collected. Lazarus sat down on the little ledge that surrounded the fireplace. While I struck a match, he took a few pieces of coal from the scuttle, carefully setting them amid the blooming flames.

"This baby…It wasn't my idea in the beginning, but I went along with it, because it seemed like the next logical step. To tell you the truth, the idea terrifies me, especially after seeing all the different ways in which things can go wrong. But now…Adler, I didn't realize how much I wanted it until it seemed possible it might not happen at all. Does that make sense?"

"Yes," I said. A little too much sense, actually. But that was neither here nor there. Standing, I clapped him on the shoulder. "She's in the most capable hands in all of London. If your best isn't good enough, Doctor, then it's just not meant to be right now."

Lazarus cocked his head. "That's very philosophical of you, Ira."

"I'm not just a handsome face, you know."

"No," he said, quite seriously. "You're much more than that. And I hope you never forget it."

"So I'm not a shallow insect with the attention of a mayfly?"

He frowned. "What? Oh, that. I was just frustrated when I said it. You were being deliberately obtuse. Probably for the best, though. And it was a peppered moth, not a mayfly. Now before I forget, this came for you this morning by way of that ginger-haired chap."

Watkins—Goddard's man. As he handed me the envelope, my anger stirred again. "I told him no more deliveries," I muttered under my breath.

"No, this was for you. The man was very clear about that."

Anger gave way to curiosity. Goddard wouldn't send a written apology. He certainly hadn't offered a verbal one. Besides, the envelope was thick with paper. What on earth could it be?

"Thanks," I said. "I'll open it at home, once I'm sure it won't bite."

"Snakes in paradise?" he asked, a smirk in his voice but his expression kind.

"Vipers. Good luck in the classroom, Professor."

❖

The morning was cool and clear. Folding Goddard's envelope into the inner breast pocket of my coat, I straightened my hat and continued up the cobblestone lane. Raven Row was shaking itself awake. Two women were carrying on a lively conversation over my head, while they hung their laundry on a line that stretched between their windows on opposite sides of the street. Up ahead, Mr. Wilks was propping open the door of his tobacco emporium. I paused briefly in front of the shop, breathing in the exquisite aromas of his wares while pretending to admire the window displays. I wasn't a habitual smoker—it was far too expensive. But, like Goddard, I did enjoy a nice Egyptian cigarette from time to time.

I was approaching the end of Raven Row when it occurred to me that I didn't have to twiddle my thumbs while St. Andrews drew his conclusions about Goddard's involvement in the deaths. I hadn't asked the man to investigate, after all. Nor was I paying him to do so. There was no reason I couldn't poke around on my own. Though the police had no doubt arranged for Mr. Backer's body to be removed—most likely to a pauper's grave at St. Bride's—I doubted they'd waste a moment tidying the flat afterward. They'd probably left behind an abundance of clues. God knew, St. Andrews's hero Sherlock Holmes could draw all sorts of conclusions from his observations of a crime scene. It couldn't be that difficult. And besides, what else was I going to do with the interminable stretch of hours that lay between me and my dinner at the American Bar?

The street ended abruptly at a T-shaped intersection. Turning sharply, I aimed myself southward and headed down Bell Lane toward Backer's flat.

❖

The tenement door was still hanging crookedly from its hinges when I arrived. Ducking inside, I made my way up creaking stairs to the second floor. The hallway was as dim and foul smelling as it had been the last time I'd been there. However, no one peered out of his doorway at the sound of my approach. I noted the flat from which Mr. Geary had appeared—several doors down from Backer's flat. Jack had said Geary and Backer had worked together at one time, but not anymore—and that Geary had a lot of free time to lurk about. Which meant Geary had very likely lost his position and not yet found another. Backer had been a foreman at the refinery. Had he, personally, given Geary the sack? People had killed for less. I'd seen it. But I'd have to see where the murder had happened before coming to any sort of conclusions about it.

I approached Backer's door and, glancing quickly up and down the hall, took out my trusty picklocks. In seconds, I was in.

As I'd predicted, the body had been removed, but the police hadn't bothered to tidy up the place. Not that tidying would have done much toward remedying the chaos. To say there was evidence of a struggle would have been a gross understatement. It looked more like the Blue Coat Boy pub after a particularly nasty brawl. The dining table lay on its back, three legs up like a dead horse. The fourth leg was nowhere to be seen. The tattered curtain that been pinned in a corner to hide the chamber pot lay in a pile on the floor. Shreds of fabric still hung from the nails from which the curtain had been torn, and the pot itself lay on its side, thankfully empty. The one picture hung askew on its hook, its glass spiderwebbed by impact. A chair lay in pieces on the floor, the splinters of wood interspersed with the wilted ruins of Goddard's flowers.

I closed my eyes, trying to imagine how the apartment had looked when Jack and I had fled. The flat would probably never have been described as tidy, but the furniture had been intact—this I remembered. The picture might have hung crookedly, but there'd been nothing wrong with the glass. Someone else had come. That person and Backer had fought, and from the blood—which I assumed was Backer's—and the dents in the wall, I surmised that Backer had died in the fight.

Which, as I turned the images over in my mind, came as no small relief.

Let me explain.

Backer had been a large man—tall, broad, and hardened from physical labor. Jack was slight. Moreover, Backer had been tossing Jack about since Jack was small. If Jack were to kill his father, it was unlikely he'd attempt to physically overpower the man. It was more unlikely still that if he'd tried, he'd have succeeded. Although I'd not entertained the idea for more than a second, it was clear now that Jack was completely innocent of the act. What's more, it would have been clear to Jeffries and Dixon. Even if they'd wanted to make a case against Jack, the evidence would have proved otherwise. I let out a sigh of relief.

A sigh that echoed softly behind me.

I whirled at the sound. It wasn't my imagination—someone was there. Though the flat consisted of only one room—every inch of which I'd searched—my skin was prickling with the sensation of being watched. Slowly, I raked my eyes over the debris until I came to the hole in the wall—another casualty of the battle that had taken place after Jack and I had left—and the eye peeping through it. The eye spied me at the same time and quickly pulled away.

"Wait!" I cried. I dropped to my hands and knees, but before I could put my face to the hole, a piece of furniture slammed against the wall.

I sprang to my feet and tore out into the hall. "I'm not with the police, I swear!" I battered the neighboring door with my fist, then put my ear to the thin wood. Someone was creeping about inside, as if trying to pretend they weren't home. Couldn't blame them, really. More often than not it's best not to get involved in other people's tragedies.

"I'm trying to help Kathe," I said.

The silence behind the door gradually lost its tension. After a pause, footsteps scuffled softly to the door. The knob turned and the same watery eye appeared in the crack—this time at the height of my shoulder.

"You a friend of little Kathy's?"

The old woman's clean silver hair was pulled back neatly behind her head. Her simple dress hung from birdlike limbs. But her blue eyes were bright and canny, and her expression showed concern now, rather than fear.

"That's right," I said. "She and I are friends."

"Is she well? There were such a terrible row, and then her father…"

"She's safe."

Nodding, she looked me up and down. "You don't look like a Peeler. Don't look like no bludger, neither." She glanced up and down the hall. "All right, then," she said, motioning me inside. She gestured toward a settee that had seen better days. The same could be said for the rest of the flat, though, in contrast to Backer's domicile, everything was clean and well cared for. The floors had been swept recently, and a modest coal fire burned in the grate.

"Did that other bloke send you, then?" the old woman asked. She locked the door behind herself before sitting slowly, painfully down onto a spindly chair.

"What other bloke?"

"That one wot were here yesterday. First the police, then him—a great, tall scarecrow of a man in a Scottish coat and deer-huntin' cap, of all things. Odd fellow, but a real gentleman."

"St. Andrews?" I asked.

She smiled, and a twinkle danced in her eye. I could imagine St. Andrews would have that effect on the lace-doily set. "That were his name, yes. Right charming he were. I imagine he has to fight the ladies off every time he leaves the house. You know him, then?"

"You might say we're working together. After a fashion."

Her smile widened. "Ain't that nice? I'm Mrs. Whitby, by the way." She extended her hand.

"Mr. Adler," I said, clasping it gently. Beneath the cool, dry skin, the bones felt thin and brittle.

"Only I'm sorry I prolly can't tell you nuffin' you don't already know, Mr. Adler."

"Why don't you try? Sometimes repeating the story stirs up memories you thought you'd forgotten."

She considered me for a moment, then said, "All right. Like I told Mr. St. Andrews, I didn't see nuffin'. That hole in the wall, that were from the fight. I didn't see nuffin', but I heard it all right."

"Who was it? A man? A woman?"

"A man. And a big one at that. Heavy footsteps. Rough voice. Didn't talk nice—not like you and that Mr. St. Andrews."

"What were they fighting about?" I asked.

She cocked her head. "Couldn't rightly say. I'm a bit hard of hearin'. They was angry, but I couldn't make out the words. Old age ain't no picnic. Only do you know, it just occurred to me. They must've known each other, 'cause when the other man knocked, Mr. Backer let him right in."

"And this was approximately what time?" I asked.

"Exactly two and a half hours after little Kathy left wiv' her friend."

That would be me.

Mrs. Whitby nodded toward the clock on the mantel. "Time passes so slowly when you're my age. I must look at that clock a thousand times a day." She sighed. "She'd been gone at least a year before that, had Kathy. She and her da always rowed somefin' terrible. Don't know why she'd go back there, but she did, and they was at it again. Then she left wiv' her friend. It were quiet for two and a half hours exactly before the other man come. They was civil enough when Backer let him in, but soon they started arguin', then shoutin', and then they was tossin' each other about like barroom brawlers."

I leaned back against the settee and crossed my arms. Mrs. Whitby's recollections, along with the aftermath of the fight that I'd found in Backer's apartment, underscored Jack's innocence. Interestingly, they also suggested that Goddard had been telling the truth about his own lack of involvement. This hadn't been an execution. There'd been no quiet knife to the throat, no elegant garrote. Not even a pistol shot in the night. Backer had died in a fight—a loud, messy, conspicuous fight. And I knew for a fact that if any of Goddard's assassins had undertaken his work in such a sloppy, risky, manner, Goddard wouldn't have hesitated to dispatch him as well.

All of which was fine and good for Jack, for myself, and for Goddard. Perhaps I should have been satisfied with that. The question was, would it satisfy St. Andrews?

"Did you know Mr. Backer well?" I asked.

"Not to talk to. He weren't much for talk. Sometimes I watched his little Kathy when she were younger. But we wasn't friendly like, Mr. Backer an' me. Always felt sorry for that Kathy, wiv' her mother gone and all."

"How did Mr. Backer get on with the other neighbors? Were there any longstanding arguments you were aware of?"

"If there were, they kept it to themselves." She shrugged, smoothing her skirt over her knees. Then she looked up, a sly look crossing her features. "'Course...well...it were prolly nuffin'...'"

"Go on," I said, smiling as if in anticipation of a juicy piece of gossip. She returned my smile with a confidential smirk of her own. "Only a few weeks back, it seemed he come into some money. And he weren't so very modest wiv' it, if you know wot I mean."

"Splashing it around, was he?"

"A new silk hat!" She crowed. "Then the next day some boots. Then a few days after that, a great heavy walkin' stick wiv' a brass lion's head on it, and I could swear that lion had *ruby eyes*. An' I remember finkin', *I wonder where he got the money*."

The money had come from Goddard, I'd have wagered, in the course of whatever business they'd been doing at the sugar refinery. And the message of Goddard's bouquet had included a rebuke for indiscretion. The showy cane was certainly the mark of an indiscreet character.

But where had the cane gone? I'd put a new hat on Jack's head before I'd led him out the door, and I'd given him the boots. But a brass-headed cane...I hadn't seen that either time I'd been in the flat. Ruby eyes or not, such a cane was valuable. Could the motive for the killing have been robbery? *Where is it, you little minx?* Backer had shouted. The only thing Jack had taken was the railway map. Surely no one would get so enraged over a penny map. Backer had to have been talking about the cane. Had it been stolen before Jack arrived? And did any of it have to do with the fight Mrs. Whitby overheard?

"Have you noticed anything else recently, Mrs. Whitby? Anything at all? Perhaps another of your neighbors also coming into money?" A cane like that would be cash in someone's pocket. I made a note to check the pawnshops.

Mrs. Whitby cocked her head and thought about it. "No, I can't say that I have. And that's exactly what I told your Mr. St. Andrews, and the police as well. Now." Standing, she smiled. "Would you care for a spot of tea, dear?"

I very much would have cared for one, but I didn't want to take advantage of what would surely have been an extravagant gesture for a person of Mrs. Whitby's means.

"Thank you, but I must be going. Before I do, though, I was hoping to talk to your neighbor, Mr. Geary. Do you know if he's at home?"

"Oh, well, I'm not sure now. Don't have too much to do with that one meself. I've seen him now and then, skulkin' around, but I've never had cause to exchange words with the man."

"All right, thank you. Good day."

I stood in the hallway for a moment after taking my leave. I really ought to speak to Mr. Geary. He might not have been connected to Backer's murder, but he was connected to Backer. What's more, he'd been leaving his flat when I'd come to deliver Goddard's flowers, and when he saw where I'd been heading, he'd ducked back inside. I wondered if Geary had been the one Mrs. Whitby had overheard arguing with Backer. They knew each other, and if Backer had dismissed him, Geary had cause to quarrel with him. It looked suspicious, but even if it wasn't, he might have heard or seen something of the argument that resulted in Backer's death.

I knocked on the door of Geary's flat. Nobody answered, and if anyone were inside, they were keeping silent and still. I knocked again. After another few moments of silence, I fingered my picklocks. Then I thought better of it. What on earth was I hoping to find there? And how would I explain my presence to Geary—or worse, to the police—if he walked in before I left? No—much better to come back and try to catch the man at home. Letting my picks drop back to the bottom of my pocket, I turned on my heel and walked toward the stairs.

CHAPTER NINETEEN

After a well-deserved afternoon of slumber in the lumpy, sprung paradise that was my own bed, I arrived at the Criterion at nine o'clock sharp. I'd washed, dabbed on a bit of cologne, thinned out my beard as best as I could with my razor, and put on my very best clothes. It wasn't that I was hoping to impress St. Andrews—or anyone at all, really. But over the years I'd found that when one is feeling downtrodden, dressing to the teeth can be remarkably uplifting.

The American Bar, one of the Criterion's many different-themed dining rooms, was already abuzz with sharp-looking young men in expensive clothing. I was wearing my silk shirt, my most colorful waistcoat, my most fashionably cut trousers, and my one and only frock coat. Nonetheless, despite garnering a few interested flicks of the eye, I felt underdressed and out of place. Piccadilly had been too high-toned for me in my younger years. One who sleeps in doorways isn't welcome in these busy halls of brass, etched glass, and polished wood. Neither had I come here when I'd been the recipient of Goddard's lavish attentions. The Criterion in general, and the American Bar in specific, was the unspoken haunt of men who preferred the company of men. And such places were anathema to Goddard, whose discretion bordered on the pathological. It went without saying that most of the diners that night spent more on cologne than I did on rent. I was used to that. The galling thing was how much younger they seemed.

I ordered a glass of Islay malt at the bar. St. Andrews hadn't arrived yet, but he did have a running account, as I'd suspected he would. Leaning against the smooth wood, I scanned the crowd for any sign of a familiar face.

"Sir?" The bartender handed the glass toward me through a thicket of well-groomed heads and shoulders.

"Thank you. Oh, pardon me," I said, as my arm brushed that of a young man in a dark-green frock coat and clover-colored cravat.

"Nothing to pardon," he said with a flirtatious glance from beneath his eyelashes. He looked me over unabashedly. "Absolutely nothing." His features were appealing—pointed nose and chin, a heart-shaped face with well-defined cheekbones, and a mouth that curved on the perpetual verge of laughter. He was clean-shaven and had a mop of blond curls. A charming little leprechaun. "Don't tell me you're here alone."

"Quite alone, I'm afraid."

"What a crime."

I returned his smile but my own hid nervousness. I was out of my element. Pleasantly. Though part of me knew it was only a matter of time before something gave away the fact that I didn't actually belong there.

"Mr. Adler!" St. Andrews's voice boomed from the doorway.

And there it was.

"Blast," I muttered. I turned to my would-be companion. "Forgive me."

"Another time, perhaps."

"With any luck."

St. Andrews was waving me over to a table, where two breadbasket-bearing waiters were elbowing each other out of the way to get there first. In addition to being a regular, I'd wager St. Andrews was also generous with the gratuities. The taller waiter reached the table first and set down his basket, while the shorter took the consolation prize of pulling out my chair.

"Now, then, my good man," St. Andrews said, waving away the proffered menus. "We'll start with the consommé. Then two steaks, medium rare." He looked at me, as if suddenly remembering that I, myself, might have something to say about my own dinner. "Forgive me, Mr. Adler. You really must try the steaks."

"I defer to your expertise."

While St. Andrews chose a wine and ordered the rest of the meal, I watched the white-jacketed bartender mix drinks in tumblers with ice, an impressive wall of varicolored bottles behind him. It was a show in itself, as was the grill where the kitchen staff slaved over thick slabs of sizzling beef, with only a large sheet of transparent glass between them and the dining room.

"Thank you for supper," I said preemptively.

"I consider it a business expense. You do intend to pay me once I find your killer?" He laughed at my expression. "Don't worry, Mr. Adler. You were exactly right about my 'Irregulars' turning up business. I have so many new cases—all relatively small and inconsequential, but one has to start somewhere—I hardly have time to breathe! Settling your case will be my way of saying thank you."

"Yes," I said, with a distinct lack of enthusiasm.

St. Andrews cocked his head. "You do still want me to find Mr. Backer's killer?"

"About that..."

At that moment the consommé arrived in two steaming bowls. All thoughts fled my mind in the presence of the rich, peppery broth. I tucked in as if I hadn't eaten in days. In the embarrassingly short time between the first spoonful and the last, the soup thawed me from the inside out and left me feeling a bit more optimistic. St. Andrews enjoyed his grub with the infectious enthusiasm with which he seemed to approach everything. He must have been a phenomenal lover—or at least a very exuberant one.

"You'll be happy to know," St. Andrews said, the moment his mouth and bowl were empty, "that in addition to clearing your name in the unpleasant matter that brought us together, I've come up with some promising leads."

As he went on, my pulse began to race. St. Andrews had spoken to Mrs. Whitby. It was possible he'd viewed the wreckage in Backer's flat. But had he done any research that might have led him to connect Backer's death with the explosion at the other refinery?

And would he find reason—or an excuse—to connect either crime to Goddard?

"While you were home sleeping off your troubles, I tracked the unfortunate corpse to St. Bride's. They do the paupers' burial every Wednesday, so I had to act quickly if I wanted to look at the body."

"And?"

St. Andrews's expression went grim. "He died in battle, Mr. Adler. A long, violent struggle. He'd been brutally beaten, and seeing how big he was, I'd imagine his assailant didn't come away unscathed, either."

"That fits with my own observations," I said, though I hadn't thought about the injuries the victor might have sustained. I should have asked Mrs. Whitby if she'd seen anyone walking about who looked like they'd been in a fight. "Do you think the assailant would have been hurt badly enough to seek help at a clinic?"

"My 'Irregulars' are looking into that. Though I'm not sure they'll turn up anything of use. The clinics patch up a lot of brawlers toward the end of the week."

"Perhaps not so many on a Sunday night, though," I said.

"That's true."

"So that rules out Backer's daughter completely."

"Oh, I should think so."

"What do the police say?"

"She was never a serious suspect, for that reason," St. Andrews said. "They wanted to talk to her to see if she would admit to hiring you to do the job. But thanks to me, you're also in the clear. No, what I suspect, and what I told the police, is that something larger is going on here."

"But—"

"Ah, the meat! Bring it here, my fine fellow!"

The steaks were gorgeous, and so big I was surprised it hadn't taken two waiters to carry each one. But my appetite had fled. He could have meant only one thing by "something larger." He'd somehow connected the two refinery deaths and come up with Goddard. Which shouldn't have bothered me, all things considered, except that I was pretty certain Backer hadn't actually met his end at Goddard's command.

Across the table, St. Andrews tore into his steak with lusty ferocity.

"Fantastic!" he cried, washing down his mouthful with a slug of wine. "Mr. Adler, you must try it!"

"I'd rather hear what you've discovered," I said.

"Oh, very well." He chewed thoughtfully. "I was a little worried how you would take this. I know you're no longer living at York Street, and though I'd never pry regarding the reasons for your move, I imagine that..."

I closed my eyes. When I opened them again, he still hadn't arrived at the point.

"The truth is, Mr. Adler, I've been keeping an eye on Dr. Goddard's business. Never interfering. Goodness knows, I don't want a war with the man. But old habits die hard, and, well, frankly, someone should—"

"Mr. St. Andrews," I said through clenched teeth.

"Yes, well, last week I came across a report concerning the death of another refinery worker, a Rudolf Lothar, just before poor Mr. Backer. Lothar was a manager at the factory on Flower and Dean Street."

"I heard about that. The boiler exploded or something."

"As boilers do, I know. But don't you find it odd that two refinery workers, a foreman and a manager, died within a week of one another?"

"The explosion was an accident."

"That's what the police believe. But my observations led me to a different conclusion. I think the two men were working together with Goddard. I'd seen that man of his, that ginger-haired chap, lurking near Backer's factory before. And I spied him poking about the place on Flower and Dean Street just after the explosion."

Yes, I almost said. *They were working together. Goddard told me that himself, about an hour before he pushed me up against a wall in that wretched alley off Fleet Street.* I wanted to suggest he tell me something I hadn't figured out myself. At the same time I was terrified he would.

St. Andrews continued. "Actually, I thought you were in on it, seeing as how Goddard had approached your landlord about purchasing the Turnbull House building."

"What?"

The room, at that moment, paused in one of those rare, spontaneous occurrences of unanimous silence, leaving the word to clatter, alone, to the glazed tile floor. St. Andrews smiled mildly.

"You didn't know about that?"

The dining-room sounds resumed—a soft, cautious crescendo of silver and china—while I scrambled to collect my thoughts. The group at the next table pointedly looked away.

"Well, your reaction is certainly consistent with that of an innocent man," St. Andrews said with shrug.

"Thank you ever so much."

My head reeled. Goddard had been the mysterious factory owner for whose sake Mr. Porter had been willing to throw us out on our ear? The same Goddard who had counseled me to find a way for Turnbull House to become self-sufficient? The same Goddard who had happily lent me an unfathomable sum to *buy the building myself*, then proceeded to woo me back into his bed, no doubt laughing behind my back the entire time?

"Mr. Adler, you're gripping your knife so tightly, I fear for the silver."

I let the knife drop.

"It's a rather grand scheme just to draw you back into his circle, if that's what he was trying to do. Though, knowing him as we both do, I'd imagine he'd been working on the refinery project for some time and only later saw the opportunity to bring you into it."

"Have you any idea what he was working on?" I asked numbly.

Goddard could have had his pick of buildings in the area. The only reason to have chosen Turnbull House was because of its connection to me. If I'd had any doubt after the alley that Goddard and I were well and truly finished, this would have settled it. Yes, between the refinery workers and his conversation with Sudworth—*factory...centrifuge...chloroform*—it was clear that he was embarking upon some large industrial endeavor. Part of me wanted to run as far away from it as I possibly could. Another part was incapable of turning away.

"Are you well?" St. Andrews asked.

"No." I drained my wineglass. St. Andrews refilled it, and I drained it again.

"Are you planning to eat your steak?"

I pushed my plate away and watched as, his face lighting up with pleasure, he deftly scooted his own empty plate beneath my untouched one. I scoffed in revulsion. Only a true aristocrat could undertake such a staggering breach of etiquette, in public, as if it were nothing at all. I wondered if he next intended to trim his toenails onto my bread plate.

"As for your question, I've no clue what Goddard might be planning. But we can be reasonably certain it involves some sort of chemical process. This is why he sought out the expertise of the two sugar refiners. Mr. Adler, do you know how sugar is made?"

"No." As he sliced into my dinner my stomach began to grumble.

"Neither did I, until I began to talk to the refinery workers. Raw liquid sugar is extracted from stalks of sugar cane. After that, they add different chemicals and centrifuge away the impurities. They do this numerous times, each time resulting in a purer—"

"Centrifuge?" I interrupted.

St. Andrews and I locked eyes. "Does that mean something to you, Mr. Adler?"

"Yes." How much to reveal? It was a little too late to be worrying about that now, though, wasn't it? In for a penny and all that. "Last night I overheard a conversation between Goddard and Rupert Sudworth. A centrifuge was involved."

"Mmm. Goddard and Sudworth. Now there's a nasty combination. You were with Goddard last night, you say?"

Yes. No. In a manner of speaking. Ugh.

"I was having supper. He and Sudworth were at the bar. I only caught bits and snatches, but I definitely heard the words 'centrifuge' and 'chloroform.'"

"Chloroform." He mused. "That's not used in sugar production."

"What is it?"

"Hospitals use it as an anesthetic, especially in childbirth. Tim Lazarus has been quite critical of the practice. Very toxic, apparently. Easy to overdose the patient. I can't fathom what its industrial applications might be, though."

"Perhaps the good doctor might have an insight," I said. "I'll ask him tomorrow."

St. Andrews was plowing through my steak with industrial efficiency. Bite by bite, I watched it disappear down his gullet. He seemed so guileless just then. But I knew how deceptive appearances could be. His jovial exterior hid a fierce intellect and, until recently, an equally fierce grudge. He was, as we all are, perfectly capable of deceit.

"Just out of curiosity," I said, running a finger over the silver knife handle. "When you said Goddard had approached Mr. Porter about buying the Turnbull House building—how did you know it was him? Mr. Porter told me he was under strictest orders to keep the identity of the buyer a secret."

St. Andrews's smile was tinged with pity. "Your Mr. Porter was, I believe, instructed to keep the name of the business secret from anyone associated with Turnbull House. However, with a small bribe and copious assurances, I—a person with no connection to the shelter whatsoever—was able to ascertain the name of the business. Does the name Mephistopheles Enterprises mean anything to you?"

I hung my head.

St. Andrews shrugged. "Shall we return to the subject of Mr. Backer's untimely demise?"

"Please."

"The thing of it is, although I'm certain the victims of the deaths are connected—connected by Goddard—I'm not at all convinced that he's responsible for their deaths."

"You must be disappointed."

"Very funny, Mr. Adler. Holding a grudge is bad for the digestion." He popped the last bit of my steak into his mouth, savoring it for a moment. "I examined the victim's flat with the police. It was clearly not the scene of an execution."

"Yes. That was my conclusion as well."

He paused. "Checking up on my work?"

"I wanted to be certain I was getting my money's worth. You spoke to Mrs. Whitby. What do you think of robbery as a motive? I can account for Backer's new hat and boots, but she said he had a fancy new cane. I didn't see it amongst his things. It sounded like a very valuable object. Not to mention something with which one could deliver a sound beating."

St. Andrews nodded slowly. "It's possible, it's possible."

"I'd really like to speak to the neighbor, Mr. Geary."

"Who?" St. Andrews asked.

I chuckled. "Ah, so the great detective missed a clue? Mr. Geary is another neighbor. He worked with Backer at the refinery for a while but is currently unemployed. My theory is that Backer, being the foreman, dismissed Geary for some reason—which would have been bad enough. But according to Mrs. Whitby—"

"Let me guess. Backer was prancing about, rubbing Geary's nose in his sudden windfall. Yes, I could see how that would provoke an argument—a violent argument, if Geary was desperate enough. I agree. One of us should speak to him."

"If we can locate him. For someone who supposedly spends his days lurking about that corridor, he's proved remarkably hard to find."

"Drinking away his sorrows, perhaps?" St. Andrews suggested. "An early morning visit might be just the thing. I'll see to it myself tomorrow. In the meantime, I've had a brainstorm. As long as you're checking up on my work, do you have further plans tonight, or would you be up for a spot of housebreaking?"

CHAPTER TWENTY

I first came here a few days ago, after it occurred to me that the two refinery deaths might be related," St. Andrews said as his carriage pulled to a stop on Flower and Dean Street, near the sugarhouse where Rudolf Lothar had met his untimely end.

We stepped out of the carriage into an eerie and silent darkness. It had been several days since the explosion, but the tenants hadn't yet been allowed to return to the surrounding buildings, and the factory would likely remain shuttered until someone tore it down. The refinery occupied almost an entire side of the street, and the explosion and subsequent fire had destroyed fully half of it. If I covered one eye, the untouched brick walls and smokestack on the right side gave the impression that workers would be streaming back in the very next morning. Covering the other eye, I saw by moonlight a black crater plunging down two stories and surrounded by charred rubble and the jagged remains of walls.

"The papers speculate that the sugar dust in the air made the explosion so violent," St. Andrews said as we approached the pit. "You can see for yourself that it started in the basement. That's where they do the melting and refining. It's incredibly hot and not at all well ventilated. Well, not before the explosion, anyway."

"Sugar dust?" I asked.

"Once they bleach and dry the raw sugar, they put it in piles— huge piles, all the way up to the ceiling—until it can be packed for market. That basement had to have been filled with dust."

"They pile it *on the floor?*" My thoughts turned immediately to rats, insects, and the street-filth brought inside on the soles of workers' boots. "I'll take my tea without from now on."

"A wise course of action in any event. But I suggest we keep our eyes open for things that *don't* belong in a sugar refinery—things which might give us a clue about what Lothar, Backer, and Goddard were doing."

I nodded. "Chloroform. A centrifuge. That's what Goddard told Sudworth. Weird residues, maybe. Chemicals."

"Assuming their little project even caused the explosion," he said.

"It happened late at night. No one should have been running machinery at that time."

"All the same, the blast destroyed half the building. I shouldn't put my hopes up too high. How do you propose we make our way down?"

That was a good question. I glanced over the vertiginous drop just inches from my toes and began to sway. St. Andrews closed a hand around my shoulder and pulled me back a step.

"Perhaps we should let ourselves in through the back entrance. If I remember correctly, the blast may not have affected one of the central staircases."

I followed him around the remains of the walls to the outbuilding attached to the rear of the refinery. The door was chained shut and secured with a stout padlock.

"Don't suppose you have a match," I said, feeling for my picklocks.

St. Andrews grinned. "Never fear. I came prepared."

Of course he had. Because one cannot flit about in a deerstalker cap and Inverness cape without also carrying a mahogany-and-porcelain calabash pipe and its associated accessories. Fortunately for both of us, the pipe wasn't just an affectation. Putting the stem between his teeth for safekeeping, St. Andrews lit a match and held it while I addressed myself to the padlock securing the door.

The lock looked stronger than it was, but I popped it on the first try, then eased the chains down quietly and let us inside. A lantern hung on the wall inside near the door. I took it down and lit it. The flame flickered to life, casting a dim glow onto walls black and sticky with sugary residue. Even after five days, the air was clammy and sweet, and smelt of damp, chemicals, and char.

"Are those icicles?" I asked, raising the lantern toward the sharp stalactites hanging from the blackened ceiling beams.

"Sugar," St. Andrews said. "Though I shouldn't break it off and eat it, if I were you."

We passed a great copper cauldron so large it required a ladder to peer over the top, then walked into the narrow, low-roofed passage that led to the main building. The walls and ceiling of the passage were covered in coils, ducts, springs, and sprockets—mysterious machinery now still, which looked vaguely sinister by lantern light. I tickled open the lock securing the main building, and we tiptoed inside.

"Look over there," St. Andrews said, pointing to the great yawning gap through which I could see the moonlight straining against clouds. "You can see where the flames came up through the floor."

I moved the lantern in the direction he indicated and saw, indeed, that the blast had forced its way up through the floorboards, leaving a gaping, splintering hole that extended over one-third of the floor. Scorch marks blackened what remained of the adjacent walls. St. Andrews pointed toward the staircase at the far end of the room.

"The melting pans are downstairs, along with the boilers and centrifuges. That's where all the truly nasty work takes place."

"You seem to know your way around," I remarked.

He tipped his deerstalker cap. "Research, Mr. Adler. Now mind your way on the stairs."

The minute I entered the stairwell, I understood what he meant. My toe slipped on slick, sugar-encrusted wood. I nearly dropped the lantern in my haste to grab the handrail, which was likewise covered in a tacky black residue. Regaining my footing, I started slowly down, the crystallized deposits crunching under my boot heels.

"Careful of your—"

"Ouch!" I cried as my head struck one of the low ceiling beams. The beam was nearly twice as big around as the others and heavy with black deposits.

"Hardbake," St. Andrews explained. "Highly flammable."

"How can anyone stand to work under these conditions?"

St. Andrews shrugged. "They're paid in beer. No, really," he said in response to my incredulous stare. "The wages are low, the work backbreaking, and the hours unconscionable. But the laborers are provided with all the beer they can drink. It keeps them from passing out in the extreme heat. It also keeps them from complaining too bitterly."

"They'd have to pay me in Islay malt," I muttered.

At the bottom of the staircase, the lantern light outlined two enormous metal vats, which had toppled over in the blast. The metal was blackened and dented, the glass fronts of the pressure gauges shattered, and the spigot on the side of one of the vats had been wrenched away. The lids that had covered the vats lay half buried in dark, hardened mounds of what I assumed had once been piles of market-ready sugar. A rat scurried along the edges of the mess—which had melted in the blast and recrystallized around the debris—and stopped to sniff.

"Remember the hardbake on the ceiling beams?" St. Andrews said, noting my revulsion. "In some factories they scrape that off, filter it through charcoal, and sell it as well."

We both flinched when a door slammed overhead.

"Just the wind," St. Andrews said. He glanced over his shoulder. "Probably."

"You don't sound convinced."

"Let's take a closer look at the explosion site."

St. Andrews strode off into the sea of broken, charred beams and twisted metal. I pointed the lantern after him and scrambled through the rubbish to catch up. Someone had cleared a path—probably the firemen, when they'd retrieved Lothar's body. The cold night air seeped down from the hole in the ceiling. I glanced up to see the sulfurous clouds that sat over the city now backlit by the moon.

"This was where Lothar's body was found," I said as we emerged from the rubble into an area conspicuously cleared of wreckage. "I was passing by when they brought him out."

St. Andrews turned to me. "Passing by?"

"I was in the neighborhood."

He narrowed his eyes but apparently decided it wasn't worth pursuing. Instead, he said, "The newspapers reported several firemen succumbing to some sort of fumes."

"Yes," I said. "I saw that as well. I remember the distinct smell of grass."

"Grass?"

"Freshly cut grass. It did strike me as odd, but I didn't think much of it at the time. I had a lot on my mind right then."

I set the lantern on top of an overturned cauldron. We picked through the jagged bits and bobs, the rain-soaked pieces of charred wood, but between the dim light and our lack of knowledge of the machinery, it was impossible to tell what we were even looking at. The grass smell was gone. Now it all smelled of burnt metal, charred sugar, and wet ashes. A few moments later, my fingers found a twisted fragment of metal that might once have been a bowl of some kind.

"Part of a centrifuge, maybe?"

The outside of the dish was blackened by heat. The inside was crusted with the scorched remains of some liquid. St. Andrews came over and took the fragment gingerly between two gloved fingertips. He held it up into the dim light of the lantern, then turned to me.

"If it was, it would have been too small for production on the scale of what goes on in this factory."

"Which is exactly what we should be looking for, if Goddard, Lothar, and Backer were working on some chemical process. They'd work on a small scale until they had it right."

St. Andrews nodded appreciatively. "That's true. Let's find the rest of it, then." While he picked through the piles, I scraped a fingernail over the surface of the bowl, scratching a line through a black, crystalline residue. "There's something burnt onto here."

"Don't touch it," St. Andrews called over his shoulder. I quickly wiped my fingers on my coat. Suddenly he stopped and stared at something in the mess, practically quivering like a retriever. "What's this?" He snaked a long arm toward the debris and carefully teased out several pieces of glass held together by a paper label. "Ac2O," he read.

"What the devil is that?"

"I don't know. I'm no chemist. From the size of the label, I'd say at one point there was a lot of it, though."

Another crash from above. A creak.

"Could be the building settling," St. Andrews said.

"Or someone coming to clear up evidence. Let's get out of here. We'll ask Lazarus our chemistry questions in the morning."

We moved, quickly and quietly, back through the mountains of ruined equipment toward the sugar-slick stairs. I paused at the bottom, raising my lantern.

"Anything?" St. Andrews whispered.

"I can't tell."

We crept slowly up the stairs, mindful of the sagging, encrusted beams and hearing every crunch and creak as if it were amplified a thousand times. By the time we reached the top, my every muscle was taut with expectation, and my palms were sticky and black with sugar. Stepping out onto the landing, I glanced toward the back door. A sudden gust of wind lifted it on its hinges and slammed it against the outside wall. I nearly laughed with relief.

"Well, looks like you were ri—"

The brass head of the cane swung out of the darkness so quickly, it barely registered on a conscious level before my right arm circled up to block it. Not the first time Goddard's fighting-arts training had saved me. The cane was heavy—almost a club—and had been swung with great force—force that sent my attacker staggering when I redirected it. Unfortunately, it also sent the encrusted centrifuge fragment clattering back over my shoulder and down the stairs.

"It's Geary!" I jumped aside. What was he *doing* there? Clearing up evidence? Or perhaps searching for something Lothar might have left behind?

Geary regained his footing and turned back toward me. St. Andrews emerged at the mouth of the stairwell. A truly useful person would circle around behind Geary at that point. Unfortunately, I'd no idea how useful St. Andrews was in a fight. He was tall and vigorous, yet soft in a way that suggested the most lethal thing he'd ever wielded was a strongly worded letter.

Geary launched himself at me again.

I've never enjoyed fighting and had avoided whenever I could the fighting-arts practices Goddard had held at the sports hall for his most trusted employees. However, I couldn't deny how useful that training had proved on several occasions since then, nor that this would likely be another.

As Geary brought the brass lion's head down toward my head, I caught a glimpse of missing teeth and a nose that had been broken more than once. Souvenirs from his fight with Backer, I surmised. I blocked the cane with my lantern arm and managed a jab to his ribs before the lantern flew from my grip. Geary doubled over, and I darted back into the shadows. Off to the side the lantern crashed to the floor near the staircase. For a split second the flames danced on a mound of crystallized sugar residue and then shot up one wall with a *whoosh*.

"St. Andrews!" I shouted.

I couldn't see him. Where was he? The flames circled the entrance to the stairwell, casting the entire room in hellish shadows. Someone cried out. I whirled just in time to see St. Andrews burst out of the flames and leap onto Geary's back. It would have been funny—St. Andrews, so tall and gawky, riding the ox-bodied Geary like a jockey—if the sugar-encrusted staircase weren't now absolutely engulfed in fire.

"We've got to get out of here!" I shouted. "This whole place is about to go up!" Geary was spinning around wildly, while St. Andrews dodged blows from the cane. "Now!" I cried.

Geary ran backward, ramming St. Andrews as hard as he could into one of the scorched walls. After a loud crack, something large and heavy fell across St. Andrews's back, crushing them both to the floor like insects.

"St. Andrews!" As I rushed across the floor, the flames licked out from the staircase, tasting the residue that coated the wall above. Smoke tinged the air and burned my eyes and throat.

"I'm unhurt, Mr. Adler, but I'll need your help."

The beam lay across St. Andrews's side, and he himself lay across Geary, holding him fast between those long legs of his. He claimed to be uninjured, but the beam was heavy, even though the earlier fire and the intervening days of rain had weakened it. He winced as Geary thrashed against his grip. Geary's right side appeared intact, but his left arm was pinned at an unnatural angle beneath the beam, and he, too, looked to be in pain.

"Let me go," Geary growled as I drew near. He lashed out at my ankle with the cane. I jumped over it, landed, then jumped again as he tried to sweep my feet out from under me.

"The beam fell across his shoulder," St. Andrews said. "I'd put money on a dislocation, or even a break."

"Too bad it didn't break his neck," I muttered as I stepped to the side to avoid the cane once again.

"I'll break your neck!" Geary swung the cane again, hard, crying out as his body twisted against his pinned arm.

I stepped down on the cane and wrested it from his grip. Giving him a warning look, I knelt. Even in the fire's orange light, Geary's skin looked pale, and he was gritting his teeth. Up close, St. Andrews didn't look so well himself. He was trying to hide how much the weight of the beam was hurting him. I'd have put my own money on at least one broken rib.

"What are you doing here, anyway?" I asked Geary as I tested the weight of the beam. Heavy. Very heavy. "You worked at the refinery on Osborn Street, not this one."

"Don't have to tell you nuffin'."

"Clearing up evidence? Or perhaps trying to find out what your former foreman was up to?"

He glared.

"Suit yourself. You can explain it to the police."

St. Andrews's eyes, bright in the light of the flames, followed me as I stood and stepped around the other side of the beam, tapping the cane thoughtfully on the ground. Though the beam was bloated and cracked, it had been part of a load-bearing ceiling support. St. Andrews and Geary were very lucky indeed.

Tucking the cane under my arm, I tried to lift the broken, splintering end of the beam. St. Andrews sucked in a painful breath. "All right?" I asked, my arms already beginning to tremble under the weight. He nodded. I stepped to the side, trying to shift the beam, but even in its current state, it was impossibly heavy. "Can you roll out from under it?"

"I don't want to let him go, Mr. Adler."

"If he moves, I'll drop it on his head. Hurry. I don't know how much longer I can hold it." The air was getting hotter by the minute and burned as it went down. I took quick, shallow breaths, which left me a little light-headed. The room blurred as stinging wetness filled my eyes. "Anytime you're ready, Mr. St. Andrews," I said through clenched teeth.

St. Andrews kicked himself free of Geary and rolled out of the way. At that moment, the air shook with a tremendous wooden crack. I jumped, and the beam slipped from my fingers. Geary screamed.

"Sorry."

The beam had fallen hard across his knees. Looking around frantically, Geary tried to push himself up on his good arm, but his hand kept slipping on the sugar-slick floor. St. Andrews staggered to his feet, a determined look on his face. A thick, ominous smoke had begun to billow from the staircase.

"I thought you said you were unhurt," I said.

"In a relative sense, Mr. Adler. Now let's help him up."

I glanced at Geary. "Perhaps we should just leave him."

"You're joking, I hope. It's not funny."

A line of flame darted across the ceiling, eliciting a series of wooden pops and cracks.

"For God's sake, help me!" Geary cried.

"Like you helped Backer?" I snapped. "He had a daughter, you know."

Where had that come from? I'd have happily left Backer to die in a burning building myself, after witnessing how he'd treated

Jack. And yet the thought of someone killing Jack's remaining family made my blood boil.

"I didn't mean to…" Geary's words disappeared into a racking cough. "I just meant to teach him a lesson." He paused to breathe, wincing. "Prancin' about wiv' his new hat and cane after givin' me the sack. Didn't want no English workin' under him once he got to be foreman." A metallic groan cut through the air. Geary looked at me wide-eyed. "But I didn't mean to kill him! You can't leave me here!"

When all was said and done, I doubted I'd have been able to abandon a man—even a killer—to die in a hell of sugar, flame, and smoke. At the same time, St. Andrews was wobbling around, hugging himself as if his insides might spill out, and I wasn't convinced I'd be able to support both of them for more than a few steps.

"You killed Backer, and you'd have killed us, too," I said.

St. Andrews's hand came down on my shoulder. His voice was tired but rang with truth. "And if we leave him, Mr. Adler, we'll be murderers as well. Stop wasting time and help him."

I glared, but he was right. "Fine. Give me a hand, then."

Working together, we managed to roll the beam away and raise Geary to his feet. His right leg was injured, but I doubted it was broken. The way he held his left arm, though, appeared rather abnormal, and his shoulder looked as if it had been torn away and carelessly replaced. Together we shambled, slowly and painfully, toward the back door and through the outbuilding. Finally we collapsed against the back wall—filthy, sticky, and gulping greedy mouthfuls of the cold night air.

"This man needs a doctor," St. Andrews said, coughing out a lungful of smoke and ash. He hissed a painful breath, clutching again at his side. In the light of the moon, I could see Geary had gone pale and his teeth were chattering.

"I suppose you'll want to send for the fire brigade as well," I said.

"Of course."

"They'll ask what we were doing here."

St. Andrews shot me an exasperated look. "We were on our way home from supper. We saw the flames. Neither of those is a lie."

I snorted. "Who knew the Holmes of St. John's Wood was also a master prevaricator?"

"Must be your influence. Now let's go find my hansom. The driver will take you and Geary to Lazarus's clinic. I'll fetch the fire brigade." He winced again.

"On foot? You won't make it three blocks." He opened his mouth to protest. I cut him off. "We can all fit in the hansom if I ride on the footboard. It won't take Lazarus more than a moment to bandage your ribs, give you a swallow of brandy, and then see to Jack the Tripper, here. No arguments," I said, as he visibly fortified himself for just that purpose. After a moment he swallowed painfully and nodded. I fixed Geary with a hard stare. He stared back but didn't fight.

As we struggled back into our tottering formation—St. Andrews on my right, Geary on my left—I grasped the brass-headed cane in my hand. It had cost a pretty penny, sure, but at the end of the day I was rather sure Jack would appreciate one last souvenir of his father.

Chapter Twenty-one

Lazarus's Stepney Street clinic was tucked into a tight little alley of mud and broken cobblestones half a mile northeast of Miller's Court, in the heart of Spitalfields. The clinic itself had been established some time ago under the New Poor Law, but had really come into its own once Lazarus had taken it over upon his return from Afghanistan. He'd been spending a lot less time there since establishing Turnbull House, though, and it showed in the broken window that had been sloppily boarded over instead of replaced, the splintering edges of the door, and the rubbish that had gathered near the step, which, at an earlier time, Lazarus would never have let remain.

Even before St. Andrews's two-seater pulled up to the curb, I could see that the windows were dark and the front door was padlocked shut. Two years ago, it would have been unthinkable, but that evening it made perfect sense. Lazarus was home fussing over Bess. Pearl, who would usually have kept the clinic open, was most likely at Turnbull House, where I should have been. No relief doctor had been available.

Once the two-seater stopped, I unfurled myself from my position on the footboard, where I'd wedged myself between St. Andrews's and Geary's feet and the horse's hindquarters, and turned around. The two men inside were quiet. Geary, who was cradling his arm against his chest, looked ready to pass out from pain. St. Andrews, seeing the situation as I did, looked alarmed.

"Don't panic," I said. "I may have another idea."

St. Andrews gave a long-suffering nod. Geary was pale and shivering. I wondered if I shouldn't just dump him off with the police and let them sort him out. At the same time, if I did, his injuries, whatever they were, would likely go unaddressed. Worse, St. Andrews would never let me hear the end of it.

"Sir?" the driver called.

I jammed my hands into my pockets. And then the answer came to me in a sharp jab of cardstock. I walked back behind the vehicle and motioned for the driver to lean down from his perch.

The card Dr. Doyle—Dr. Arthur Conan Doyle—had given me listed his address in South Norwood, more than an hour away. Fortunately for me, the good doctor had scribbled another address on the back—the room where he stayed when business kept him in town. It wasn't the best of all possible solutions, but it was the best I could do at a moment's notice. The clinic was closed, and the nearby hospital would ask too many questions.

Besides, I thought, sighting St. Andrews's ridiculous tweed cap through the back window of the hansom, even in his current state, St. Andrews would be over the moon to meet the creator of the character upon whom he attempted to model his life. It might even make up for the injuries he'd himself sustained while technically in my employ.

"Take us to the Langham Hotel," I said, as, in the distance, the great clock struck half-eleven. "Leave us off, then send the fire brigade to the sugarhouse on Flower and Dean Street as quickly as possible."

❖

When Dr. Doyle had handed me his card in Stoker's theatre, instructing me to call on him if I needed anything, I doubted he meant I should bring him an injured murderer in the middle of the night after breaking into and inadvertently setting fire to a sugar refinery. Less still, I'm sure, did he mean I was to bring him a second man who, though a good soul, dressed like Doyle's literary creation and styled himself "the Holmes of St. John's Wood." It took quite a bit of quick talking to make it past the doorman at the Langham, but in the end, I found myself standing on an immaculate Chinese-patterned runner in the quiet, softly lit hallway outside Doyle's room, while St. Andrews and Geary waited in the lobby, caked in sugar and ash, and trying not to bleed on the furniture.

"I'm so sorry to disturb you, Dr. Doyle," I said as he, clad in striped pajamas and a heavy dressing gown, blinked at me from the doorway of his elegantly understated room. "I'm not sure if you remember me, but—"

"Of course I remember you, Mr. Adler," he said, smiling to make up for the uncomfortable silence that had passed before he actually had. Then the smile turned rueful. "I also remember issuing generous, if ill-advised instructions to call on me at any time. Well, come in, I suppose. What can I do for you?"

"I need a doctor."

"I see. And the hospitals are closed?"

"Well..."

Sighing, he ushered me inside, closing the door behind me. He listened while I described my companions' injuries, kindly refraining from asking too many questions about how we had come to find ourselves wrestling and rolling about inside a burning sugarhouse. All the while he bustled from one end of the room to the other, tucking instruments into a well-made leather bag. Finally, he excused himself to the back room. When he emerged a short time later, he was properly clothed, and a hint of optimism had replaced his resigned expression. He'd even managed to comb that magnificent moustache of his.

"We'll go to my office," he said.

"I'm terribly sorry for the inconvenience."

"Nonsense. I'm happy for the opportunity to put my training to work."

"You can't mean that," I said. But from the new glint in his eye, I suspected that at some level he might have.

Taking his bowler and a heavy wool coat from their pegs by the door, Doyle motioned me out into the hall, then followed, locking the door behind him. When we reached the stairs, he handed me his hat and bag, and shrugged on his coat.

"Mr. Adler, it's been nearly a year since I opened my ophthalmological practice. In that time, well, let's just say I've had many, many hours to devote to my writing."

"A fact for which legions of Sherlock Holmes devotees are no doubt grateful," I replied, handing back the hat and bag.

His expression darkened. "Don't speak to me of Holmes. Lately I've been considering pushing the man off a cliff. He keeps my mind from more important things."

St. Andrews's tweed-topped visage danced in my mind's eye, and I suppressed a laugh. "I know someone who would beg to differ."

"Hmph." He screwed the bowler down onto his massive head. "I should very much like to meet someone other than my editor who believes that a handful of silly stories can be more important, or more needed, than a sound ophthalmological practice. Shall we?"

We descended the stairs in silence. When we emerged in the lobby, St. Andrews looked up from his chair by the door. Seeing Dr. Doyle, he rubbed his eyes, as if Doyle might be a trick of the gaslight. Realizing this was not the case, he scrambled to his feet. Geary glanced toward the door, as if calculating the likelihood of fleeing. Pointedly, I placed myself in his path, meaningfully slapping the brass-headed cane against my palm.

"Dr. Doyle," I said, trying not to smile at St. Andrews's happy-puppy expression. "May I present my associate, Mr. St. Andrews?"

"Dr. Arthur Conan Doyle!" St. Andrews cried, leaping forward in an embarrassing show of enthusiasm. "Can it really be you? I can't tell you how much your stories have meant to me!"

Doyle stopped. Blinked. For a moment I worried that he might be offended. The moment after that I wished the floor would open up and swallow me. Or better yet, that it would swallow St. Andrews. Then I saw the edges of Doyle's lips twitch in the hint of a smile.

"What an amazing coincidence!" St. Andrews gushed, shaking Doyle's hand like a water pump. "Oh, I have so many questions for you! For instance, to what degree did you base Watson's character on your own life? And, in *The Adventure of the Red-Headed League*, how did Holmes…" Suddenly dropping Doyle's hand, he winced and clutched his side.

Doyle's amusement turned to concern. He caught the doorman's eye. "Do find us a cab, my good man."

"Sir." Tipping his hat, the doorman slipped outside.

Doyle turned back to St. Andrews. "Mr. Adler thinks you may have a broken rib or two."

"It's nothing." St. Andrews gasped. "But regarding the diary page in *The Five Orange Pips*—"

"We'll go to my office on Upper Wimpole Street. It'll be a nice change to have patients." He nodded toward Geary. "I suppose this is the man with the dislocated shoulder?"

"In my uneducated opinion," I replied, not taking my eyes from Geary.

Dr. Doyle nodded. "We'll see you right, sir, never you worry." Lowering his voice, he leaned toward me. "I'll have the police meet us at my office."

After a moment, a four-seater cab pulled up to the curb. While I helped Geary and the still-babbling St. Andrews inside, Dr. Doyle spoke with the doorman, no doubt instructing him where to send the police. Glancing toward the doorway once more, I settled myself on the bench across from Geary and St. Andrews, while Doyle had a word with the driver. Geary leaned back against the padded bench and closed his eyes. A moment later, Doyle slipped in beside me. He closed the door and the cab began to roll.

As the vehicle glided down the smooth pavement, relief settled over me like a cool sheet. The police would sort Geary out, and in the meantime, his injuries would be off my conscience. However Jack ultimately felt about his father, he'd be pleased to know that the man's killer had been brought to justice—and to have something to remember the man by—or to sell, if he preferred. As for me, I suppose I felt a modicum of relief that Goddard had been telling the truth when he'd said he'd had nothing to do with Backer's death. Whether he'd had a hand in the explosion that had killed Lothar remained to be seen. Given how quickly the remains of the refinery had caught fire this evening, though, I was willing to believe in accidents.

But what had Goddard, Lothar, and Backer been working on?

Factory. Chloroform. Centrifuge. And Ac2O, whatever that was. They had to be doing some sort of chemical production that involved processes similar to those performed in sugar refining. Perhaps Doyle would have an insight. Beside me, Doyle and St. Andrews were carrying on an animated conversation about the process of deduction. They caught me watching and, as if embarrassed, lowered their voices.

Before long the carriage stopped, and we emerged in a quiet, clean neighborhood of white stone, brown brick, and evenly paved sidewalks—just a stone's throw from Cain Goddard's front door, as a matter of fact. The driver opened the door, and Doyle climbed down, slipping him a few coins. St. Andrews and I helped Geary out, half supporting him and half restraining him as Doyle opened the front door of his office.

Inside, the good doctor lit a lamp and hung up his coat and hat, gesturing for me and St. Andrews to do likewise. He showed St. Andrews to a chair, then led Geary behind a fabric screen. There was a bit of noise as Doyle helped Geary off with his shirt, but Geary didn't resist. Perhaps the possibility of pain relief outweighed his fear of justice. Or perhaps his injuries had simply taken the fight out of him. I watched the shadows the lamp cast against the screen: the doctor gently palpitating Geary's shoulder, Geary flinching, then Doyle coming around to have a look from the front.

"You have a broken clavicle," Doyle announced, while he helped Geary back into his shirt. I watched the doctor, silhouetted against the cloth screen, remove a large square bandage from a drawer and fold it into a triangle. "There's not much to be done except to immobilize it and hope for the best. In the meantime, I can give you something for the pain."

Geary pulled back suddenly. "You're wiv them, ain't you? How do I know it ain't some kind of trick?"

"Or you can try to set it yourself at home."

After a moment, Geary relented and allowed Doyle to draw near. Carefully, Doyle placed Geary's arm in the sling and knotted the bandage around the far side of his neck. As he did, his fingers slipped. Geary flinched and pulled back. His subsequent yelp was pathetic. I could almost feel the pain radiating from him from where I was standing.

"Are you certain you wouldn't like something for the pain?" Doyle asked.

Geary whimpered and nodded.

I watched Doyle's shadow pick up a syringe, fill it from a bottle, and jab it into the bicep of Geary's good arm.

"There. You should start to feel better in a moment. Why don't you take a seat over there?" Doyle said, indicating a low bed against the wall. Geary sank down on it, gratefully. After a moment he pulled his legs up and lay down. A few moments later, he was softly snoring.

Doyle emerged from behind the screen, looking pleased with himself. "Morphine is a wonderful thing. Next patient, please." He rubbed his hands together, as if relishing the idea. As St. Andrews stood, Doyle quickly crossed the room. He helped St. Andrews to remove his jacket, waistcoat, and shirt, then proceeded to examine him thoroughly.

"Painful when you breathe?" he asked.

"Excruciating."

"M-hm. Excuse me." He ducked back behind the screen, then emerged with a contraption consisting of two rubber tubes with a metal horn at their junction. Inserting a tube into each ear, he placed the horn in different places along St. Andrews's chest and abdomen. Then he ran his hands gently along St. Andrews's sides, noting the places that made St. Andrews wince. "Congratulations, sir," he said, removing the tubes from his ears and settling the stethoscope around his neck. "You have two fractured ribs."

"Is that serious?" St. Andrews asked.

"Seriously painful, yes, but you'll survive. I would recommend against any further exploration of abandoned buildings for the time being, however."

"Duly noted."

"And stay off your feet as much as possible. Catch up on your reading, perhaps. I'm working on a new story at the moment. Perhaps you'd be so kind as to read it and tell me what you think."

"I'd love to!" St. Andrews cried, then winced again.

Doyle laughed. "Don't hurt yourself. I'll send the manuscript in a day or two. Now, let's get you bandaged up. Would you like a drop of morphine?"

"No, thank you," St. Andrews said through clenched teeth. "Opiates don't agree with me."

Opiates?

Goddard had made much of his fortune importing and selling opium. One of his business associates had experimented with breeding poppies with an exceptionally high alkaloid content. Though that associate was two years cold in the grave, Goddard had built a greenhouse in his garden and was putting a lot of effort into breeding different sorts of flowers. Was he picking up where his late associate had left off? And did his dealings with the sugar bakers have anything to do with it?

Doyle nipped back behind the screen and emerged with a new roll of bandage cloth. He gestured for St. Andrews to raise his arms. Holding one end of the fabric to St. Andrews's side, he slowly unrolled the bandage around his torso. After he'd unfurled the entire roll and tucked in the edge, he said, "You might be tempted to wind the bandage tighter. Don't. It'll decrease the pain for a short time, but I've found it increases a patient's chance of developing pneumonia. Try to breathe naturally, and take a deep breath every now and then to clear your lungs. And if you change your mind about pain relief, I'll be happy to write you a prescription."

"Dr. Doyle, could you tell me how morphine is made?" I asked.

Doyle turned, stroking his moustache thoughtfully. "It's derived from opium, though I'm sure you already knew that. The alkaloids are chemically removed, then refined and purified—"

"With chloroform?"

He frowned. "Chloroform is used to remove alkaloids from opiate plants, yes. Why do you ask?"

"Are the chemicals centrifuged at any point?"

"Yes. But I don't understand why—"

"What about..." St. Andrews gestured for a pen and paper. He scribbled the sequence of letters and numbers he'd found on the label in the basement of the refinery. *Ac2O.* "It's a chemical formula, I think. What does it mean?"

"Acetic anhydride?" Doyle's frown deepened. "Truly I couldn't tell you." He looked from one of us to the other. "Does this have anything to do with your adventures in a burning sugar refinery?"

Without being overly specific, I gave him a thumbnail sketch of what we'd found and the conclusions taking shape in my mind. When I was done, Doyle sat down on the edge of his desk and exhaled thoughtfully. Then he pulled out his pipe, filled it, and lit it.

"About fifteen years ago," he said, as the comforting smell of expensive tobacco wafted across the room, "a chemist named Dr. Charles Wright created something called diacetylmorphine by boiling morphine and acetic anhydride together. He was trying to invent an alternative to morphine—something less potent and less addictive. But the result was exactly the opposite, so he abandoned the idea. But I've read that some German chemists have revived his work recently and are building on his ideas as we speak."

"German?" I asked.

Like the owners and most of the employees of the sugar refineries. It couldn't be a coincidence. I imagined if I dug deeply enough I'd find that either Lothar, or Backer, or perhaps both of them had connections to these chemists. It all made sense now. Goddard had gone as far as he could with opium. How much more money could he make by creating something similar but dramatically more potent?

"If someone was careless with these chemicals, could it cause an explosion?" I asked.

Doyle's eyes went wide. "Goodness, yes. Acetic anhydride has a very low flash point. What's more, it reacts violently with both air and water, and releases toxic vapors when heated."

"Vapors that smell like grass?" I asked.

He frowned. "No. Chloroform would do that, though. The phosgene it releases when it burns—also highly toxic—it smells of grass."

"Good God."

That's what I had smelled the morning of the explosion. That's what had killed the firemen who had rushed into the sugarhouse expecting only burning sugar and wood. Goddard had been trying to make diacetyl-whatever. Naturally, he'd been working through proxies—not dirtying his own hands. And conveniently enough, they were both dead. Goddard was responsible for those deaths—indirectly, perhaps, but undeniably—not to mention the deaths of the firemen. Though any traces of Goddard's connection to any of it had been carefully erased within moments of the explosion.

"Have I answered your question, Mr. Adler?" Doyle asked, peering at me with an expression of concern.

I nodded. "Indeed. Thank you, Doctor."

"Well, then. I suggest you both go home and get some rest. I asked our cabbie to remain outside. You should find him on the street where we left him. As for me, I shall wait with our sleeping guest until the police arrive. You'll forgive me for not releasing him into your custody, Mr. Adler. Though I don't doubt your word, this man is my patient, and I'm duty bound to ensure he receives proper treatment, both medically and under the law."

"I wouldn't have it any other way, Dr. Doyle. You've been ever so generous. How can I repay you?"

He smiled, offering me a square, solid hand. "You already have. I think there might be a story in this, somewhere."

I shook my head. "Thank you. By the way, you expressed interest in Dr. Lazarus's work with Turnbull House. We're having an event of sorts on Saturday morning—a test run of our messenger service. Teach the residents a trade, earn money for the organization, that sort of thing."

"Ah, yes. Stoker mentioned he intended to employ a pair of your young people in his theatre. I'd love to attend."

"Do extend my invitation to Mr. Stoker as well, then. Dr. and Mrs. Lazarus would be honored, as would I."

"I'll do that."

We shook hands again. Then I let myself outside into the cool night air, to let St. Andrews bid his hero a good night in peace.

CHAPTER TWENTY-TWO

THURSDAY

How things had come full circle, I reflected as I walked up Raven Row toward Turnbull House, a box of raisin buns under my arm. The tang of impending rain danced in the air, and the atmosphere was thick with moisture and grit. My boot splashed down in a mud puddle that had formed between two broken sections of pavement. My ankle buckled, and I nearly went over.

The last time I'd left Cain Goddard, I'd sworn it was the end. Though I'd recently held hopes to the contrary, it was clear my original judgment had been correct. The changes to my own psyche had been so incremental that I didn't feel substantially different from the man who had left York Street behind all those years ago. And yet though Goddard and I had once fit together like interlocking puzzle pieces, now this was no longer the case.

It wasn't merely that he'd failed to abandon his criminal ways. I hadn't asked that of him, and I would never expect him to do it of his own accord. Goddard was the man his experiences had made him—and I was as well. And though it would have been impossible for me to go through the things I had over the past few years and remain unchanged, he'd not experienced those things—at least not in the extremely personal way I had. He'd not encountered anything, as far as I knew, that would have made him question who he was or how he was making his way through this world. It had been a mistake on my part, or perhaps just wishful thinking, to think that time alone would have changed this fact.

Likewise the details of his recent endeavors didn't bother me as much as they might have. Goddard had paid two people to create a more potent opiate—legal, though unethical. One of those people had caused a tragic accident, and the second had been a victim of an unrelated murder. Sad, preventable, and wrong—but considering the depravities that transpired daily in the alleys and back streets of London, it wasn't at the top of the scale of dastardly deeds.

I might even have forgiven his assault, in time, had he shown a spark of remorse.

What ultimately doomed our reconciliation was the fact that he still looked upon me as a cog in his machine. A functioning sprocket is oiled and polished. A wobbly one is bashed with a spanner until it either straightens out or is destroyed and replaced. It wasn't how I wanted to live my life.

Enough. It was over, and, like it or not, Cain Goddard was gone once again from my life. I was back among my true family.

As I reached toward the familiar doorknob, the front door of Turnbull House opened. Jack stood there.

"Oh, it's you!" he cried. He glanced over his shoulder toward the open door of the classroom. Bess Lazarus had returned but was teaching from her chair. A fire was burning in the grate, and even the scant warmth that made it out into the hallway was welcome.

"You sound disappointed," I said as he reached around me to shut the door.

"Relieved, actually. That lot were startin' to act like openin' the door was me job."

Behind him, I saw Bess crane her neck to see who had arrived. I waved. She smiled and gestured for me to come inside.

"Good morning, Mr. Adler." The students greeted me in unison as I walked through the door.

"Good morning, class."

They were sitting in pairs that morning, unlike their usual grouping by academic progress. One member of each pair held a slate and chalk, and as I entered, they returned to their excited scribbling and chatter. Bess sat facing them from behind her desk. Her cheeks had some of their color back, and her eyes were bright and clear.

"This morning we're studying the railway map," she said. "I've challenged each of the pairs of messengers to find the quickest way across Central London. The pair that gets the message from one end of the designated area to the other fastest tomorrow will win a prize. Ooh!" Her eyes widened as I approached. "Are those raisin buns?"

I set the box on the desk before her. The warm smells of cooked fruit and spices rose in a mouth-watering cloud. She inhaled deeply, an expression of ecstasy spreading across her face.

"I expect you'll want to wait until luncheon," I said.

Her eyes turned sharp. "Bite your tongue. Jack, go downstairs and find some plates and a knife."

"Yes, Missus."

"Please!" she called belatedly.

Jack returned quickly with the implements, and Bess divided her treasure among her charges. The last piece, she offered to me.

"Oh, no," I said. "I wouldn't dream of it."

Grinning, she devoured it in three greedy bites.

"I see your doctor has allowed you back to work," I said.

"He's not happy about it, but in the end, he had to admit defeat. He's not cut out to be a teacher. He doesn't understand that the subject matter is only one small part of the job. The rest is teaching wild little animals to *sit up and eat their raisin buns like human beings*," she called toward a young man who was stuffing his gob as if he'd never seen food. Looking back at me, she smiled.

"And where is the good doctor now?" I asked.

"Enjoying a well-deserved day off at the South Kensington Museum. There's a new exhibition of British painters opening this morning and a lecture on geometry in art this afternoon."

I snorted. "I always knew he had a wild side."

"Be nice, Ira. I think we'll all benefit from his elevated spirits once he returns."

"Of that I have no doubt. Are you all right by yourself? Would you like me to stay and help?"

"Thank you, but I have everything under control." She frowned. "Unusual to see you before noon. Did you need something?"

I looked around the room, noting the pairs of busy students. It was a good thing there was so much enthusiasm for the messenger project. The way things stood with Goddard, he wouldn't have a lot of tolerance for late payment. I shuddered to think where I'd be if I failed to meet the terms of the contract. Damn it! And I wouldn't be in this position if Goddard hadn't put me there. I quickly pushed back my anger when Bess's relaxed expression turned to concern.

"Actually, I thought I might borrow Edmund and Martha. Mr. Stoker is still interested in hiring two of the older students to work in the theatre. I thought I might introduce them this morning and, if everyone agrees, to determine their hours and compensation."

She thought for a moment, then nodded. "They'd do well there. Edmund is nearly ready to be out on his own, and Martha will be soon. They're both capable and hardworking. Yes." She nodded. "You can take your bus fare from the coffee can on Tim's desk."

While she called Edmund and Martha, I let myself into Lazarus's office. He had tidied recently, swept and dusted. The room was calm, uncluttered, and smelled faintly of the vinegar used to wash the windows. Peace was settling once again over the house, and I was glad.

When I emerged with a pocket full of coins, Edmund and Martha were standing at the front door, wearing their coats and looking eager for adventure. They almost appeared to be brother and sister, in their slightly outsized secondhand clothing, faces scrubbed and hair combed to Bess's standards. Jack was standing nearby, leaning against the doorjamb, trying hard to hide some insecurity behind his usual cocky façade.

"Mind if I tag along?" he asked.

"Aren't you needed here?"

He shrugged. "Nah, we got it all sorted this mornin'. I could disappear and them messages would run themselves." He glanced around, fidgeting. "Only I'm feelin' restless. I could use some air."

I smiled. "Come on, then. You can join us."

❖

The sun was shining weakly behind the clouds as the four of us stepped off the omnibus and walked up the Strand toward the Lyceum Theatre. Everything was tinted a watery gray. But it wasn't as bitterly cold as it had been, nor was it raining. Martha and Edmund were lagging a few steps behind Jack and myself, gawking at the well-dressed crowds and the white stone facades of the long, tall buildings that lined the street.

"So who's this bloke takin' away two of me messengers?" Jack asked.

"Mr. Stoker, the manager of the Lyceum. Weren't you listening when I went over it on the bus?"

"I was listenin'. It's just, well, I know Mr. St. Andrews is a friend of yours and the doctor's, but I don't know this Stoker fellow. If anything happened to Eddie or Martha, I'd feel responsible, that's all."

I cocked an eyebrow. Not only a natural leader and organizer, but someone who would look after those in his employ. The very sort who should be managing something somewhere. And he was right, I realized guiltily. If he'd attired himself in the clothing befitting his born gender, he'd likely never have the chance to try. I gave him a surreptitious once-over. Jack had a young man's build and passed well enough amid the hurly-burly everyday of Turnbull House. But he'd been there less than two weeks, and during that time, Tim and Bess had been, shall we say, distracted. The truth would come out at some point. I wondered what would happen when it did.

"I've only met Mr. Stoker a few times," I said, "but I'll vouch for him."

The imposing white columns of the Lyceum Theatre came right to the edge of Wellington Street. The gold lettering on the façade stood out in shining contrast to the darkening skies above and the smooth black pavement below. Behind me, Martha gasped.

"Cor," Edmund echoed. Jack looked unimpressed.

It was late morning, and the front door was open. As we entered, the thick carpeting on the floors and the tapestries on the walls swallowed up the sounds of the street. When the door closed behind us, the silence was complete.

"This where we gonna be workin'?" Martha whispered.

"With any luck," I replied. I looked up and down the corridor, but not a soul was about. I remembered what Stoker had said about things being quiet during the day. The auditorium was unlocked. Looking quickly over each shoulder, I gestured for the others to join me in the doorway.

"Blimey!" Martha exclaimed.

"I'd say so," I said as they gaped at the expanse of velvet-covered seats that swept over the floor below, swung out on the balcony overhead, and lined the walls on three levels, the boxes framed by ornate curlicues of iron and painted plaster. Edmund and Martha were duly awed with the theatre's grand appearance, but it was Jack who really seemed to be taking an interest in the place. Eyes narrowed, brow furrowed, I could almost hear him calculating, judging, assessing. When he caught me smiling at his wide eyes, he straightened.

"Might be all right," he said.

"*All right?*"

He cracked a tight smile. "Could even see meself workin' here one day."

"Mr. Adler!"

Stoker's greeting kept me from giving that idea any further thought. Stoker was smiling and wearing a well-made suit cut to his generous proportions. I couldn't help smiling back at him, though my charges appeared daunted by his looming presence.

"And you've brought friends," he said.

"Mr. Stoker, please allow me to present Miss Martha Wells and Mr. Edmund Hill, two young people who are excelling in our program."

Stoker's smile widened. "Very pleased to meet you. And who might you be?" he said, turning his keen eyes on Jack.

"May I present Mr. Jack Flip?" I said. "Jack is the architect of our messenger service."

"Pleased to meet you, Mr. Flip," Stoker said as they exchanged a handshake.

"Likewise, I'm sure," Jack said distractedly. "Listen, how many seats is in this place?"

"Two thousand, one hundred," Stoker replied proudly.

"An' you fill them seats every night? All of 'em? How much do a ticket cost?"

Stoker chuckled. "We endeavor to fill the seats, but—"

"What's your expenses like, wiv' a place this big?"

I chided him. "Jack. This is hardly the time or place—"

Jack turned to me. "Only it's just if Eddie and Martha is gonna be workin' here, I want to make sure they's paid fairly, that's all."

Stoker laughed again. "I don't mind, Mr. Adler. These are valid questions. I respect a…a man who looks out for his friends."

Jack and I exchanged a glance. He, too, had heard Stoker stumble over the word "man."

Stoker continued as if it were nothing to him. "So are Miss Wells and Mr. Hill to be my new messengers?"

"I thought we might make an appointment to discuss that," I replied.

"Well, there's no time like the present. Please, let's retire to my office. As for you, young man," he said as Jack fell into step with him, "if you have any further questions, please don't hesitate to ask." He turned to address Martha and Edmund as well. "And that goes for you, too, Miss Wells and Mr. Hill. Honesty and transparency are the foundation of any sound business."

He walked a few more backward steps before turning, as if by instinct, through the door of the office I remembered. The entire time, Jack continued to pepper him with questions, while Stoker attempted to answer them before being hit with another volley. But Stoker didn't seem offended in the least. In fact, his enthusiasm for the subject seemed to blossom under Jack's interrogation.

"Here we are, then," Stoker said, gesturing for us to enter. "You want to work, I need workers, and you seem to have brought along a skilled negotiator. I don't see any reason why we all can't leave this room satisfied. Would anyone care for tea?"

CHAPTER TWENTY-THREE

SATURDAY

The sun came out the morning of the messenger-service test. It didn't stay out, of course. But the weather was as pleasant as it ever was this late in November. The air was crisp and clean, and, though the streets weren't exactly dry, at least they weren't running shin-deep with cold, black runoff. I'd slept away the rest of Thursday and had spent most of Friday mooching around my flat with a couple of magazines and a pouch of Egyptian tobacco. By the time I walked up the front steps of Turnbull House, the Great Clock ringing half-eleven in the distance, I was well rested and in a buoyant mood.

"He's here!" Ruth threw open the door as I reached for the knob. "Come quick, Mr. Adler!"

She took my elbow and pulled me into a classroom buzzing with excitement. There, the residents stood together in pairs, each clutching what I assumed was their plan to carry their test message across the designated area quicker than their counterparts. Bess sat behind her desk examining a potted orchid. She smiled when she saw me. Quite a few pots and vases with fresh flowers were arranged around the place. Someone had made an effort with the decorations, it would appear, though where an orchid might have come from that time of year, I couldn't say. Over by the fireplace, Lazarus stood, regarding the spectacle with the air of a proud father. I raised my hand to greet him, but before I could call out, Ruth nearly pulled me off my feet again.

"Over here! Look! They just come this mornin'." She dragged me toward a stack of paperboard boxes—eight of them arranged across two classroom benches. Moving a vase of pink carnations to the side, she continued excitedly. "Only nobody knows who sent 'em! The doctor said we had to wait to open 'em until you come, 'cause it had to be you. Was it you, Mr. Adler?"

"No," I said, confused.

The boxes were pristine white and bore the gold insignia of a well-known—and rather expensive—clothier. I looked at Lazarus and shrugged.

"Well, let's open 'em, then!" cried Ruth.

"Carefully!" Lazarus said. "I'm sure we'll find plenty of uses for the boxes later."

He was trying to sound authoritative, but his own voice was taut with excitement. As the students gathered around, I handed my coat and hat to Ruth and wiped my hands on my trousers.

"Well, go on!" someone said.

"I'm afraid to touch them," I said.

Lazarus rolled his eyes. "Let me do it, then."

"No, no, I have it."

The room went silent as I eased the top off one of the boxes and peeled back the thin paper below.

"Oh, my," I said. The box contained a jacket—a stunning jacket in red-dyed wool, with a crest bearing the letter "T" on the right breast. "Let's open the rest of them. Carefully, like the doctor said."

In addition to a jacket, each box contained a white shirt, a matching red cap, and either a pair of black wool trousers or a long, black skirt. Gasps rose around the room. None of the residents had likely ever received new clothing, not to mention such fine specimens. Come to think of it, I'd never possessed anything of that quality myself, not, I realized with growing apprehension, since I'd lived with Goddard at York Street.

"Why only eight?" someone asked. "There's thirteen of us."

"It's for the messengers," I said, suddenly understanding. "Isn't it obvious? They're uniforms. People will trust us if we look official.

And they'll know how to find us. And when they think of sending messages, they'll think of us first. It's very clever."

"I thought you said you didn't send them," Lazarus said.

"I didn't."

"Then who did?" He frowned. "St. Andrews has the money. And Ruth and Daisy are already working for him. He could have learned the sizes from them, and how many skirts and trousers."

"He didn't say nuffin' to me about it," Ruth said.

A knock on the door interrupted further speculation.

"Oh, dear, I hope it's not more flowers," Bess said. I glanced over and saw a number of containers on the floor beside the desk. "We're running out of places to put them."

"You didn't buy them?" I asked.

She shook her head. "They began arriving this morning after breakfast."

"Oh, hell."

That now-familiar feeling of dread confirmed my suspicions. Of course Goddard had sent the uniforms. He'd certainly sent the flowers. Orchids only grew in hothouses. As for the rest of them—azaleas, white heather, different kinds of lilies—"out of season" was putting it mildly. "Was there any message?" I asked, trying to hide my dismay.

Lazarus said, "Only that the flowers are for Bess. But beyond that, not a single word. Ira, are you sure you don't know anything about this?"

"Another one!" Ruth called, saving me from having to respond.

"Give the man a penny and bring it inside," Lazarus called.

"No, never mind the penny. He won't take it. None of them would." Lazarus turned to me. "It is the most curious thing."

"Rain lily!" Ruth crowed as she set the flowers down on the already-crowded desk and reached for her copy of *The Language of Flowers*. "Rain lily can mean either 'I'll never forget you,' or… wot's that word, Mr. Adler?" She pointed to the page.

"Atonement," I said. "Righting a wrong."

"Then there's white heather. That's protection. An' the carnations is for a mother's love. The 'zaleas mean 'look after yourself,' and the orchid—"

"Is a very expensive, very rare flower that doesn't generally grow in London," Lazarus said. "Looks like you have quite an admirer, Bess." He looked pointedly at me.

"I swear I don't know anything about it, Tim."

"And *I* swear, Adler, if *that man*—"

"Please don't argue," Bess said.

Lazarus looked at her, then looked at me and sighed. "No, no, of course not. Forgive me. We should just accept these blessings and enjoy them for what they are. Isn't that right, Adler?"

"I agree. And I really did have nothing to do with it."

Bess was still a bit pale and fragile-looking, but Lazarus had said the danger had passed. She probably could have carried all the boxes upstairs herself if she wanted to, but she was humoring her physician. And he looked grateful. They were going to be fine.

As for Goddard, I didn't know what sort of game he was playing. Atonement, indeed. I was thankful, of course, for the uniforms. All the same, once the loan was repaid, I planned to stay as far away from Cain Goddard as possible. That mistake, at least, could be rectified.

"Jack's comin'!" someone called from the front window. "An' he's got someone wiv' him!"

A moment later, Jack walked through the front door with Stoker at his side. Jack was wearing a well-cut coat and new bowler that made him look two feet taller and several years older. His hair was freshly cut, and he'd used a bit of theatrical paint to conceal the remnants of the bruises his father had given him. He was carrying the lion-headed cane. When he saw me, his face broke into a grin. He greeted me with a hearty handshake.

"It's your day, Jack," I said. "Glad you could make it."

"I feel a bit guilty comin' up wiv' the idea, then leavin' it to someone else, but Mr. Stoker wanted me to start right away."

Stoker squeezed Jack's shoulder with a heavy paw. "I couldn't ask for a more competent assistant," he said. "You'll make a fine theatre manager one day. Now go say hello to your friends." Once Jack had stepped away, Stoker said, "Mr. Adler, how can I ever thank you for introducing me to that remarkable young woman?"

"Ah...yes...well...er..."

"No need to explain. I'm in the theatre. And that's where Jack should be as well. He has a real future there, and I'm in a position to help him."

"Then it's I that must thank you," I replied. "I trust your two messengers are earning their keep?"

"I do believe I've ended up with the better part of that bargain." Stoker smiled.

He went on in praise of Edmund and Martha, but his words faded in my ears as, glancing through the front window, I caught sight of a familiar silhouette in the shadows across the street. Tailored coat, silver-headed cane, silk topper—Cain Goddard was bold showing his face that day, even if he was only showing it to me. My instincts told me to turn my back to the window, but my heart told me I wouldn't sleep until I'd severed our connection like a man.

"Excuse me," I said.

"But we're about to begin the test, Mr. Adler," someone called behind me as I quickly made for the door.

"I'll only be a moment."

Raven Row was bustling that morning with vehicles and pedestrians taking advantage of the calm weather. Goddard didn't step out of the shadows when I emerged from Turnbull House, but I could see him watching me, fingers tapping the head of his cane.

"You do have a nerve turning up here," I called before a passing carriage came between us. Once it had rumbled by, I stepped across the cobblestones to meet him.

"Sorry," Goddard said. "I thought you said the test was today."

"It is. But why are you here?"

He straightened his cravat haughtily, but I spotted a new insecurity in his eyes. Guilt, perhaps. Or perhaps the vaguest flicker of conscience. But as quickly as I'd seen it, it was gone.

"As the primary investor, I have an interest in seeing that your organization carries out its plans. But don't worry. I've no intention of forcing my company on any of you. Walk with me?"

Without waiting for a response, he started toward Crispin Street. His bruises were fading, and his lip was no longer swollen.

He wore the expression of a man who had seen much worse—which, of course, he had—though his gait was devoid of its customary arrogance. Curious. I knew I wasn't imagining the new crack in his confidence. He, too, was sensing the irrevocable change between us and had not yet decided how to approach it.

I walked with him to the corner, where we stopped and turned to watch as the pairs of students emerged from Turnbull House. Lazarus gave the word, and they took off running in all directions.

"Thank you for the uniforms and flowers. It was very generous."

"You knew I sent them, then?"

"Even Lazarus figured it out. He was not best pleased."

"Pleasing Dr. Lazarus isn't my concern. What did you think?"

I considered my words carefully. "I'm grateful on behalf of Turnbull House, but it doesn't change anything between us."

"Ah." A shadow passed over his face. At the same time, the sun passed behind a thicker bank of clouds, casting a chill over the entire street. "No, I suppose you're past being won over by grand gestures."

"You crossed a line. I'm not your employee. I'm not your possession. I may not be your social equal, but I deserve your respect."

In the brief instant he allowed himself to meet my eyes, I saw remorse. And in that instant, I wondered if I would ever truly want it to be over between us.

"You were right when you said it was my decision to contact you again," I said. "That was a mistake, and I'm sorry. I suppose I thought things might be different, now."

"I've never deceived you about the nature of my work."

"No," I admitted.

"Would it change anything if I apologized?"

Sighing heavily, I looked out over that narrow cobblestone lane. After a long moment I said, "Probably not."

He nodded, gazing off into the distance. "Then for what it's worth, I'm sorry. You were hoping I'd changed, and I was hoping you hadn't. But it was unforgivable to take my frustration out on you in that particular way."

While I stared, speechless and slack-jawed—the Duke of Dorset Street never apologized, for anything, unless he meant to gain a clear advantage—Cain Goddard turned on his heel and began to walk up Crispin Street. Shaking my head clear, I followed.

"How is Mrs. Lazarus?" he asked as I jogged to catch up with him. "I heard about the accident."

"Such concern is unlike you, Cain."

"Don't be cruel. I'm trying to demonstrate that I'm not a complete bastard."

I smiled grimly. "Bess is taking it easy, but she should be pushing us all around again in no time."

"And the baby?"

"The heartbeat is strong. Tim thinks it'll be fine."

"I'm glad."

Was he? I couldn't tell. It didn't matter, I supposed. It was the polite thing to say. Imagine Cain Goddard giving a hang about politeness. Perhaps he really was trying. The thought somehow made me sad. Him, too, from the set of his mouth. We came to the corner and stopped to let a heavily laden lorry shamble past.

"You may not believe it, but I am happy about the messenger service. It seems a very likely means of securing your organization's financial independence."

"Even though you were the one who put us in the position of needing financial independence."

"The question would have come up eventually."

"I suppose."

"On that note, I also came to give you this." Producing a large envelope from beneath his coat, he handed it to me. "The last time I handed you an envelope, it sat on your desk for two years. This time I want to watch you open it."

Shrugging, I inserted my finger beneath the flap and carefully pulled the edges apart. Inside was the contract I'd signed for the loan to purchase the leasehold.

"Burning, I find, is the most effective way to destroy a document," Goddard said. "Only you might consider tearing it up first. I learned that lesson the hard way."

"Oh, no," I said, handing the papers back. "I prefer my obligations written down in black and white, with no opportunity for misunderstanding."

He pushed the document back toward me. "There will be no further obligation, Ira. If you destroy the contract, you destroy the debt. If you insist on paying me back, that's your right. But I'd really like to do this."

"Why?" I asked suspiciously.

He shifted his weight from one foot to the other and glanced around impatiently. "Do you mind if we step into the alley?"

"I'd really rather not."

"Yes. Of course. The thing is, Ira, most men in your position would jump at the chance to take advantage of my generosity. But you've rejected it twice."

"I need more," I said. "Not materially, but..."

"I know. And I can't say that I understand. But I want to."

I stared, wondering if he was making fun of me. But gone was the condescension, that I-know-best smirk. He seemed to genuinely be considering the question.

"It's an experiment," he said. "I'm happy to be generous when I know it will pay off in the end. But you...you seem to derive a distinct satisfaction from helping people who can't do anything for you. I find it incomprehensible."

"It's pretty basic, Cain."

"Is it?" He frowned. "I sent the flowers because I wanted to understand. Mrs. Lazarus is in no position to help me, nor would she, I'm certain, if she had the opportunity. So I sent her a gift— anonymously—to see if I could perceive the supposed benefits of pure altruism."

I stifled a laugh. This conversation was taking a turn for the ludicrous. "And?"

"And..." He looked up into the clouds, as if searching there for the right words. "It didn't hurt."

I did laugh at that. "So, are you going to send me down to the butcher, now, to buy a goose for Bob Cratchit?"

"I think the Cratchits are doing well enough for themselves, don't you? Their building is secure, and now they have a way of bringing in a regular income. Not to mention some rather flash new uniforms."

"Were those part of the experiment, too?" I asked.

"Those were to help the business. I figured if you were obstinate about the contract, the uniforms would give the messenger service an extra measure of professionalism that would ultimately help you to meet your obligations faster."

I shook my head. "You do think of everything." I turned my attention back to the documents. "And there's no implied obligation here? You won't be trying to press me into roughing up your business partners or taking them weird flowers?"

"If you tear up that contract, you'll never have to deal with me again on any level." He met my eyes. "Unless you want to."

I swallowed hard. After all that had happened, I found the very idea inconceivable. At the same time, the very thing I had wanted—a fresh start with him, uncomplicated by the patterns of our past, and with every hope of a future of equality and mutuality—that very thing was dangling in front of me, daring me to take it.

I dared not.

Smiling sadly, I tucked the papers into the breast pocket of my coat. "Thank you, Cain," I said.

The sun passed out of the bank of clouds, casting a rare warm glow down onto the crooked, crowded streets of Spitalfields. Several doors down, a shopkeeper stuck his head out the door as if to investigate the origins of this alien glow. The Great Clock struck in the distance.

"Well. That's half an hour passed," Goddard said. "You should be getting back to Turnbull House to see if your little urchins have passed their test."

"I suppose."

"And do read that monograph I sent. I think you'll find it enlightening."

"Monograph?"

He frowned. "I sent it to Turnbull House with Watkins the other day."

"Oh, yes, of course," I said, remembering the envelope Lazarus had handed me the morning I'd gone to see Mrs. Whitby. It was currently sitting on my desk atop my notes for one of Wilde's unfinished stories. "Lazarus did pass it on."

"But you haven't opened it. Do. Please."

As he reached over to straighten my scarf, I simultaneously wanted to flinch and to lean forward into his touch. Once the task was finished, he pulled his hands away quickly, as if realizing he'd overstepped. I missed these tiny intimacies—the things that seem insignificant until they're gone. I missed him—at least the part of him that wrote monographs and sent flowers to pregnant women. The steel and vengeance I'd be happy to do without.

He cleared his throat. "I'm leaving the door open, Ira. If you walk back through it, it'll be on your terms."

"Cain—"

"Don't say it." He smiled bravely, turned around, and began to walk. "Leave an old man some shred of hope, hmm?"

"Diamorphine!" I called after him. He stopped. When he turned back, a smile was twitching at the corners of his lips. "But tell me, did you choose Lothar and Backer because of their technical knowledge or because they had connections to the German chemists currently working on the same thing?"

"Why don't we meet at the American Bar next week and I'll tell you over drinks?"

He waited for a breath to let me know the offer was serious, then laughed to show he already knew the answer. Bowing my head, I waved my farewell.

CHAPTER TWENTY-FOUR

I returned home to find a fist-sized package on my doorstep. It wasn't from Goddard. It was too clumsily wrapped, for one thing. For another, the greasy paper that enclosed it had been reused a number of times. Shrugging, I tucked it into my coat pocket and let myself in.

The room was chilly, but I had coal in the scuttle and a rather nice bottle of brandy that had arrived for me that afternoon at Turnbull House. In the accompanying note, Dr. Doyle had written that our nighttime adventure had inspired a handful of new stories, and for this he would remain in our debt. Shucking off my coat, hat, and boots, I laid a fire, then dug out Goddard's monograph to read while the room warmed up.

The monograph was a scientific treatise from an independent scholar. Neither the author nor the publication was affiliated with any academic institution—a fact that would probably doom the idea to obscurity. I'd seen many such monographs cross Goddard's desk in my time. Given his own troubled history with the academic establishment, Goddard held a special place in his heart for independent inquiry.

The Latin and Greek made my eyes cross, but, the brandy burning a pleasant path through my core, I persevered. This wasn't some trinket or a book of dirty poems. For some reason Goddard thought it important to share this bit of knowledge with me. And he considered my mind up to the task. After a moment or two, his reasoning became clear.

The monograph concerned a letter written some twelve years earlier by an Albert Brydges Farn to Charles Darwin—a name that even I, in my ignorance, had heard. In his letter, Farn noted color variations of the Annulet moth and postulated that a new, black variation had arisen due to the layers of ash deposited on the chalk cliffs by the limekilns situated below them. Farn suggested that the increase in the black moths supported Darwin's idea of the "survival of the fittest."

Darwin never responded to the letter, but the author of the monograph agreed with Farn and went on to suggest that the same process had resulted in the dramatic change in the coloring of the peppered moth—a species common enough in London that anyone of a certain age couldn't help but notice how they had once been white with black speckles, but now were almost entirely black.

It was also the species to which Lazarus had compared me, most unfavorably. Though to be fair, I don't think Lazarus was thinking of Darwin's theory when he said it.

The article made me smile. I wasn't so dense that Goddard's meaning wasn't immediately clear. The moths, according to the author, changed color over time in response to their environment. Evidence that species change, develop, adapt, and improve over time, rather than being doomed to the inherent weaknesses with which they were created. Just as my experiences, good and bad, had tempered and improved me, Goddard was saying. Taken in this context, it was quite a compliment.

Could he, perhaps, also be suggesting that he was himself undergoing some sort of metamorphosis? I'd believe it when I saw it. And yet, hadn't I already witnessed the beginnings of change?

As long as people existed, they would need someone to cater to their vices. Goddard had positioned himself uniquely to fulfill this role. It had made him a very wealthy man. But had it made him a happy one? Was this really all he wanted from life? His pursuit of the life of the mind suggested that, at one time, at least, he'd harbored higher ambitions. And how many common thugs experimented with breeding hothouse orchids in their spare time? Would the Duke of Dorset Street one day retire to write monographs and potter around his greenhouse? And in that unlikely event, would I be tempted to join him at the Criterion for that drink? Bess had forgiven Lazarus for a number of things many would consider unforgivable. But Tim Lazarus was as far removed from Cain Goddard as a person could possibly be.

Shaking my head, I downed my brandy and poured myself another. What Cain Goddard did or thought or did not do was no longer my affair. The fire was burning merrily in the grate, and the room had become pleasantly warm. Pushing myself to my feet, I retrieved Goddard's contract from the pocket of my coat. After a moment, I also took out the grimy little package. Leaning against the mantel, I carefully tore it open.

Firelight flashed across a bit of silver glinting through the paper. I laughed as my shaving scissors slid out, and with them a note.

Sorry.—M

I smiled as I returned the scissors to their drawer. Apparently London was filled with evolving creatures. And speaking thereof...

I held the contract in my hands. Traced the familiar loops of Goddard's signature with my finger. Destroying the document would destroy my debt. Would destroy any reason I might have to maintain contact with the Duke of Dorset Street.

It was the right thing. It was time.

Swallowing hard, I tore the paper into little bits, sprinkled them into the grate, and watched them burn.

—END—

About the Author

Jess Faraday is the author of several novels, including the Lambda finalist *The Affair of the Porcelain Dog*, and the steampunk thriller *The Left Hand of Justice*. She lives and writes in the American west. Visit her at http://www.jessfaraday.com.